James A. Little

From Kirtland to Salt Lake City

James A. Little

From Kirtland to Salt Lake City

ISBN/EAN: 9783337405991

Printed in Europe, USA, Canada, Australia, Japan

Cover: Foto ©Andreas Hilbeck / pixelio.de

More available books at **www.hansebooks.com**

FROM

KIRTLAND

— TO —

SALT LAKE CITY,

BY JAMES A. LITTLE.

———

WITH ILLUSTRATIONS.

———

JAMES A. LITTLE, PUBLISHER.

PRINTED AT THE JUVENILE INSTRUCTOR OFFICE,

SALT LAKE CITY, UTAH.

1890.

DEDICATORY.

With feelings of heartfelt gratification and esteem, and by permission,
this book is respectfully dedicated to

PRESIDENT WILFORD WOODRUFF,

The only living Apostle Pioneer.

THE AUTHOR.

PREFACE.

IT WAS not designed to make this little volume a detailed history of the Church of Jesus Christ of Latter-day-Saints, in the early stages of its growth. A consecutive narrative of its most important movements, the policies involved in them, the potent influences that forced them to a culmination, and some of their more immediate results is all that has been aimed at.

Only sketches have been made where volumes might be written, and the subject is far from exhausted even in the general way in which it has been handled.

It is hoped, that what is written will be found interesting and instructive to the reader and, what is of much importance, that all who may desire to peruse the book will find it easily within their reach.

History should not only give a correct narrative of events but, as well, the influences and motives that stimulated the actors. For this reason whenever they have left a record of their acts and motives, they should be permitted to speak for themselves. Hence, this book may be considered an epitome of the motives and experiences of the Saints who rejoiced and suffered in the persecutions and exoduses attending the early growth of the Latter-Day Work.

THE AUTHOR.

INDEX.

CHAPTER VI.

CHAPTER VII.

CHAPTER VIII.

CHAPTER IX.

CHAPTER X.

CHAPTER XI.

CHAPTER XII.

CHAPTER XIII.

CHAPTER XIV.

CHAPTER XV.

CHAPTER XVI.

CHAPTER XVII.

CHAPTER XVIII.

CHAPTER XIX.

CHAPTER XX.

CHAPTER XXI.

CHAPTER XXII.

CHAPTER XXIII.

CHAPTER XXIV.

CHAPTER XXV.

CHAPTER XXVI.

CHAPTER XXVII.

CHAPTER XXVIII.

CHAPTER XXIX.

CHAPTER XXX.

FROM KIRTLAND

— TO —

SALT LAKE CITY.

CHAPTER. I.

EARLY RECOLLECTIONS—THE ORGANIZATION OF THE CHURCH
—THE POLICY OF MOVING "TO THE WEST" REVEALED—
THE OBJECT OF THE GATHERING TO KIRTLAND—TIME
SPECIFIED FOR REMAINING THERE—THE MOVE TO THE
ROCKY MOUNTAINS FORESHADOWED.

IN THE spring of 1846, the writer was a soldier in
the Army of Occupation, on the Rio Grande, under
General Z. Taylor, ready to contribute his mite in the
expected contest with Mexico, towards redressing the
wrongs of American citizens and enlarging the public
domain. There reports reached him of the expulsion of
the Mormons from Nauvoo, accompanied with the suggestion that they would probably perish in the storms of
winter on the bleak prairies of Iowa.

In the spring of 1849, he joined their fortunes by
embracing their doctrines. The same season, in company
with many others, he followed the trail of their pioneers
across the desolate wastes between the Missouri river
and the shores of the Great Salt Lake. The first object
on the route that particularly interested him was a collection of dilapidated, tenantless houses, on the west

1

bank of the Missouri river, near where the town of Florence now stands. On inquiry he was informed this had been the resting-place of the Mormons after their expulsion from the beautiful city of Nauvoo; the rest denied them in their own homes in Illinois they had sought from the mercy of savages, beyond the confines of civilization.

Near this way-mark of civilization was a place of sepulchre where rested, in the secure repose of death, stern, enduring manhood, elastic youth and prattling innocence, alike the victims of relentless persecution. No fence protected this humble mausoleum from the tread of the reckless emigrant, the prowling savage, and the wild beasts who found protection in the very desolateness of its surroundings. No costly monuments, with finely chiseled epitaphs, ornamented the ground and reminded the passer-by that here rested the opulent and influential. The humble condition of surviving friends was evident from the rude pieces of timber and the ill-shapen stones at the head of graves. There was a sameness in their appearance that required the recollection of surviving friends to indicate where wounded affection might drop a few parting tears, when the still operative forces of persecution compelled the remnant of this shattered people to bid adieu to the resting-places of departed loved ones and seek a home in the solitudes of the great desert.

A fast age and the great continental railways have made the trail of Mormon migration to the interior of the continent a thing of the past, but the dusty road, the dreary plains, the rocky heights, the almost impassible canyons, the stampedes of cattle, the lurking savage, the nights of sleepless vigils, the days of watchfulness and of dreary labor, the dying friend who had long hoped to enjoy a season of rest in a desert home, the grave by the wayside, hastily dug but deep to protect the debris of humanity from ravenous wolves, will forever remain fresh in the memories of those to whom they have been a living reality.

With these scenes vividly photographed on his mind for forty years, the writer's interest in the early history of the Saints has constantly increased.

A latter-day dispensation in which should culminate the redemption of the race, has been expected by seers and prophets down through the ages. A leader of that dispensation was also prepared, in whom should first be planted the principles of the Latter-day work. That leader is Joseph Smith, the Prophet of the nineteenth century.

The Church of Jesus Christ of Latter-day Saints first assumed organized form in Fayette, Seneca County, New York, the 6th of April, 1830. Its journeyings from there to the Salt Lake of the Rocky Mountains was the filling up of a grand prophetic outline.

In October of that year Parley P. Pratt and Ziba Peterson were required, by revelation, to accompany Oliver Cowdery and Peter Whitmer, Jr., into the wilderness among the Lamanites.

After necessary preparations, they bade adieu to brethren and family friends, and preaching by the way, continued their journey to Kirtland, Ohio, where they tarried awhile and labored, and, as a result of that labor, organized a branch of the Church of about one hundred and twenty-seven members. They were mostly from the followers of Sidney S. Rigdon, an influential Campbellite preacher.

The latter part of January, 1831, the Prophet Joseph Smith and family, accompanied by S. S. Rigdon, who had been visiting them, moved to Kirtland, where they arrived about the first of February. This made it the headquarters of the Church, and a nucleus around which to gather its increasing numbers.

Soon after the arrival of the Prophet in Kirtland, the Lord said to him in a revelation, "And from this place ye shall go forth into the regions westward; and inasmuch as ye shall find them that will receive you, ye shall build up my Church in every region, until the time shall come when it shall be revealed unto you from on high, where the city of the New Jerusalem shall be prepared, that ye may be gathered in one, that ye may be my people and I will be your God." This indicated that still further "to the west" would be the center of future empire and another objective point towards which the movements of the Church would be directed. This view was further emphasized by a subsequent passage in the same revelation: "And behold it shall come to pass that my servants shall be sent forth to the east and to the west, to the north and to the south; and even now, let him that goeth to the east, teach them that shall be converted *to flee to the west*, and this in consequence of that which is coming on the earth, and of secret combinations."

In this we see a declared policy, which developed in the subsequent movements of the Church until they culminated in colonizing the Great Salt Lake Valley.

Elder P. P. Pratt and companions faithfully performed their mission and Elder Pratt in his Autobiography, sums up general results as follows:

"After much fatigue and some suffering we all arrived in Independence, in the county of Jackson, on the extreme western frontiers of Missouri, and of the United States.

"This was about fifteen hundred miles from where we started, and we had performed most of the journey on foot, through a wilderness country, in the worst season of the year, occupying about four months, during which we had preached the gospel to tens of thousands of Gentiles, and two nations of Indians; baptizing, confirming and organizing many hundreds of people into churches of Latter-day Saints."

Thus early was the way marked out for a future stride of the Church to the west of one thousand five hundred miles. Events proved that "the Ohio," with Kirtland as a center of operations was, from the first, only designed as a way station at which to gather strength for carrying out the policy of continuing "to flee to the west;" for, as early as September 11th, 1831, the Lord declared through his Seer, that it was His "will to retain a stronghold in the land of Kirtland, for the space of five years," and after that He would "not hold any guilty that shall go with an open heart up to the land of Zion."

An important factor in the gathering of this strength was the building and dedication of a temple. For ages the Priesthood in heaven and on the earth had been awaiting, with deep interest, the ushering in of "the dispensation of the fullness of times." The Seer, the circumstances of whose coming had been a subject of recorded prophecy, came. A suitable place, in which he could be clothed with authority for the fulfillment of his mission, was a necessity. That the Kirtland temple was the place in which this grand purpose was accomplished is evident from *Sec. 110, Doc. and Cov.*

That the Church was organized, a people gathered, a town built up, a temple erected and dedicated in which a great event of the ages was consummated, within the short period of six years, evidences the rapid growth of the Latter-day work and the toils and sacrifices of the Kirtland Saints.

Even in this primary gathering place the location in the Rocky Mountains began to develop from the shadows of the future. Doubtless, many evidences of this might be gathered up, but the following will answer our purpose. Elder Lorenzo D. Young states in his Autobiography that, when very sick in Kirtland, Father Joseph Smith promised he should recover, live to go with the Saints to the Rocky Mountains and there receive many blessings.

We may reasonably assume that when the Prophet received the revelation counseling those that should be converted "to flee to the west," the idea was well defined in his mind that the culmination of the policy would be in the valleys of the Rocky Mountains.

While there was a grand purpose in the temporary occupation of Kirtland, it was, at the same time, necessary they should establish themselves in Missouri for a central gathering place when it became necessary to evacuate it.

CHAPTER II.

DISARMING THE SAINTS—THE EXPULSION FROM JACKSON
COUNTY—"ZION'S CAMP"—THE NEW COUNTY OF CALD-
WELL IS ORGANIZED, TO WHICH THE SAINTS GATHER—
THE PRESIDENCY OF THE CHURCH DRIVEN FROM KIRT-
LAND—THE KIRTLAND EXODUS—ITS ORGANIZATION—
SCARCITY OF FOOD—NECESSITY FOR LABOR—MUCH SICK-
NESS IN CAMP.

IT IS a singular fact to contemplate, that the first ground
from which the Saints were driven, was that on which
will be built the chief city of the Western Hemisphere.
Fifty-five years after that sad event they are still wanderers from their heritage, and the longing eyes of the faithful are directed towards the place, as are those of Judah
to the Jerusalem of their fathers.   When they will
realize the fruition of their hopes remains an unanswered
query.

The bitter feelings engendered by the slavery question between the people of the Northern and Southern
States, made the slave owners of Missouri, like others,
jealous and suspicious of northern people.   This, with
other causes, operated from the first, to give the Saints
but little rest among these rude people of the frontier.
Those in Jackson county had suffered almost constant
annoyance, culminating in expulsion from their homes.

Preparatory to the accomplishment of this barbarous
act, with the assurance of the Lieut. Governor of the
state and others, that the object was to disarm the com-
batants on both sides, with the hope of insuring peace,
the Saints surrendered about fifty of their weapons of

defence. The mob, then secure from injury, were like savages let loose on women and children. They went about well armed in companies, on foot and on horse-back. They frightened the distracted women and children with threats of what they would do to their husbands and fathers if they could catch them, and warned them to flee immediately or they would demolish their houses and massacre them before night.

Christian preachers acted a conspicuous part in these cruel proceedings; called the Mormons "the common enemies of mankind" and exulted in their afflictions.

Sunday, the 24th of November, 1833, about one hundred and fifty of these harassed people were driven from their homes in Jackson county. Some went into Van Buren county, others fled into Clay county and camped on the banks of the Missouri river. The exiles subsequently made every possible exertion to recover their property, but without success. The citizens of Van Buren county would not let the Saints rest in peace among them. This was a double hardship after having built themselves houses and provided food for winter.

In 1834, a military body, called "Zion's Camp" marched from Ohio to Missouri for the relief of the Saints. After a short time spent among them, Joseph Smith and others, on the 9th of July, commenced their return journey to Kirtland where they arrived the 1st of August. There the Prophet found the elements of discord and apostasy in several leading elders. Much opposition had been aroused against him by false reports and accusations. All of which disappeared before the light of investigation.

When driven out of Jackson county the Saints

scattered into several counties, but perhaps more of them settled in Clay than in any other county, as they there met more kindness and consideration than elsewhere. Besides, it was the most convenient county for the exiles to gather to in their great distress.   In time, however, causes similar to those in Jackson county operated to make the citizens uneasy at their presence. The success and influence of the Jackson County mob also assisted in developing the spirit of persecution in the surrounding counties.

The first general move made in Clay county, for the expulsion of the Saints, was on the 29th of June, 1836.   In accordance with previous notice a respectable number of citizens met at the court-house in Liberty. The meeting was organized and a committee appointed to give expression to the object of the meeting, and the sentiments of the citizens of the county, with regard to the residence of the Mormons among them.

In perusing the minutes of this meeting we are struck with the open-hearted candor with which it gave expression to the public sentiment and the total want of consideration which popular prejudice engenders with regard to justice and constitutional rights.   An excited populace regards no law that stands in the way of the gratification of its blind fury.

The Saints were required to remove from the county, and a committee of ten was appointed to wait on them and receive their answer.   The 1st of July a considerable body of the elders of the Church in Clay county assembled and organized.   The proceedings of the citizens who met on the 29th of June were read and a Preamble and Resolutions adopted in answer to them.

The Preamble expressed the gratitude of the Saints for the kindness shown them by the citizens of Clay

County, and said: "Being desirous for peace, and wishing the good rather than the ill-will of mankind, we will use all honorable means to allay the excitement, and so far as we can, remove any foundation for jealousies against us as a people."

A committee of three was appointed to present the Preamble and Resolutions to an adjourned meeting of the citizens. This meeting accepted the reply of the Saints to their resolutions passed on the 29th of June. It was also urged upon the citizens to carry out, in good faith, the arrangements made between themselves and the Mormons. The meeting also recommended the Mormons to the good treatment of the people of the surrounding counties.

The Saints in Clay county selected a new location on Shoal Creek in territory attached to Ray county, and commenced moving on to it in September, 1836. Thus this move from Clay county was accomplished without much violence. The Saints gathering on Shoal Creek, petitioned the Missouri Legislature to incorporate a new county from territory attached to Ray county. This petition was granted about the middle of the following December and the new county was called Caldwell.

The mob in Davies county gave notice to the Saints in that county to leave by the 1st of August, 1837. At this time there were about one hundred houses in Far West, the chief settlement of the Saints in the new county.

In the autumn of 1837, the spirit of apostasy began to develop with much power in Kirtland. The Prophet had been to Missouri to aid in the direction of affairs by his presence and counsel. Returning to Kirtland about the 10th of December, he found several of the quorum of the apostles in open rebellion, and these with others,

united for the overthrow of the Church.   So bitter did
this spirit become that there was a show of armed force
to destroy those who sustained the legitimate authority
of the Church.   So great was the pressure that Elder
Brigham Young, a staunch supporter of the Prophet, left
Kirtland for Missouri the 22nd of December, 1837.

The apostate power continued to increase until Joseph Smith and Sidney S. Rigdon were compelled to flee
in the night.   They left Kirtland on the evening of the
12th of January, 1838.   They were joined by their families on the 16th, and pursued their journey to Missouri
in wagons.   They arrived in Far West the 14th of the
following .March.   The' head quarters of the Church
were now removed from Kirtland to Missouri, and it was
the signal for the evacuation of the former place.   It had
filled its mission and was no longer needed for the progress of the Saints "to the west."

The 6th of March, 1838, the seventies met in the
temple in Kirtland to devise the best means of removing
their quorum to Missouri.   On the 10th of the month it
was made manifest by "vision and prophecy," that they
should go up in a camp, pitching their tents by the way.
On the 13th, they adopted rules for their journey, which
were signed by one hundred and seventy-five men.   The
privilege was given for any persons to go in the company
provided they would abide the laws for its government.
A Board of Commissioners was appointed to lead the
camp, which was divided into companies of tens with a
captain over each.   A clerk, historian and treasurer were
also appointed.

Elder Joel H. Johnson says in his journal: "On the
6th of July, 1838, I started from Kirtland, with my family,
in company with the camp called 'The Kirtland camp,'
numbering in all, men, women and children, five hundred

and fifteen souls ; with fifty-eight wagons and a large number of cows.   It consisted, principally, of the poor Saints of Kirtland, the sick, lame, blind, etc., with all who

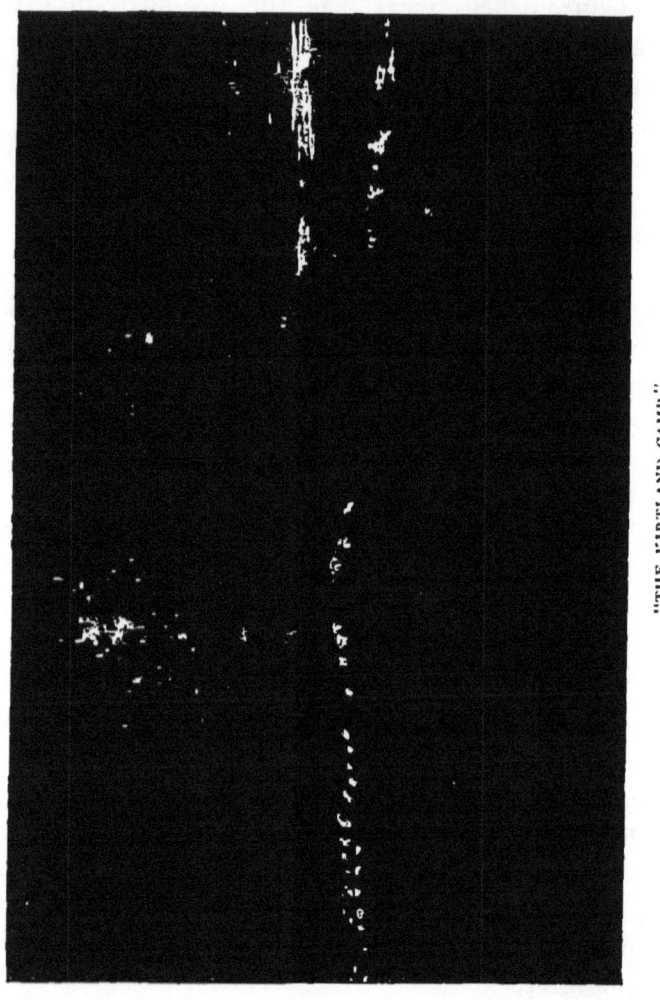

"THE KIRTLAND CAMP."

could not move without help." . Kirtland was the first place the Saints had gathered to and the third they evacuated in less than five years.   Zion's camp was essentially a military organization not burdened with

families. The "Kirtland camp" was the first company
of Saints, of any considerable magnitude, that was an
emigrating one, burdened with women and children,
household goods, cattle, etc.

Traveling among avowed enemies organization for
defence was a necessity. The following circumstance
illustrates the temper of the people in many places.
Near the town of Mansfield, Ohio, three of the company, Josiah Butterfield, Jonathan Dunham and H. Hall,
were, for some supposed connection with the "Kirtland
safety society money," arrested and lodged in jail.
Threats were in circulation that the camp should not pass
through the town; but as they continued their journey
the next morning nothing disturbed them, except the
repeated firing of cannon to frighten their horses as
they passed the court-house. The court was in session
and the case of the imprisoned brethren was called up,
but no bill being found against them they were discharged a little after one o'clock p. m. This was on the
20th of July.

On account of a heavy rain, which had thoroughly
wet the camp the night before, on the 21st the roads
were muddy and traveling bad. To seriously increase
the difficulties food was scarce, there not being half
enough in camp for dinner. There was some appetite
for raw corn before a supply could be obtained. Sunday
the 22nd of July, the camp was one hundred and eighty-
eight miles from Kirtland.

In these early times of trying experiences cleanli-
ness was, as now, a part of the religion of the Saints.
At proper times the company was halted at a convenient place for fuel and water, and the "Sisters" were
notified that time would be given for cleansing linen, etc.

The 24th of July, while in camp for this purpose, the

men obtained a job and performed labor to the amount of nineteen dollars. Some difficulties were thrown in the way of the people because they were Mormons. For this reason, in one place they could not buy forage and one man threatened to shoot Captain Dunham, the engineer.

About the 1st of August, the Kirtland company halted in their journey to recruit their teams. The men engaged in such labor as they could obtain in order to get means to continue their journey. No rations were issued to those who could not give a reasonable excuse for absenting themselves from labor. The doctrine that "the idler shall not eat the bread of the laborer" appears to have been rigidly enforced. Three brethren were appointed to settle minor difficulties. For some time the camp did not make much progress. Many were sick, and the evening of the 8th of August was spent by several of the Elders in visiting the tents and rebuking diseases and evil spirits. Elder Byington's child died, but many of the sick were healed.

Division crept into the camp and they did not properly improve their time in labor. The 20th of August the company began to break up. Two men who had been cut off from the Church left it with their families. About this time two children were born in camp. The men continued to labor as they had opportunity. They burned charcoal, erected a forge, and the blacksmiths repaired wagons, shod horses, and prepared to resume their journey.

Every man was expected to fill his place in the organization. For not honoring his office of tent-master a Mr. Hammond was cut off from the company. It was the duty of a tent-master to see that prayer was attended to at the proper time, that no iniquity existed in his tent, and also to draw the daily rations for those belonging to his mess.

At three o'clock in the morning of the 29th of August, the trumpet sounded to wake up the sleepers to prepare for the journey. The people appeared weary of inactivity, for "every heart leapt with joy, and even the children were so delighted that they appeared like a lot of playful lambs."

CHAPTER III.

THE COMPANY LEAVE THEIR ENCAMPMENT OF A MONTH— SEVERAL BURIED BY THE WAY—HUNGER IN CAMP—THE ECONOMIC METHODS OF THE SAINTS—ENTRANCE OF THE COMPANY INTO MISSOURI—GREAT EXCITEMENT AMONG THE PEOPLE—THE COMPANY ARRIVE IN FAR WEST.

AT NINE o'clock the camp ground which had been occupied for a month was vacated. The company traveled eighteen miles and that night was two hundred and seventy miles from Kirtland. The enmity of the people was shown in various ways. On Sunday, the 2nd of September, a malicious stage-driver turned out of his course and broke up a wheel of one of the wagons. The following day the company passed through Indianapolis, the capital of the state of Indiana. Although there were some threats from the people, no demonstration was made except hurling a brickbat at one of the men which did no harm.

There was much sickness in the country the company were passing through, and several of its members died and were buried by the way. It was autumn and winter was approaching. While it was still thought advisable for the company to try to go up to Zion in a body, a few families were counseled to find places to work through the winter, and get means with which to help themselves.

In accordance with this counsel the 10th of September, nine or ten families remained behind. On the 14th of September the company passed through Springfield in the state of Illinois. Much enmity was manifested in the countenances and conduct of the citizens. Fever and ague were prevalent in the country, and on account of sickness and destitution, many families had found stopping places before arriving at this place. The people of this camp had learned what it was to be hungry, as they were often short of food for man and beast. For the last one hundred miles of travel their food had consisted of boiled corn and shaving pudding. The latter was made by shaving the new ears of corn on a jointer or foreplane. It was pronounced excellent with a little milk, butter or sweetening. An occasional mixture of pork, flour, potatoes, etc., made it approximate quite a comfortable living. The cobs and refuse were given to the horses so that nothing was lost.

At this early period of church history the economic methods and patient endurance of the Saints made the following sentiment proverbial: "The Mormons would starve a host of enemies to death, for they will live where everybody else would die." At this time the company had become reduced from five hundred and fifteen to two hundred and sixty persons. They were five hundred and forty-six miles from Kirtland, and had been a little over five months on the way. Destitution, severe toil, sickness and death caused murmurings and division, and they had scattered along the route.

September 20th, 1838, the Kirtland Saints crossed the Mississippi river into Pike county, Missouri, and pitched their tents one mile west of the town of Louisiana, six hundred and fifty-six miles from Kirtland. The Saints in Missouri were in serious difficulty with the mob, and the travel-worn remnant of the Kirtland Exodus found no place to rest. They fled from the fires of persecution in Ohio to find themselves in a furnace of affliction in Missouri.

The following incident partially illustrates the temper of the Missourians. Elder John D. Tyler had charge of the loose stock of the company. The third day after crossing the Mississippi river, in passing through the town of Paris, those having charge of the herd were hailed and asked to what place they were driving the cattle. They were answered, "Towards the Rocky Mountains." "Well, you are going into trouble." Elder Tyler replied, "We have been in that place before and know how to take it." It may justly be said of the Missourians "they grumbled and growled like wolves."

In passing through the town of Madisonville the company met all sorts of exciting stories about the Mormon troubles. They encamped at night on the west side of the north branch of Salt river, on the ground occupied a few days previous by Elder Page's company from Canada. They were told that the governor of the state was just ahead with a military force to stop them. It was only one of the many flying reports that they so often heard.

The 28th of September, 1838, the company found themselves on Parson's creek, Lynn county, Missouri. The country was a natural paradise. It was well sup-

2

plied with wild turkeys, prairie hens, quails, partridges, wild geese, ducks, snipes, deer, raccoons and squirrels. From this profusion of game some food was obtained for the camp. The following day a couple of wagons upset and hurt several persons, and there were also some sick in camp.

Sunday, the 30th of September, the camp traveled fifteen miles and encamped in Caldwell county, on the farm of Brother Oliver Walker who gave each one a large pumpkin and some shelled beans. The company began to enjoy the kindly hospitality of the Saints, and these friendly associations made them feel as though they had, indeed, entered the "Land of Promise."

The 2nd of October the company approached Far West. The Prophet, Joseph Smith, Elders Sidney S. Rigdon, Hyrum Smith, Isaac Morley and George W. Robinson met them a few miles out and escorted them into the city. They encamped on the public square where friends greeted friends in the name of the Lord. Isaac Morley, Patriarch at Far West, furnished a beef for the camp, and Elder Rigdon provided a supper for the sick. The people needed the kind hospitality of friends for they had eaten but little for several days. By the way they had traveled, they were distant from Kirtland eight hundred and sixty-six miles. They had now reached the "Land of Zion," the headquarters of the Church, and the Kirtland exodus had culminated, but we will accompany them to their destination.

The 4th October, 1838, was an important day to the "Kirtland Camp." It ended their long and trying journey, "for they arrived at their destination and began to pitch their tents about sunset, when one of the brethren living in the place proclaimed with a loud voice—"Brethren, your long and tedious journey is now

ended, you are now on the public square of Adam-ondi-
Ahman.   This is the place where Adam blessed his
posterity, where they rose up and called him Michael,
the Prince, the Archangel, and he being full of the Holy
Ghost predicted what should befall his posterity to the
latest generation."

The town of Adam-ondi-Ahman had been located
in June of that year on the north side of Grand River, in
Davis county, twenty-five miles north of Far West.

CHAPTER IV.

THE EXODUS FROM MISSOURI—THE COVENANT OF ASSISTANCE
    —SUFFERINGS OF THE SAINTS AS ILLUSTRATED IN A
    SKETCH OF THE LYTLES—KINDNESS OF THE PEOPLE OF
    QUINCY—HOW LEVI HANCOCK GOT OUT OF MISSOURI—
    BLESSING ON THE GREEN CORN.

MISSOURI was a "Land of Promise" to the Saints,
to be retained only on condition of keeping
the law of consecration which had been in part revealed
in Ohio.   This law was applicable to all members of the
Church, and without its observance an inheritance could
not be obtained upon the land of Zion.   For evidence
that the conditions were not fulfilled the reader is referred to *Sec.* 110, *Doc. and Cov.*

With divine requirements unfulfilled the Saints had
not faith to contend with surrounding antagonisms, and
the land of Missouri proved an uncongenial soil for
their growth.   Even with their failure in coming up to

the standard of excellence required of them, the purity of
their principles, their progressive spirit, and their unity of
action, were too much for the crude intellectual and moral
capacity of the average Missourian, and he made frequent spasmodic efforts to eject from his surroundings
elements so antagonistic to his nature..

As before stated the Saints in Missouri were subject
to great annoyances and, in the autumn of 1833, were
expelled by mobs from their homes in Jackson county.
They scattered out into Clay, Daviess, and De Witt counties.   They were not permitted to rest in these places;
they gathered into Caldwell county and located the town
of Far West.   These persecutions were a constant
accumulation of unredressed wrongs heaped upon them
by the Missourians.   These wrongs generally culminated
in confiscation of property, and often in imprisonment
and death.   Death sometimes by personal violence, but
oftener by dieases caused by exposure to the elements
and want of the necessaries of life.

When the Prophet, Joseph Smith, arrived in Far
West, in March, 1838, it became the residence of the
leading authorities of the Church, and it and the surrounding country, the gathering place for its members.
The Missourians feared the Saints on account of their
thorough organization, their unity of purpose and action,
and offered violence to oppose their voting at the August
election.   At the town of Gallatin a knock down fight
occurred between the parties in which the Mormons were
victorious.   This roused the popular excitement to fever
heat.   From that time antagonisms seemed to strengthen.
Mobs became legalized military bodies under State authority; the judiciary instead of defending the injured became a mere tool in the hands of a vindictive populace.

The climax of tyranny and wrong was finally reached

by the governor of the State, Lilburn W. Boggs, issuing a decree that the Mormons must either leave the State or be exterminated. The Saints were disarmed and their leaders imprisoned. In this defenceless condition they were robbed and abused by as graceless a set of villains as ever claimed connection with Christian civilization.

The crisis had come, and it was death or expatriation. The memorable exodus of the Saints from Missouri commenced in the autumn of 1838, and culminated the ensuing winter under circumstances of extreme destitution and suffering. It was a dark day. They were leaving their "Land of Promise" to which they had clung with great tenacity and there was no other in sight. There had been no prophetic utterances to indicate where should be their next gathering place. Only those who have passed through a similar experience can conceive of their sufferings, and they will never be written unless it is done by the recording angels.

They left ample evidence of their sufferings along their trail to the west bank of the Mississippi river, opposite the town of Quincy, Illinois, a distance of about one hundred and seventy-five miles. There hundreds encamped in winter storms with little protection except the forest along the river bottom, which furnished abundant fuel for their fires.

In fulfillment of a covenant made by the Elders, that they would not cease their exertions until their people were gathered out of Missouri, when those who owned teams had accomplished the deliverance of their families, they, and their scanty stock of household goods were unloaded and the team returned to Missouri to deliver others from perils and death.

Some Missourians living on the road traveled by

the Saints, in their vindictive hate, ignored their usual
customs of hospitality, and at night denied women and
children shelter from the rigors of a northern winter, the
icy air of which was often breathed by new born babes;
others, with warm sympathies for suffering humanity,
offered them such shelter and comfort as was practicable
under the eyes of some vindictive neighbor.

Let it be recorded to the honor of the citizens of the
town of Quincy, that they liberally administered to the
wants of the fugitives from Missouri.   •

The misfortunes of a people are often best illustrated by individual experiences.

With the slender outfit of a wagon and a pair of
horses Mr. John Lytle, his brother Andrew, and their
families, in all ten persons, arrived on the west bank of
the Mississippi river, opposite the town of Quincy, Illinois, in the month of February, 1839. In fulfillment of
a covenant before referred to, their effects were at once
unloaded and the team returned to assist others. After
bringing out its owner and his brother, it made two trips
bringing two families each time, when it was too exhausted
for further labor in that direction. The Lytles encamped
in the timber on the river bottom, with many other fugitives. At the time of their arrival the river was open
and no arrangements had been perfected for crossing the
people.

Their shelter from the chilling winds of winter was
what the timber afforded, with quilts and wagon covers
drawn over poles. In a day or two the weather turned
severely cold, the river froze over, and the people crossed
on the ice. Mr. John Lytle and family, with five other
families, found shelter in a room about 18x20 feet. The
only advantage of this crowded condition was protection
from the cold. The first and only night this shelter was

enjoyed, Mrs. Lytle gave birth to a son. Even in this extreme of destitution they were not permitted to rest, for the following day the owner ordered them to vacate the house as he had an opportunity to rent. A cabin was found barely large enough to shelter the two brothers and their families. To it the suffering wife and new-born babe were removed.

This miserable shelter was occupied but one night for they were again ordered to vacate. Fortunately another shelter was found, but at a considerable distance. To it, families and effects were removed. Under these hardships the tender infant sickened and died. The mother, destitute of every comfort woman is supposed to need in her condition, also sickened but finally rallied and recovered.

Hoping to find some relief and rest, Mr. Lytle and family made a visit to Pike county, Illinois. They found their relations embittered against their people, and a cool reception was the result. In a day or two they returned to the neighborhood of Quincy, and soon after continued their journey to Commerce where their people were already gathering. There they found a hearty welcome from fellow-sufferers as destitute as themselves. Levi Hancock was well known in the Church as one of the First Seven Presidents of Seventies. Many will be interested in the following account of how he got out of Missouri. It may be considered an extreme case but doubtless, there were many others nearly paralleling it.

Levi Hancock arrived from Ohio in Far West, Missouri, in March, 1838, in company with the Prophet, Joseph Smith. He settled on Plum Creek, a short distance from the town. There he remained until the time had nearly expired within which the Saints were to leave the State. Up to that time he had spent his energies in assisting others to get away. The New Year of 1839 found him nearly destitute of the means of moving, or of providing ordinary necessities for his family. The mob had killed his only cow, robbing his family of even that limited source of sustenance.

He had a blind horse, but no vehicle to carry his little children and the few household goods still retained for family use. He had a small foot lathe. This he fitted up with belts of rawhide from the skin of his cow. With this crude machinery he turned hubs for two cart wheels, split spokes out of fence rails, and cut out felloes from the hewn puncheons of his cabin floor. From the puncheons he also made a box for his cart, and over a semblance of bows, an old quilt was stretched to shelter the contents of the box from storms.

Several inches of snow covered the ground when this destitute family were forced to leave the shelter of their cabin, to dare their fate in the cold of winter. It consisted of husband, wife and three children, the oldest a lad of about five years. The children were shoeless and the mother nearly so, having on her feet the tattered remains of a pair of shoes which afforded her feet but little protection from the cold snow.

To intensify the sufferings of the lad, and to add to the keen edge of those of the father and mother, a short time previous to starting, while out after the cow, he was met by a couple of Missourians and because he was a Mormon boy, was whipped with hickory withes until his back and legs were covered with welts and cuts, from which the blood trickled down to the ground. Exposure and traveling made these partially healed wounds very painful. The mother with wet chilled feet and limbs, and her deep sympathies for her little ones, about reached the extreme of human suffering and found some relief in tears. The husband and father, still trusting in a kindly Providence appeared as cheerful as an aching heart made it possible.

He prophesied to his suffering companion that she should be provided with a pair of shoes in a remarkable manner. In the middle of the first day's travel they stopped to rest and warm. A good fire was made, for wood was plentiful. The mother stripped the ragged, saturated shoes and stockings from her feet and placed them by the fire to dry. The dinner, consisting of parched corn—quite inadequate of itself to sustain the human frame, especially under such circumstances—was eaten. Preparing to resume the journey the mother reached her hand down to take her tattered shoes, and to her astonishment she held a new pair in her hand. Both husband and wife expressed their heart-felt gratitude for this gift of a kindly Providence, so opportunely supplying a serious want.

When it stormed mother and children huddled together under the old quilt cover of the cart. At night the meagre bed was made by the camp fire, with a log at the foot and one at the head to keep off the wind. On the single quilt that covered them was spread such outside garments as they could divest themselves of, and, by sleeping together, a considerable degree of warmth and comfort were obtained.

They traveled the well-worn track of those who had preceded them and arrived on the bank of the Mississippi river, opposite the town of Quincy sometime in the month of February. An idea of the severity of the weather may be formed from the fact that the Mississippi river was frozen over and they crossed it on the ice.

Although the people of Quincy had shown much

kindness to the destitute Saints, Elder Hancock continued his journey to the new location then called Commerce, now Nauvoo.   There was enacted the closing scene in this family drama. It was still winter and the fact had a serious significance to the poorly sheltered, half-clad and famishing Saints. The faithful blind horse had nearly dragged out his life in the service of his master. That master could not feed him, and his heart rebelled against turning him out on the common with the certainty that he must gradually starve to death.

One day the lad, Mosiah, saw his father leading the faithful brute towards the river, with a wisp of provender under his arm and an axe in his hand. Curiosity prompted the boy to follow and inquire of the father what he intended to do with the horse. Without answering his question the father ordered him, somewhat sharply to return. As he did so, the last he saw of the horse he was quietly eating the provender and the master was cutting a circle in the ice around him.

CHAPTER V.

LOCATION OF NAUVOO—CAMP OF THE EXILES—THEIR SUFFER-
ING CONDITION—THE LOCATION MADE HEALTHIER BY
DRAINING—JOSEPH SMITH IN VISION PROPHESIES THAT
THE SAINTS WILL REMOVE TO THE ROCKY MOUNTAINS—
THE TWELVE LABOR TO CARRY OUT HIS PREDICTIONS
—THE COMMENCEMENT OF THE EXODUS.

AN UNHEALTHY location, called Commerce, on the east bank of the Mississippi river, was the only gathering place available for the Saints. It was a commanding site for their future city near the head of the Lower Rapids, and one hundred and ninety-two miles above the city of St. Louis. The ground is regular and rises gradually from the river, with a plain at the summit. The first land was purchased for the Saints May 1st, 1839. The 10th of May the Prophet Joseph, lately delivered from a Missouri prison, moved on to the ground with his family in a condition of extreme destitution. Leaders and people occupied a common level. Burnings, plunderings and drivings had been a common lot. Leading men had suffered in Missouri prisons, and broken constitutions were the heritage of many of the people.

The camps of the Saints occupied the lower ground along the bank of the river. They presented a general appearance of great destitution. Houses, covered wagons and tents were luxuries enjoyed by few. There was slight protection from the scorching sun by day or from chilling dews by night. Their food was poor in quality and meagre in quantity. In a state of semistarvation, alternately chilled to the marrow with ague or burning with fever, death reaped a bountiful harvest among these victims of religious persecution.

On the bottom lands along the river, and extending a considerable distance above the camps, were a succession of ponds of stagnant water filled with decaying vegetation. In the heat of summer miasmatic vapors from these stagnant pools filled the air with seeds of disease and death. It was soon evident to the people that these sloughs must be drained by cutting ditches from them to the river. So urgent did this labor appear that men who suffered from chills and fever alternate days, labored on these drains the days they were free from these attacks. This labor was completed in the summer of 1840 and, from that time, there was a marked improvement in the health of the place.

The following from the recollections of Elder Mosiah

Hancock vividly illustrates the great needs of the people: He says, although then only a lad the circumstance made too powerful an impression on his mind to be ever forgotten. In the summer of 1839 his father and family lived with the Prophet Joseph. The first green corn of the season was greeted with much satisfaction, as the fruit of their labors in their new location. It was boiled on the cob and placed in the center of the table. Around it were the Prophet, Joseph Smith, Sen., Levi Hancock, and others of his family. Joseph asked his father to bless the food. The Patriarch grasped an ear of corn between his thumb and two fingers. Holding it up from the table he said, "Oh God, the Eternal Father, we thank Thee for this corn, and we ask Thee in the name of Jesus Christ to bless and sanctify it, and strengthen our stomachs that we may be able to receive the same to the nourishment of our bodies, until Thou canst provide something better for us, this we ask Thee in the name of Jesus Christ, Amen." This blessing was asked with the tears trickling down the face of the aged father. He evidently keenly sensed his own needs and those of his people; more especially the wants of the sick and of delicate women and children. Another year of suffering and this Patriarch of the House of Israel passed away the 14th of September, 1840.

Nauvoo proved only another way-side station where the Saints might gather strength for the culminating move in this succession of exoduses. For advancement in the ordinances of the gospel, it was necessary that another temple should be built. The land of Missouri was so thoroughly under antagonistic influences, that progress in that direction was limited to selecting sites and laying corner-stones.

The corner stones of the Nauvoo temple were laid

the 6th of April, 1841, less than two years after the first
purchase of land for the new city. Within five years
that temple was so far completed that the object of its
construction was realized, and it was the chief object of
interest in a beautiful and populous city. Considering
the extreme poverty to which the Saints were reduced,
by the Missouri persecutions, these historical facts
evidence their wonderful vitality and recuperative powers,
and modern history will scarcely parallel them where the
chief incentives to action have been embodied in a religious faith.

There are many events in the history of the Saints
bordering on the miraculous. Personal experiences are
often surrounded with a halo of romance, and again
others are enveloped in the dark shadows of tragedy.
Faith in God and their mission have given them wonderful
powers of endurance. Opinions may differ as to the
character of that faith, but with it they have faced the
fires of affliction, overcome the difficulties of the ever
present, and found strength and comfort in assurances
of a better future. In the shifting scenes the Church
was passing through the Prophet Joseph, and those
immediately around him, did not lose sight of the objective point in the command "to flee to the West."

At a meeting of Freemasons in the town of Montrose, on the west side of the Mississippi river, Joseph
Smith, while conversing with his brethren, uttered the
remarkable prophecy that the Saints would be driven
to the Rocky Mountains. Elder Anson Call was present
on the interesting occasion and in his autobiography,
gives a more detailed account of the circumstance than
the writer has found elsewhere. On the 14th of July,
1843, the Prophet Joseph, with quite a number of
his brethren, crossed the Mississippi river to the town of

Montrose, to be present at the installment of the masonic
lodge of the "Rising Sun."   A block school-house had
been prepared for the occasion with a shade in front,
under which was a barrel of ice water.   Judge George
Adams was the highest Masonic authority in the State of
Illinois, and had been sent there to organize this lodge.
He, Hyrum Smith and J. C. Bennett, being high Masons,
went into the house to perform some ceremonies which
the others were not entitled to witness.   These, including Joseph Smith, remained under the bowery.   Joseph,
as he was tasting the cold water, warned the brethren
not to be too free with it.

With a tumbler still in his hand, he prophesied that
the Saints would yet go to the Rocky Mountains.   Says
Anson Call: "I had before seen him in vision, and now
saw, while he was talking, his countenance change to
white; not the deadly white of a bloodless face, but a
living, brilliant white.   He seemed absorbed in gazing at
something at a great distance, and said, 'I am gazing
upon the valleys of those mountains.'   This was followed
by a vivid description of the scenery of these mountains
as I have since become acquainted with it.

"Pointing to Shadrach Roundy and others he said :
'There are some men here who shall do a great work in
that land.'   Pointing to me, he said: 'There is Anson, he
shall go and shall assist in building cities from one end
of the country to the other, and you,' rather extending
the idea to all those he had spoken of, 'shall perform
as great a work as has been done by man, so that the
nations of the earth shall be astonished, and many of
them will be gathered in that land, and assist in building
cities and temples, and Israel shall be made to rejoice.'

"It is impossible to represent in words this scene
which is still vivid in my mind, of the grandeur of Joseph's

appearance, his beautiful descriptions of this land, and his wonderful prophetic utterances, as they emanated from the glorious inspirations which overshadowed him. There was a force and power in his exclamations of which the following is but a faint echo. 'Oh, the beauty of those snow-capped mountains! .The cool refreshing streams that are running down through those mountain gorges!' Then gazing in another direction, as if there was a change of locality! 'Oh, the scenes that this people will pass through! The dead that will lie between here and there!' Then, turning in another direction as if the scene changed again: ' Oh, the apostasy that will take place before my brethren reach that land!' Not an iota of this prophecy has failed of being fulfilled.'' This narrative, in part is a testimony of that fulfillment. Elder Call continues, ''Although I felt that Joseph was wrapt in vision, and that his voice was the voice of God, little did I realize the vast significance of those prophetic declarations compared with what I do now, with the experience of forty-five years that has intervened since they were uttered. As he drew to a close, the door of the house opened and we entered the building to transact the business for which we had gathered.''

The following, from the *History of Joseph Smith*, indicates the development in his mind of plans for the fulfillment of what he had seen in vision:

"On Sunday, the 25th of February, 1844, in a meeting at the assembly room of the Saints in Nauvoo, Joseph prophesied that within five years the Saints would be out of the power of their old enemies, whether apostates or of the world, and he asked the brethren to record the prediction.

"About this time he was inspired to direct the glance of the apostles to the western slope, where he said the people of God might establish themselves anew, worship after their own sincere convictions and work out the grand social problems of modern life. This subject was present in his mind and often upon his lips during the brief remainder of his earthly existence. Frequent councils were held and he directed the organization of an exploring expedition to venture beyond the Rocky Mountains.   *   *   *   *   *   *

"His purpose was not to sever the Saints from this sublime republic by any emigration; he saw that this country's domain must soon stretch from ocean to ocean. *   *   * And though he did not live to see the exodus of the Saints nor to send out the first pioneer party of explorers, his inspired suggestion was carried out, and through it his prediction was fulfilled that the Saints in five years would be beyond the power of their old enemies."

The career of the Prophet was drawing to a close. He had appointed and endowed others with authority and power to carry out his inspirations, and he and his brother Hyrum were assassinated in Carthage on the 27th of June, 1844.

A short time before the death of Joseph and Hyrum, being hard pressed by their enemies, with a few friends they crossed to the west bank of the Mississippi river, with the hope of yet leading the way to the fastnesses of the Rocky Mountains, and of assisting the Saints in realizing the bright, prophetic visions of their future. But through the over persuasion of his supposed friends, the Prophet was induced to return to Nauvoo to meet his fate.

He saw the crisis and met it with the following sentiments welling up from the very depths of a strong but keenly sensitive soul : "If my life has ceased to be of value to my friends, it has ceased to be of much value to myself." "I am going like a lamb to the slaughter."

He was succeeded by Brigham Young, the Presi-

3

dent of the Council of Twelve Apostles, and under his leadership the plans of Joseph were perfected and carried out.

In Illinois, as in Missouri, the Saints suffered a long series of persecutions. They were the cause of much sorrow and suffering, of which the present and future generations will get only an occasional glimpse from what is recorded of them. Under the culminating pressure of these the Saints commenced their long-contemplated move to the Rocky Mountains on the 5th and 6th of February, 1846, by beginning to cross the Mississippi river and forming an advanced camp on Sugar creek, a few miles from Nauvoo.

CHAPTER VI.

THE TWELVE IN CAMP—EXTREME COLD—A LAST VISIT TO
NAUVOO—EXPERIENCE OF ELDER MEEKS—THE HEROISM
OF THE SISTERS—DEATH OF EDWIN LITTLE—BRIGHAM
YOUNG vs. NAUVOO—SIXTEENTH ANNIVERSARY OF THE
ORGANIZATION OF THE CHURCH—GARDEN GROVE—
MOUNT PISGAH.

THE 15th of February, 1846, Brigham Young, Willard Richards and George A. Smith, with their families, moved across the river to the camp on Sugar creek, and the following day began to organize the people for the march westward. Previous to this the thermometer had indicated 20° below zero, and the Mississippi river had frozen over so that teams crossed on the ice.

About the same date that the movement from Nauvoo commenced, the ship *Brooklyn* sailed from the harbor of New York for the Bay of San Francisco with two

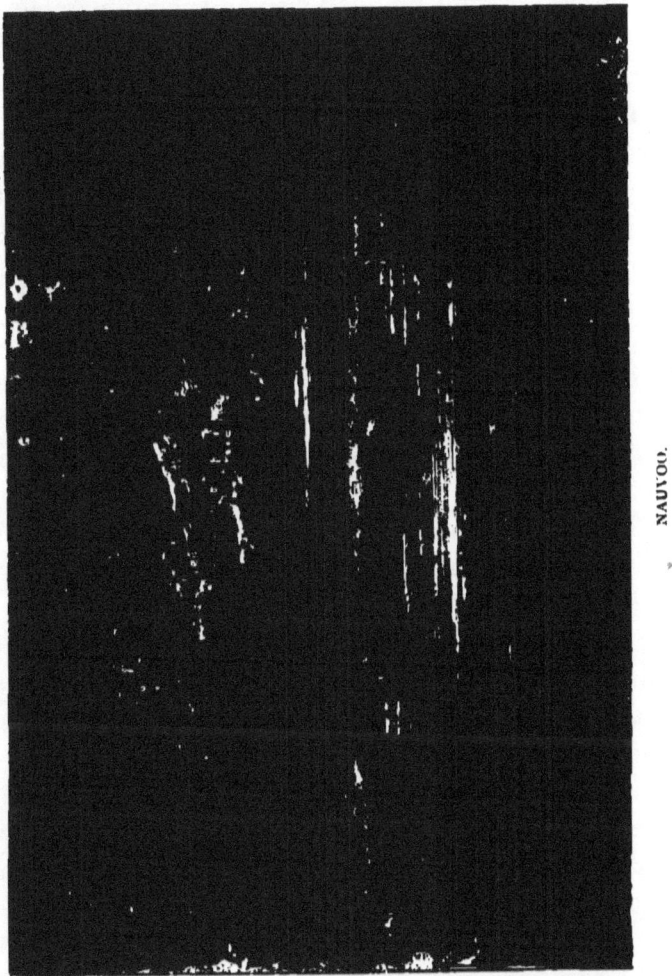

NAUVOO.

hundred and fourteen Saints, under the charge of Elder Samuel Brannan.   The object was to plant a colony on the Pacific coast.

Before leaving Christian civilization and launching out

onto the prairies of Iowa, Brigham Young, and others of
the Council of the Twelve, returned to Nauvoo to see
the deserted homes of their people for the last time, and
to bid adieu to their beloved city and temple. There was
much suffering in the camp on Sugar Creek. Violent
storms, excessive cold and fatiguing labor made heavy
drafts on the energy and vitality of the people, in many
cases thinly clad and poorly fed. It is safe to assert,
that the sum of suffering in getting away from Nauvoo
and in crossing the prairies of Iowa will never be footed
up by mortals, nor a tithe of the interesting and instructive experiences written.

The following narrative, showing how Elder P. Meeks
got out of Nauvoo will illustrate some of the difficulties
of the situation. It is dated Orderville, March 4th, 1882.
"I am now eighty-six years of age. My faculties are
more or less failing, and my memory with the others.
But there are some events of my life which I shall never
forget, for they are so thoroughly impressed upon my
mind that they seem a part of myself.

"The persecutions of Nauvoo I endured with the
Saints. I gave up my gun to a brother who, I thought,
could make a better use of it. For a substitute I fastened a strong table-fork on to the end of a pole about
six feet long. With this, when the alarm was given that
our enemies were approaching, I repaired to the temple,
prepared to do the best I could to defend myself and the
Saints.

"About the time the latter were crossing the Mississippi I had been east and was returning home. I passed
through Carthage where Joseph and Hyrum Smith were
martyred. Some Mormon-eaters of the place, took my
horse from me and, with oaths and imprecations, asserted
that they could cut my heart out. They confined me in

Carthage jail and in the room where Joseph and Hyrum
had been shot.   There I was compelled to remain in
sight of the stains made by their blood.   This was very
unpleasant and caused many sorrowful reflections.   I
remained there eight or ten days, when it was very necessary that I should be in Nauvoo to care for my family
and go west with the Saints.

"In these things was the extreme cruelty of the mob
manifest.   They were not willing to give us reasonable
time to get ready to leave, and when we were making
every possible exertion to do so would perplex, detain
and sometimes rob us, as they did me of my horse.   The
sheriff of the county knowing that I was innocent of any
crime, and that I wished to get away with my people,
favored me all he could.   Having occasion to go to
Nauvoo, he drew up some bonds for my appearance at
court, induced an irresponsible person to sign them, in
order to give him some excuse for letting me go, brought
out a horse from one of my friends in Nauvoo, got me
on to it and told me not to look back, for fear of exciting suspicion, until I reached a piece of timber a little
distance from the town.   I did as directed although it
was very difficult to not look back to see if I was pursued.
From the timber I made all haste to Nauvoo.

"I had been engaged with brother Wm. McCleary,
the Prophet's brother-in-law, getting up a wagon with
which to go west.   It was well along towards completion
when I was under the necessity of parting with my
interest in it for a barrel of flour.   I then succeeded in
trading a little, one horse wagon for a light, two horse
wagon.   My principal dependence for a team to haul
this was a pair of three-year-old, unbroke bullocks.   Their
chief characteristic was a wonderful ability for using their
hind legs without any regard to the convenience or safety

of those around them.   These unmanageable beasts were put on to the tongue of the wagon and, for a time, an old pair of oxen were used ahead of them to prevent their getting away or doing damage.

"I had a small flock of sheep which I had not time to sell.   These I left, together with my house and lot, the former containing my furniture and books.   With my rickety old wagon, and the little it would carry, I crossed the Mississippi river and joined the camp on Sugar creek.   I had an interest in a wagon shop which I left with Brother McCleary to turn over to some brother who needed assistance.   My right of ownership in the horse, which was taken from me in Carthage, I assigned to lawyer Edmunds for keeping me clear of legal process, until I could cross the river out of the immediate reach of such process from Illinois.

"I thought if I could get my old wagon to a blacksmith shop and expend about twenty dollars on it, it would enable me to get to the Missouri river.   In going from Nauvoo to Sugar creek, a short distance from the ferry across the river, the road passes over a hill.   The top of this hill, I was aware, was the last point from which I could see the Nauvoo temple   I have no words with which to convey a proper conception of my feelings when taking a last look at this sacred monument of the living, faith of the Saints, and which was associated in their minds with the heavenly and holy.   After the lapse of thirty-six years I can scarcely restrain my feelings when I write of it.   The rain and mud so swelled the timber and tightened the irons on my wagon, that without the aid of a blacksmith, I was able to continue my journey westward."

The first of March, 1846, the "Camp of Israel" on Sugar creek commenced its weary march for the Missouri river. It comprised nearly four hundred wagons, traveled five miles in a north-west direction and again encamped on Sugar creek. A well-known writer says: "The survivors of that journey will tell you they never suffered so much from the cold in their lives as they did on Sugar creek. And what of the Mormon women? Around them circles an almost tragic romance. Fancy may find abundant subject for graphic story of the devotion, the suffering, the matchless heroism of the 'Sisters,' in the telling incident that nine children were born to them the first night they encamped on Sugar creek, February 5th, 1846. That day they wept their farewells over their beloved city, or in the sanctuary of the temple in which they had hoped to worship till the end of life, but which they left, never to see again; that night suffering nature administered to them the mixed cup of woman's supremest joy and pain."

As a fitting continuation of the above, Eliza R. Snow says: "I was informed that on the first night of the encampment, nine children were born into the world, and from that time as we journeyed onward mothers gave birth to offspring under almost every variety of circumstances imaginable, except those to which they had been accustomed; some in tents, others in wagons—in rainstorms and in snow-storms. I heard of one birth which occurred under the rude shelter of a hut, the sides of which were formed of blankets fastened to poles stuck in the ground, with a bark roof through which the rain was dripping; kind sisters stood holding dishes to catch the water as it fell, thus protecting the new-comer and its mother from a shower bath as the little innocent first entered on the stage of human life."

The following is another picture from the same pen illustrating the situation: "Many of our sisters walked

all day, rain or shine, and at night prepared suppers for
their families, with no sheltering tents ; and then made
their beds in and under wagons that contained their
earthly all.   How frequently, with intense sympathy and
admiration, I watched the mother, when, forgetful of her
own fatigue and destitution, she took unwearied pains to
fix up, in the most palatable form, the allotted portion of
food, and as she dealt it out was cheering the hearts of
her homeless children, while, as I truly believed, her own
was lifted to God in fervent prayer that their lives might
be preserved."

In the midst of suffering there was comfort and con-
solation to these people in the thought that they were
leaving their enemies.   All were cheerful and happy in
anticipation of finding a resting place from persecution
somewhere in the solitudes of the Rocky Mountains.
Welling up in every heart to stimulate to exertion, to
nerve up to endurance was the hope, aye, the abiding
faith that in the mountains and deserts they would find
shelter from the pursuit of relentless enemies.

Exposure to the elements, excessive labor, want of
proper food and comfortable clothing forced many to lay
down their weary bodies in unmonumented graves, the
location of which has passed from the knowledge of
the living.   Among these was the eldest brother of the
writer, Edwin Little.   He left Nauvoo with his wife and
child with President Young.   He was a strong man,
physically, with a heart overflowing with kindness, he
assisted all who needed help if possible.   In this way he
wore himself out, took cold and died with inflammation of
the lungs, at Richardson's Point, fifty-five miles from
Nauvoo.   He was buried in a rough board coffin, the
best that could be had under the circumstances, and an
effort was made by his friends to hide his place of sep-

ulchre for fear it might be disturbed by the enemies of the Saints.

At this time Joseph Young, president of the Seventies, was still in Nauvoo. From Richardson's Point his brother Brigham expressed his personal feelings on the situation as follows: "I feel as though Nauvoo will be filled with all manner of abominations. It is no place for the Saints, and the Spirit whispers to me that the brethren had better get away as fast as they can. * * * Do not think, Brother Joseph, that I hate to leave my house and home. No, far from that, I am so free from bondage at this time, that Nauvoo looks like a prison to me. It looks pleasant ahead, but dark to look back."

Yes, it was deliverance from bondage. Better, far, the freedom of the wilderness than the chances of suffering and death from a vindictive populace, stirred up with religious hate until they ignore the common rights of humanity.

CHAPTER VII.

TO PROVIDE for the inhabitants of a city driven from their homes into a wilderness, exposed to the sweeping storms and bitter cold of winter, with nothing but the slender resources of the camp itself, is a task which but few men could hope to successfully accomplish. Besides the food supply for the people, it required daily large quantities of grain to sustain the animals of the camps, and these were necessities of existence, the people's means of deliverance from the perils that environed them.

The sixteenth anniversary of the organization of the Church found the camps on a branch of Shoal creek, where they remained over two weeks on account of rain and mud. The 6th of April nine or ten teams were sent to the settlements for corn. In about three days they returned, the most of them empty. There was but little strength in the old, dry grass or in the early, succulent growth, and the animals were weak.

Many reflections crowd around this sixteenth anniversary of the organization of the Church. Its situation was quite in keeping with its wonderful, eventful history. Three times in this short period had its members been forced to evacuate their homes *en masse*, and these sweeping exoduses were interspersed with minor drivings and plunderings. The gospel had been preached extensively in the United States, in the Canadas and in Europe. Two beautiful temples and several cities had been built, hundreds of the Saints had lost their lives, the direct and indirect results of persecution, and the inspired genius, the great prophet of the nineteenth century, who had led them in the God-like struggle to plant truth and righteousness in the earth, had been slain in the meridian of life.

After petitioning the Executive of every State in the Union for a place of rest, they were now seeking a refuge in the wilderness from the vindictiveness of Christian civilization. Let one who toiled and suffered speak of the situation and sentiments of the Saints at this time:

"April 11th. During the night the mud froze hard. To any but Saints our circumstances would have been very discouraging, for it seemed to be with the greatest difficulty that we could preserve our animals from actual starvation, and we were obliged to send off several day's journey to the Missouri settlements, on the south, to procure grain. Many of the people were nearly destitute of food, and many women and children suffered much from exposure to the inclemency of the weather and from the lack of the necessaries of life, such as they were in former times accustomed to enjoy. But in the midst of all these temporal afflictions the Saints were comforted in anticipation of better days. They looked forward to the time when these light afflictions should cease. * * * They were willing to endure hardships and privations for the sake of escaping the unrelenting persecutions of Gentile Christians, from whom they had received for many years nothing but cruelty and the most heart-rending oppression.

"Their desire was to establish themselves in some lonely valley of the mountains, in some sequestered spot where they and their children could worship God and obey His voice and prepare themselves for the glory which is to be revealed at the revelation of Jesus Christ.

"With these glorious anticipations, cheerfulness and joy seemed to animate every countenance and sufferings were endured without murmuring. The Twelve and other authorities met in council and determined to leave the settlements still further to our left and launch forth upon the broad prairies of the north-west, which were for hundreds of miles uninhabited."

The 24th of April Garden Grove, on the head-waters of Grand river, was reached. There it was decided to make a way station, a place of rest for those who were unable to proceed further. It was still a seasonable time for putting in corn and other crops. The camps were organized for labor, and by the 10th of May many houses were built, wells dug, extensive farms fenced, and the place assumed the appearance of having been occupied for years. On the 11th of May, a portion of the camp resumed their journey.

Of this time P. P. Pratt, in his autobiography, says:

"We called the place 'Garden Grove.' It is in Iowa, perhaps one hundred and fifty miles from Nauvoo. After assisting to fence this farm and build some log houses, I was despatched ahead by the Presidency with a small company to try to find another location. Crossing this branch of Grand river I now steered ,through the vast and fertile prairies and groves without a track or anything but a compass to guide me—the country was entirely wild and without inhabitants.

"Our course was west, a little north. We crossed small streams daily, which, on account of deep beds and miry banks, as well as on account of their being swollen by the rains, we had to bridge. After journeying thus for several days, and while lying encamped on a small stream which we had bridged, I took my horse and rode ahead some three miles in search of one of the main branches of Grand river which we had expected to find for some time. Riding about three or four miles through beautiful prairies, I came suddenly to some round and sloping hills, grassy, and covered with beautiful groves of timber, while alternate open groves and forests seemed blended in all the beauty and harmony of an English park, while beneath and beyond on the west rolled a main branch of Grand river, with its rich bottoms of alternate forest and prairie. As I approached this lovely scenery several deer and wolves being startled at the sight of me, abandoned the place and bounded away till lost from sight amid the groves.

"Being pleased and excited at the varied beauty before me, I cried out; this is *Mount Pisgah*. I returned to my camp, with the report of having found the long sought river, and we soon moved on and encamped under the shade of those beautiful groves. It was now late in May, and we halted here to await the arrival of the President and council. In a few days they arrived and formed a general encampment here, and finally formed a settlement, and surveyed and enclosed another farm of several' thousand acres. This became a town and resting place for the Saints for years, and is now known on the map of Iowa as a village and post-office named ' Pisgah.'"

Most of the Saints who stopped at these stations were pre-disposed to disease. The hardships they had endured, the large area of rich prairie soil newly turned up to the warm spring and summer sun, and other untoward conditions rapidly developed the germs of disease already sown.

Mrs. Zina D. Young, in her written experience at the latter place, furnishes a vivid illustration, not only of her own afflictions, but of the unrecorded sufferings of a multitude of others. She says, "We reached Mount Pisgah in May. I was now with my father, who had been appointed to preside over this temporary settlement of the Saints. But an unlooked-for event soon came. One evening Parley P. Pratt arrived, bringing the word from headquarters that the Mormon Battalion must be raised in compliance with the requisition of the government upon our people. And what did this news personally amount to, to me? That I had only my father to look after me now; for I had parted from my husband; my eldest brother, Dimick Huntington, with his family, had gone into the Battalion, and every man who could be spared was also enlisted. It was impossible for me to go on to Winter Quarters, so I tarried at Mount Pisgah with my father.

"But, alas! a still greater trial awaited me! The call for the Battalion had left many destitute. They had to live in wagons. But worse than destitution stared us in the face. Sickness came upon us, and death invaded our camp. Sickness was so prevalent and deaths so frequent that enough help could not be had to make coffins, and many of the dead were wrapped in their grave clothes and buried with split logs at the bottom of the grave and brush at the sides, that being all that could be done for them by their mourning friends. Too soon it became my turn to mourn. My father was taken sick, and in eighteen days he died. Just before he left us for his better home, he raised himself upon his elbow, and said: 'Man is like the flower or the grass cut down in an hour! Father unto Thee do I commend my spirit!' This said, he sweetly went to rest with the just, a martyr for the truth; for, like my dear mother, who died in the expulsion from Missouri, he died in the expulsion from

Nauvoo. Sad was my heart. I alone of all his children was there to mourn."

When the Saints were scattered from Garden Grove to Council Bluffs, under very unfortunate conditions, that memorable call was made on them by the United States for a battalion of five hundred men for the Mexican war. It drew heavily on the strength of the camps and necessarily modified both general and individual plans. Leaving them for the present on the lands of the Pottowatomie Indians, who made them welcome, we will go back and bring up our friend Elder Priddy Meeks.

He left Sugar creek with the Saints and in continuation of his narrative says: "When I arrived at the crossing of the Des Moines river, I found many wagons already there waiting to ferry over. As this would occasion considerable delay, I felt impressed to move up the river with the hope of finding some better opportunity of crossing. I traveled up it for two or three days and saw several others who had taken the same view of the situation as myself. We found an old ferry boat lying idle. This we repaired and crossed the river. Finding no road in the direction it was necessary to travel, we followed a divide, or the high ground between two streams, for several days. It rained almost incessantly, but still we made some progress each day.

"Notwithstanding our untoward circumstances, we were cheerful and happy. We ate our water gruel when we had nothing better, which was much of the time. I had a fiddle with me in the use of which I was sufficiently proficient to grind out music for evening dances. This enabled us to diversify our lives with the merry dance around our camp fires, when the weather would permit.

"After traveling several days we discovered in the distance white objects moving slowly over the prairies.

Various were our conjectures as to what we were indebted for the unusual appearance.   Some surmised they
might be a flock of white cranes feeding, but a nearer
approach developed them into wagons.   It was President
Young's company traveling in nearly the same direction
as ourselves.

" Arriving at the wayside settlement of the Saints
called Mount Pisgah, I stopped to make a temporary
home and raise a crop.   I assisted in fencing a field in
which I planted corn and vegetables.   I also built quite
a comfortable cabin where I anticipated spending the
winter.   I farmed in connection with Brother Christian
Houtz.   After accomplishing considerable labor I was
directed by President Young to go on to the Bluffs.
I left my interest in the crops to Brother Houtz, and
directed him to let some poor brother, who might
arrive late in the season, have my cabin.   He afterwards turned it over to Joseph W. Johnson.   Soon
after I arrived at Council Bluffs the Mormon Battalion
was raised for the Mexican war.   My son-in-law Orson
B. Adams was the second man who volunteered to go
and I took charge of his family and effects."

CHAPTER VIII.

MILLER AND EMMETT COMPANY—THE CAMP ON RUNNING
WATER—THE AGED CHIEF OF THE PONCAS—BREAKING
UP OF THE CAMP ON RUNNING WATER—WINTER QUARTERS
LOCATED AND A TOWN BUILT — SISTER BATHSHEBA
SMITH'S DESCRIPTION OF THE HOUSES—TEN THOUSAND
SAINTS ON THE MOVE ACROSS IOWA.

IT HAD been contemplated, by the leaders of the
Church, to send a company of pioneers to the
mountains the same year. An unsuccessful effort was
made. The following account of that effort is from Mr.
Anson Call's Biographical Sketch in *Tullidge's History
of Northern Utah*:

"George Miller and James Emmett, under false pre-
tences, had deceived many of the Saints and drawn off
fifty-two wagons into the western wilderness. Brigham
Young and Heber C. Kimball each organized a company of seventy-five wagons for the avowed purpose of
traveling westward.

"They left Elk Horn river for the mountains by
order of the Apostles, the 22nd of July, 1846. They
traveled up the Platte river to the Pawnee missionary
station on the Loupe Fork, where they found the company of Miller and Emmett.

"When encamped on the west side of the Loupe Fork,
an express came from the Apostles, directing them not
to travel any further west that season. The express also
brought instructions for the organization of a council of
twelve men, to direct the affairs of the companies, and
they were named in the communication. The council
was organized on the 8th of August, 1846. Bishop Geo.
Miller was its president.

4

"The next move was to find a place where the companies could winter.   For this purpose the country around the Platte river and Loupe Fork were explored without gratifying results.   They counseled with two Ponca chiefs, who invited them to winter with their people on the Missouri river.   They were guaranteed protection, plenty of feed for their animals, and timber with which to build houses.   They accepted the invitation of these friendly Lamanites, and with nine days travel arrived at their camp.   A place was selected on the west side of the mouth of the Running Water river, and one hundred and twenty-five log houses were built in fort form.

"Nucanumpa, the aged chief of the nation, was taken sick and sent for the council.   He said he had told his captains not to distrust the Mormons, and they had agreed that they would not.   He wished to talk all he could before he died ; had killed his best dog, and after it was eaten he wanted to commence to talk.

"The Mormon leaders assisted the chiefs to eat the dog, when the talk commenced through the interpreter, Battese.   The chief said much about dying and another world.   He desired his Mormon friends to prepare such a stone as he had seen in St. Louis, and put it at the head of his grave with his name and title on it.   The following day this noble specimen of the aboriginal American went to his departed fathers, and a stone was put at the head of his grave as he had requested.

"Rushes were plenty for cattle, but it was a hard winter and many died.   The Poncas did as they agreed, but the Sioux stole some horses and cattle.

"George Miller, being in authority, seemed infatuated with the idea that he was the real head of the people, and that when spring came he could lead them into the wilderness away from the Apostles.

"The 27th of February, 1847, Apostles E. T. Benson and Erastus Snow arrived in camp with instructions from their quorum for the people to return to Winter Quarters, and replenish their teams and their stock of provisions preparatory to going to the mountains.   After delivering their message they departed.

"The council of twelve was called together and with its president came James Emmett, who was not a member, but who was permitted by request of Bishop Miller, to take a part in its deliberations. The president arose and addressed the council, saying in substance that he did not consider the Twelve had any right to dictate to the people of that camp; that he was their appointed leader and it was their duty to follow him into the wilderness among the Lamanites, in fulfillment of a special mission conferred upon him by the Prophet Joseph. James Emmett followed in the same strain. It then being the privilege of each member of the council to express his views, Anson Call, who had from its organization been an active member, arose and stated his, the summary of which was that the twelve Apostles were the legitimate leaders of the Saints and that he should follow their counsel. The ten members of the council who followed him were unanimous in expressing the same views.

"Bishop Miller saw the reins slipping out of his hands and vented his rage in an impetuous speech. All the council excepting its president, decided to call the people together and lay the subject before them, that they might understandingly choose for themselves whether they would stay with Miller and Emmett, or return to Winter Quarters. This was done and preparations were at once commenced for the return journey. On the 3rd of April the camp moved out for Winter Quarters, and only five or six wagons remained with Miller and Emmett.   *   *   *   *   *   *   *   *

"The action of Bishop Miller in opposing the Apostles had opened the eyes of all who had been deceived. Thus by a far-seeing policy of the Apostles, or by a chain of special providences, were many honest people saved from temporal ruin, and brought back under their legitimate leaders, to act their part in the grand scheme of empire-founding in the Rocky Mountains. Arriving at Winter Quarters the companies were broken up."

Some of the Saints remained at the way stations of

Garden Grove and Mount Pisgah. Many others settled on the Pottowatomie lands, built houses, cut hay for their animals, gathered sustenance for their families, and made every possible preparation for the coming winter. The leaders of the Church located a place on the west bank

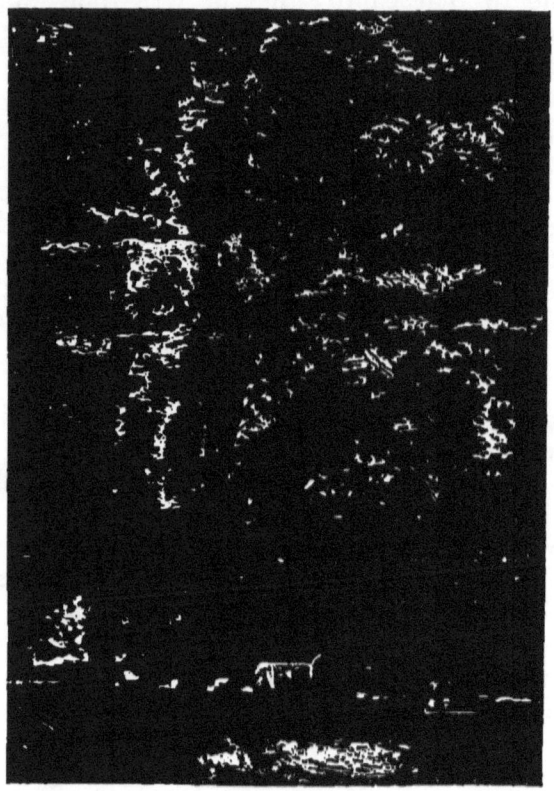

THE FERRY.

of the Missouri river which they called Winter Quarters. The name sufficiently indicates the object. There seven hundred houses were built, suggestive that that many families located there, comprising four thousand people.

The narrative of Mrs. Bathsheba W. Smith furnishes a good illustration of the make up of the houses of this

impromptu city: "Our chimneys were made of sods, cut
with a spade in the form of a brick; clay was pounded
in to make our fireplaces and hearths. In our travels
the winds had literally blown our tents to pieces, so that
we were glad to get into cabins. The most of roofs
were made of timber, covered with clay. The floors
were split and hewed puncheon; the doors were generally made of the same material, of cottonwood and
linn.· Many houses were covered with oak-shakes, fastened on with weight-poles. A few were covered with
shingles. A log meeting-house was built, about twenty-
four by forty feet, and the hewn floor was frequently
used for dancing. A grist-mill was built and run by
water-power, and in addition to this, several horse-mills
and hand-mills were used to grind corn."

In the general epistle to the Saints of December
23rd, 1847, it is estimated that in the month of July,
1846, there were more than two thousand emigrating
wagons between Council Bluffs on the Missouri river and
Nauvoo. The number of people accompanying these
wagons may be reasonably estimated at ten thousand.
Probably half as many more scattered out from Nauvoo
in various directions, to get away from enemies and
to accumulate means to follow the main body of their
people.

Winter Quarters was the third, and by far the most
important way station between Nauvoo and the objective
point of the "Camps of Israel," the valleys of the Rocky
Mountains. There, and in the surrounding country, they
were to gather up their strength and mature their plans
before grappling with the difficulties of a thousand miles
of desert travel. In log cabins and dugouts, hastily constructed under the pressure of necessity, must the
Saints endure the rigors of winter and take the chances

of life and death with bodies worn, constitutions broken
from excessive toil and exposure, often half famished
for want of proper food and chilled for want of comfortable shelter and clothing. To say that a city of the
dead increased rapidly beside that of the living is stating
the case mildly. To say that the living were decimated
would not probably be an over estimate of the mortality
during that season of struggling for existence.

CHAPTER IX.

THE REMNANT IN NAUVOO—A BRAVE DEFENCE AGAINST THE MOB—ELDER BULLOCK'S THRILLING NARRATIVE— THE HANCOCK TRAGEDY.

HAVING located the Saints who left Nauvoo in the
winter and spring of 1846, we will return and
record the fate of the poor and afflicted who were of
necessity left until teams could be sent from the advanced
camps to move them away. The vindictive spirit in the
inhabitants of the surrounding country which had forced
the main body of the Saints from their homes in midwin-
ter, could not let this helpless remnant remain in peace
until friends could assist them. In the fore part of September, 1846, the mob marched on Nauvoo in force.
There were only about one hundred and fifty men and
boys, generally poor in health and in an impoverished
condition, to defend the place against an enemy several
times their number. They made a desperate effort in
self-defence, but were overpowered.

A competent eye witness may tell what he saw others suffer and what he endured. The writer of the following letter, Elder Thomas Bullock, was known to many thousands of the Saints. The copy of the letter, from which the writer has taken these excerpts, was without date, but the letter was doubtless written the winter after the events described in it took place. It was addressed to Elder F. D. Richards, then in England.

"WINTER QUARTERS, CAMP OF ISRAEL,
"OMAHA NATION.

"*Beloved Franklin:*

"In the month of August, 1846, I was taken very sick with the ague and fever, and soon after my wife and four little children were taken with the same disease. In this condition we continued until the 16th of September. On that day a friend, George Wardell, packed up my goods on two wagons and removed them to his house to be out of danger from the cannon balls, which were flying about too thick for anyone to feel anyway comfortable. He located us behind his house out of danger. As I did not see this battle, I don't write much about it. But I know for a whole week the roar of cannon and the sharp cracking of rifles kept us in awful suspense and anxiety.

"Our devoted city was defended by about one hundred and fifty poor, sickly, persecuted Saints, while it . was cannonaded by from fifteen hundred to two thousand demoniacs in the shape of men, who had sworn to raze our temple to the ground, to burn the city, ravish our wives and daughters and drive the remainder of the people into the river. With what desperation our little band fought against such an overwhelming horde of desperadoes, I leave you to judge. My flesh seems to crawl on my bones at the remembrance of those scenes. On the 17th of September, two thousand men with five hundred wagons marched into the city. Such yelling and hooting I never before heard from civilized men, nor even from the wild savages. Terror and dismay surely for once overcame the sick, the poor women and children.

"While the leaders were haranguing their mob followers at the rope walk, by Hibbard's, such an awful and infuriated noise I never before heard, though I was in Warsaw street, more than a quarter of a mile from the scene. We expected an indiscriminate massacre was commencing. Myself and others who were sick were carried by friends into the tall weeds and into the woods, while all who were able to do so hid themselves. Many crossed the river leaving everything behind them. As night approached we returned to our shelter. But, O God, what a night to remember!

"The next morning at nine o'clock saw me, my wife, my four children, my sister-in-law Fanny, my blind mother-in-law, all shaking with the ague in one house, only George Wardell to do anything for us, when a band of about thirty men, armed with guns, with fixed bayonets, pistols in belt, the captain with sword in his hand, and the stars and stripes flying about, marched opposite my sheltering roof. The captain called and demanded that the owner of the two wagons be brought out. I was raised from my bed, led out of doors, supported by my sister-in-law and the rail fence. I was then asked if those goods were mine. I replied, 'They are.' The captain then stepped out to within four feet of me, pointed his sword at my throat, while four others presented their guns with bayonets within two feet of my body, and said, 'If you are not off from here in twenty minutes my orders are to shoot you.' I replied, 'Shoot away, for you will only send me to heaven a few hours quicker, for you may see I am not for this world many hours longer.' The captain then told me, 'If you will renounce Mormonism you may stay here and we will protect you.' I replied, 'This is not my house; yonder is my house,' pointing to it, 'which I built and paid for with the gold that I earned in England. I never committed the least crime in Illinois, but I am a Mormon, and if I live I shall follow the Twelve.' Then said the captain, 'I am sorry to see you and your sick family, but if you are not gone when I return in half an hour, my orders are to kill you and every Mormon in the place.'

"But Oh, the awful cursing and swearing these men did pour out! I tremble when I think of it. George and Edwin drove my wagons down to the ferry and were searched five times for firearms. The mob took a pistol, and though they promised to return it when I got across the river, I have not seen it to this day. While on the bank of the river I crawled to the margin to bid a sister who was going down to St. Louis good bye. While there a mobber shouted out, 'Look! Look! there is a skeleton bidding death good bye.' So you can imagine the poor, sickly condition of both of us.

"On Wednesday, the 23rd of September, while in my wagon on the slough opposite Nauvoo, a tremendous thunder shower passed over which drenched everything we had; not a dry thread left to us; the bed a pool of water, my wife and sister-in-law lading it out by basins full, and I in a burning fever and insensible, with all my hair shorn off to cure me of my disease. Many had not a wagon or tent to shelter them from the pitiless blast. One case I will mention. A poor woman stood among the bushes, wrapping her cloak around her three little orphan children, to shield them from the storm as well as she could through that terrible night, during which there was one continued roar of thunder and blaze of lightning while the rain descended in torrents.

"The mob seized every person in Nauvoo they could find, led them to the river and threw them in. I will mention one individual case. They seized Charles Lambert, led him to the river and in the midst of cursing and swearing one man said, 'By the holy saints, I baptize you by order of the commanders of the temple,' plunged him in backwards and then said, 'The commandments must be fulfilled, G— d— you, you must have another dip.' They threw him in on his face, then sent him on the flat boat across the river, with the promise that if he returned to Nauvoo they would shoot him. Such were some of the scenes that occurred when we were driven from Nauvoo."   *   *   *   *   *   *   *

Elder Bullock wrote the above under the keen sensibility of one who suffered about all that could be endured.   We might expect the picture to be overdrawn but the following from the *Mississippian*, a paper published at Rock Island, about seventy miles from Nauvoo, fittingly parallels Elder Bullock's letter in intensity of expression and vividness of coloring.   The *Mississippian* heads the article,

"THE HANCOCK TRAGEDY.

"Such is our feeling, our indignation, our burning sense of shame, of disgrace, in regard to recent affairs in Hancock county that we hardly know what to say—how to begin.   * . *   *   *   *   *   *

"The savage will relent over the infant's wail, but these infuriated men see the haggard mother with her dying infant, nerved by despair, and goaded by fear, rushing from the city, and they can laugh at her misery, taunt her as she passes, and add speed to her faltering steps by their abuse, their insults and jeers.   Aye, too, many of these helpless, dying children, these more than widowed mothers, have fathers and husbands now engaged in the service of the United States, fighting for their country.   *   *   *   And such is the protection afforded to their wives and children, turned out from their only shelter, none but heaven's canopy, with no hope but in God's mercy!   And to such a pass has mob law come in the state of Illinois.   Men deliberately taken out and shot, denied a trial, and their last appeal for mercy meeting no response.   Men surrendering themselves under the most solemn pledges and faith of the state, confined within prison walls, guarded by men under a solemn promise to protect them from all violence, basely surrendered to armed ruffians and brutally massacred while awaiting a trial under the laws of their country!   Men unsafe even with their female companions, but inhumanly shot on the highway! Men resorting to the cruelest tortures to wring from their victims confessions of crime! Men with their wives and children compelled to see their houses, their substance, all destroyed before their eyes, with their sick and dying around them, and then driven out into the wilderness to become the prey of savages, or the victims of famine.

"We turn from the picture with disgust and loathing. If such is to be the state of things, we with our brethren may next become the victims of mob violence because we are immersionists and close communionists—our Methodist friends because they shout—the Presbyterians by their infant sprinkling, the Episcopalians for reading their prayers! It is time at any expense, at any cost, for every citizen, for every officer to stand forward and defend, maintain, and obey the laws."

CHAPTER IX.

COL. THOMAS L. KANE'S GRAPHIC PICTURE OF THE NAUVOO EXPULSION—THE MIRACULOUS FLOCK OF QUAILS—KIND PROVIDENCE CARES FOR THE SAINTS—CLOSING EVENT ON THE BANKS OF THE MISSISSIPPI.

THE account of Nauvoo and surrounding country, laid waste by religious persecution would not be complete without that immortal picture of its desolation drawn by the philanthropist, Thomas L. Kane, in a lecture before the Historical Society of Philadelphia.

"A few years ago," said Colonel Kane, "ascending the upper Mississippi in the autumn when its waters were low, I was compelled to travel by land past the region of the rapids. My road lay through the Half-Breed

tract, a fine section of Iowa, which the unsettled state of
its land titles had appropriated as a sanctuary for
coiners, horse thieves, and other outlaws.   I had left my
steamer at Keokuk, at the foot of the Lower Fall to hire
a carriage, and to contend for some fragments of a dirty
meal with the swarming flies, the only scavengers of the
locality.

"From this place to where the deep water of the
river returns, my eye wearied to see everywhere sordid
vagabond and idle settlers ; and a country marred without being improved by their careless hands.   I was
descending the last hill-side upon my journey when a
landscape in delightful contrast broke upon my view.
Half encircled by a bend of the river, a beautiful city lay
glittering in the fresh morning sun, its bright new dwellings, set in cool green gardens ranging up around a
stately dome-shaped hill which was crowned by a noble
marble edifice, whose high tapering spire was radiant
with white and gold.   The city appeared to cover several
miles, and beyond it, in the background, there rolled off
a fair country chequered by the careful lines of fruitful
husbandry.   The unmistakable marks of industry, enter-
prise, and educated wealth everywhere made the scene
one of singular and most striking beauty.

" It was a natural impulse to visit this inviting region.
I procured a skiff, and rowing across the river, landed
at the chief wharf of the city.   No one met me there.   I
looked and saw no one.   I could hear no one move,
though the quiet everywhere was such that I heard the
flies buzz, and the water ripples break against the shallow
of the beach.   I walked through the solitary streets.   The
town lay as in a dream under some deadening spell of
lonliness from which I almost feared to wake it, for plainly
it had not slept long.   There was no grass growing up

in the paved ways ; rains had not entirely washed away
the prints of dusty foot-steps.

"Yet I went about unchecked.   I went into empty
workshops, ropewalks and smithies.   The spinner's wheel
was idle, the carpenter had gone from ·his work-bench
and shavings, his unfinished sash and casing.   Fresh
bark was in the tanner's vat, and the fresh-chopped light-
wood stood piled against the baker's oven.   The blacksmith's shop was cold, but his coal-heap and ladling
pool and crooked water horn were all there, as if he had
just gone off for a holiday.   No work-people anywhere
looked to know my errand.

"If I went into the gardens clinking the wicket-latch
loudly after me, to pull the marygolds, hearts-ease, and
lady-slippers, and draw a drink with the water-sodden
well-bucket and its noisy chain, or knocking off with my
stick the tall, heavy-headed dahlias and sunflowers,
hunted over the beds for cucumbers and love-apples—no
one called out to me from any opened window, or dog
sprang forward to bark an alarm.

"I could have supposed the people hidden in the
houses, but the doors were unfastened, and when at last
I timidly entered them, I found dead ashes white upon the
hearths, and had to tread a-tiptoe as if walking down the
aisle of a country church, to avoid arousing irreverent
echoes from the naked floors.   On the outskirts of the
town was the city grave-yard; but there was no record
of plague there, nor did it in anywise differ much from
other Protestant-American cemeteries.   Some of the
mounds were not long sodded.   Some of the stones were
newly set, their dates recent and their black inscriptions
glossy in the mason's hardly dried lettering ink.   Beyond the grave-yard, out in the fields, I saw in one spot
hard by where the fruited boughs of a young orchard

had been roughly torn down, the still smouldering em-
bers of a barbacue fire that had been constructed of rails
from the fencing around it.   It was the latest sign of life
there.   Fields upon fields of heavy-headed yellow grain
lay rotting ungathered upon the ground.   No one at
hand to take in their rich harvest.

"As far as the eye could reach, they stretched
away, they sleeping too, in the hazy air of autumn.   Only
two portions of the city seemed to suggest the import
of this mysterious solitude.   On the eastern suburb the
houses looking out upon the country showed by their
splintered woodwork and walls battered to the foundation, that they had lately been the mark of a destructive
cannonade.   And in and around the splendid temple
which had been the chief object of my admiration
armed men were barracked, surrounded by their stacks
of musketry and pieces of heavy ordnance.   These
challenged me to render an account of myself and why I
had had the temerity to cross the water without a written
permit from the leader of their band.

"Though these men were generally more or less
under the influence of ardent spirits, after I had explained
myself as a passing stranger, they seemed anxious to
gain my good opinion.   They told the story of the dead
city, that it had been a notable manufacturing and commercial mart, sheltering over twenty thousand persons;
that they had waged war with its inhabitants for several
years, and had finally been successful, only a few days
before my visit, in an action fought in front of the ruined
suburb; after which, they had driven them forth at the
point of the sword.   The defence, they said, had been
obstinate, but gave way on the third day's bombardment.
They boasted greatly of their prowess, especially in this
battle, as they called it; but I discovered they were not

of one mind as to certain of the exploits that had distinguished it, one of which, as I remember, was, that they had slain a father and his son, a boy of fifteen, not long residents of the fated city, whom they admitted to have borne a character without reproach.

"They also conducted me inside the massive sculptured walls of the curious temple, in which they said the banished inhabitants were accustomed to celebrate the mystic rites of an unhallowed worship. They particularly pointed out to me certain features of the building, which, having been the peculiar objects of a former superstitious regard, they had as a matter of duty, sedulously defiled and defaced. The reputed sites of certain shrines they had thus particularly noticed, and various sheltered chambers, in one of which was a deep well, constructed, they believed, with a dreadful design.

"Besides these, they led me to see a large and deep chiseled, marble vase or basin, supported upon twelve oxen, also of marble, and of the size of life, of which they told some romantic stories. They said the deluded persons, most of whom were emigrants from a great distance, believed their Deity countenanced their reception here of a baptism of regeneration, as proxies for whomsoever they held in warm affection in the countries from which they had come. That here parents "went into the water' for their lost children, children for their parents, widows for their spouses and young persons for their lovers. That thus the great vase came to be for them associated with all dear and distant memories, and was therefore the object of all others in the building to which they attached the greatest degree of idolatrous affection. On this account the victors had so diligently desecrated it as to render the apartment in which it was contained too noisome to abide in.

"They permitted me also to ascend into the steeple to see where it had been lightning struck on the Sabbath before, and to look out, east and south, on wasted farms, like those I had seen near the city, extending till they were lost in the distance.   Here, in the face of pure day, close to the scar of Divine wrath left by the thunder bolt, were fragments of food, cruses of liquor and broken drinking vessels, with a bass drum and a steamboat signal bell, of which I afterwards learned the use with pain.

"It was after nightfall when I was ready to cross the river on my return.   The wind had freshened since the sunset, and the water beating roughly into my little boat I headed higher up the stream than the point I had left in the morning, and landed where a faint, glimmering light invited me to steer.

"Here, among the docks and rushes, sheltered only by the darkness, without roof between them and the sky, I came upon a crowd of several hundred human creatures, whom my movements roused from uneasy slumber on the ground.

"Passing these on my way to the light, I found it came from a tallow candle in a paper funnel shade, such as is used by street venders of apples and peanuts, and which, flaring and guttering away in the bleak air of the water, shone flickeringly on the emaciated features of a man in the last stages of a bilious remittent fever. They had done their best for him.   Over his head was something like a tent, made of a sheet or two, and he rested on a but partially ripped open, old straw mattress, with a hair sofa cushion under his head for a pillow. His gaping jaw and glazing eye told how short a time he would monopolize these luxuries, though a seemingly bewildered and excited person, who might have been his wife, seemed to find hope in occasionally forcing him to swallow awkwardly measured sips of the tepid river water from a burned and battered, bitter smelling tin coffee pot.   Those who knew better had furnished the apothecary he needed, a toothless old bald-head, whose manner had the repulsive dullness of a man familiar with death scenes.   He, so long as I remained, mumbled in his patient's ear a monotonous and melancholy prayer, between the pauses of which I heard the hiccough and sobbing of two little girls who were sitting upon a piece of drift wood outside.

"Dreadful, indeed, was the suffering of these forsaken beings; bowed and cramped by cold and sunburn, alternating as each weary day and night dragged on, they were, almost all of them, the crippled victims of disease.   They were there because they had no homes, nor hospital, nor poor house, nor friends to offer them any.   They could not satisfy the feeble cravings of their sick, they had not bread to quiet the fractious hunger-cries of their children.   Mothers and babes, daughters and grand parents, all of them alike, were bivouacked in tatters, wanting even covering to comfort those whom the sick shiver of fever was searching to the marrow.

"These were Mormons, famishing in Lee County, Iowa, in the fourth week of the month of September, in the year of our Lord 1846.   The city, it was Nauvoo, Illinois.   The Mormons were the owners of that city, and the smiling country around.   And those who had stopped their planes, who silenced their hammers, their axes, their shuttles and their workshop wheels.   Those who had put out their fires, who had eaten their food, spoiled their orchards and trampled under foot their thousands of acres of unharvested bread; these were the keepers of their dwellings, the carousers in their temple, whose drunken riot insulted the ears of their dying.

5

"I think it was as I turned from the wretched night watch of which I have spoken, that I first listened to the sounds of revel of a party of the guard within the city. Above the distant hum of the voices of many, occasionally rose distinct the loud oath-tainted exclamation and the falsely intonated scrap of vulgar song; but lest this requiem should go unheeded, every now and then when their boisterous orgies strove to attain a sort of ecstatic climax, a cruel spirit of insulting frolic carried some of them up into the high belfry of the temple steeple, and there, with the wicked childishness of inebriates, they whooped and shrieked and beat the drum that I had seen, and rang in charivaric unison their loud-tongued steam-boat bell.

"There were, all told, not more than six hundred and forty persons who were thus lying on the river flats. But the Mormons in Nauvoo and its dependencies had been numbered the year before at over twenty thousand. Where were they? They had last been seen, carrying in mournful trains their sick and wounded, halt and blind, to disappear behind the western horizon, pursuing the phantom of another home. Hardly anything else was known of them; and people asked with curiosity, 'What has been their fate—what their fortunes?'"

A few days after Col. Kane's visit to Nauvoo and the camp of sickness and death on the west side of the river, a number of wagons arrived from the advanced camps of the Saints for the deliverance of this forlorn remnant. Elder Bullock's letter continues:

"On the 9th of October several wagons with oxen having been sent by the Twelve to fetch the poor Saints away, were drawn out in a line on the river banks ready to start. But hark! what noise is that? See! the quails descend. They alight close by our little camp of twelve wagons, run past each wagon tongue, when they arise, fly around the camp three times, descend and again run the gauntlet past each wagon. See! the sick knock them down with sticks and the little children catch them alive with their hands! Some are cooked for breakfast.

"While my family were seated on the wagon tongue and ground, having a washtub for a table, behold they come again! One descends upon our tea-board in the midst of our cups, while we were actually around the table eating our breakfast, which a little boy eight years old catches alive with his hands. They rise again, the flocks increase in number, seldom going seven rods from our camp, continually flying around the camp, sometimes under the wagons, sometimes over, and even into the wagons where the poor, sick Saints are lying in bed; thus having a direct manifestation from the Most High that although we are driven by men He has not forsaken us, but that His eyes are continually over us for good. At noon, having caught alive about fifty and killed about fifty more, the captain gave orders not to kill any more, as it was a direct manifestation and visitation from the Lord. In the afternoon hundreds were flying at a time. When our camp started at three p. m. there could not have been less than five hundred, some said there were fifteen hundred, flying around the camp.

"Thus am I a witness to this visitation. Some Gentiles who were at the camp marveled greatly. Even passengers on a steamboat going down the river looked with astonishment."

As welcome to this famished "forlorn hope" were these quails as the heavenly manna to the hungry hosts of ancient Israel in the wilderness. What a comfort to these suffering exiles to grasp in their faith the assurance that although men tried to destroy them they were not

forsaken of their God.   Could the skeptic wish to ignore
the fact that in this visitation a kindly Providence manifested sympathy for suffering humanity?

The 9th of October, 1846, was an important day in
the history of the Nauvoo Exodus.   It was the distinct
closing of that immortal event on the banks of the Mississippi river.   The heritage of the Saints was fully in
possession of their enemies.   The poor remnant that
from the force of circumstances were compelled to
remain to the last, were on the trail of their people
towards the setting sun.   The interests of this traveling
Zion were now wholly transferred to the Missouri river.

CHAPTER XI.

THE WILDERNESS ECHOES WITH THE SOUND OF INDUSTRY
—THE PIONEERS LEAVE WINTER QUARTERS—THEIR
MILITARY ORGANIZATION—THE FIRST BUFFALO HUNT—
REPRESENTATIVE LADY PIONEERS—A PROPHET GENERAL
WITH APOSTLES FOR LIEUTENANTS — THE PRAIRIE ON
FIRE—VAST HERDS OF BUFFALO — THIEVING INDIANS.

" The time of winter now is o'er,
    There's verdure on the plain ;
We leave our sheltering roofs once more
    And to our tents again."—*E. R. S.*

WITH several hundred Saints wintering with the
Indians on Running Water river, one hundred and
fifty miles above Winter Quarters; with a large portion
of the people on the Pottowatomie lands on the east side

of the Missouri; with several thousands, including the indigent and helpless, the families of men in the Battalion who needed direct attention from the authorities; with the general supervision of large herds of animals, the preservation of which from marauding Indians was a necessity of existence, imposed very heavy responsibilities on Brigham Young and his fellow Apostles.

The Saints bore their afflictions with the fortitude characteristic of them. The long winter gave their leaders ample time to perfect their plans for the important operations of the ensuing season. As the spring of 1847 opened, this wilderness, so lately occupied by only a few Indians, resounded with the sounds of intelligent, well directed labor. There was energetic purpose in every stroke of an ax, every turn of a wagon wheel or of a plow. Those who had been selected to make up the company of pioneers and those who expected to follow them that season "to the west," were busy preparing for their advent into the wilderness. Those expecting to remain, with equally decided purpose, were fencing fields, breaking up the virgin soil and preparing to raise food for themselves and for those who might take their places when they departed for the place which all expected would be found for them in the desert.

The 7th of April, 1847, the pioneers began to move out of Winter Quarters for their place of gathering on the Elk Horn river. After organizing they started on their long-contemplated journey the 14th of April. The company consisted of seventy-three wagons and carriages, one hundred and forty-three men, three women and two children, in all, one hundred and forty-eight souls. With one exception the animals of the camp were horses and mules; that exception was a milch cow belonging to Lorenzo D. Young. Doubtless previous training had fitted this cow for the proper performance of her part as a pioneer, for she daily followed the camp without trouble to anyone. Mrs. Harriet Young was the pioneer butter-maker of the Mormon camps on the plains, for she had thoughtfully taken along a small churn, so that her husband and sometimes friends enjoyed the luxury of a taste of butter as well as milk for their tea and coffee.

It was a matter of serious consideration on the part of President Young on account of emergencies that might arise, whether any woman should accompany the pioneers. The following considerations might well decide in their favor. So far the wives and daughters of the Elders had bravely shared dangers and sacrifices with them. They were not likely to encounter any more hardships and risks than had already characterized much of their lives. When the subject was fairly considered their past record evidently entitled them to a representation in "The camps of Israel," and why should that of the pioneers be an exception? The representative ladies were Mrs. Clara Young, wife of Brigham Young, Mrs. Elleh Kimball wife of H. C. Kimball and Mrs. Harriet Young wife of Lorenzo D. Young.

This company was made up of a choice selection of Elders whose previous experiences and known abilities gave an assurance that the organization was well adapted to meet any probable emergencies that might arise. Those intending to follow them the same season, were advised to wait several weeks until the weather should become warmer, and the grass have time to grow.

The pioneers were efficiently organized as a military body of which Brigham Young was the chosen leader. A prophet-general, leading the van of his shattered people into the wilderness with Apostles for lieutenants, marking out the road for the thousands who were to follow, and selecting a location abounding in profusion with elements of comfort and wealth, where they could recruit their energies and increase in numbers until able to combat the antagonisms which they must meet in the fulfillment of their mission.

They were pioneers in the strictest sense, for there was no beaten track for them to follow. They struck out on the north side of the beautiful Platte which for five hundred miles wound its serpentine way through a magnificent country, with scarcely a mark of civilization. They crossed several small streams before arriving at the Loupe Fork of the Platte. This they found the most dangerous stream to ford on the whole route, having an ever changing bottom of quicksand.

It was necessary for the men to wade the stream in crossing their wagons. The water was up to their waists and as the weather was yet cool, this made them very uncomfortable. From the ford they followed a dividing ridge to the head of Grand Island, where they first came in sight of buffalo. This was something new in their varied experiences. The sight made a sensation for in it was a spice of romance. A buffalo hunt was at once inaugurated. Several men mounted their horses with the view of attacking a band in sight, but a considerable distance away. Coming up with them they gave chase in splendid style along the side of a ridge in full view of the camp. The hunters mingled with the noble game and all were soon enveloped in a cloud of dust. Occasionally a straggling animal was singled out and became a victim. The sport was continued until the party had killed and secured eleven bulls, cows and calves. When these were brought to camp, it presented the appearance of a lively meat market. All were busy drying their meat over smoking fires in the sun to preserve what could not be used immediately. Now fairly launched out on to the plains into the midst of wild animals

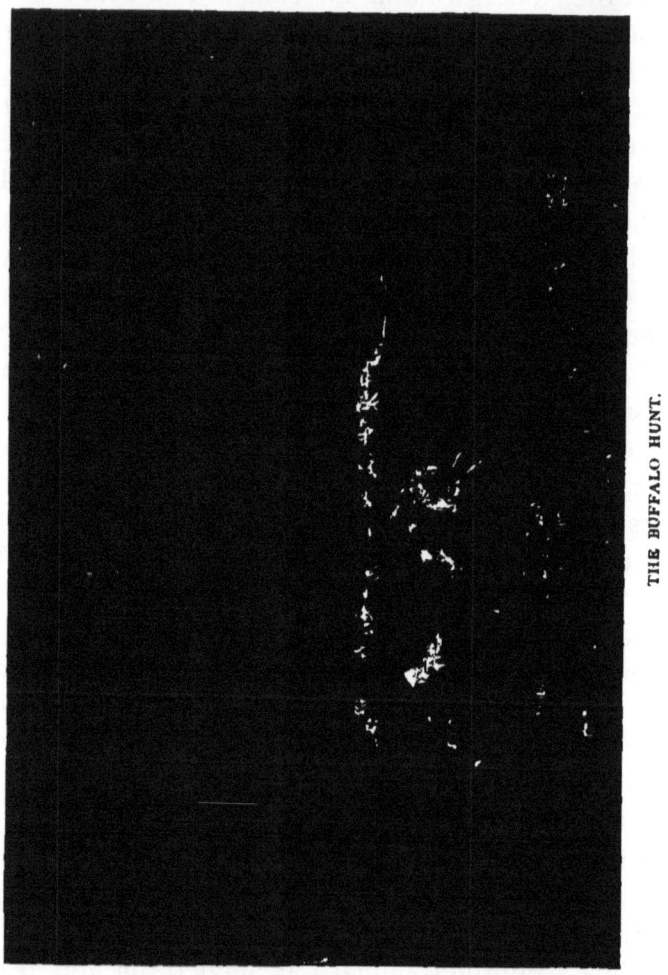

THE BUFFALO HUNT.

and roving bands of Indians, each day brought not only its legitimate labors, but its imaginary or real dangers, its novelties in animal and vegetable life and its new and ever varying scenery.

The teams being weak for want of sufficient food, on the 3rd of May the company concluded to rest for the day. Many of the men repaired wagons, harness, etc., and a company of hunters were sent out and returned with two buffalo calves and one antelope.

The morning of the 4th of May, a report having reached camp that a scouting party a few miles ahead had seen a large body of Indians, the company was directed to travel two wagons abreast, as this compact form was better suited for defence. As soon as the wagons were well out on the prairie President Young called out, "Attention, the camps of Israel. First company forward." Then the others in succession took their places until the desired formation was attained. This was a unique style of command for modern times.

During the day a Frenchman came over from the south side of the Platte. He was one of a company of nine men, with three teams, on their way from Fort Laramie to the States. By him fifty or sixty letters were sent to the families of pioneers at Winter Quarters. He remained with the pioneers about an hour, and three of their number returned with him. The Indians had been burning the dry grass which gave the country a blackened appearance, occasionally relieved by a spot of green grass mingled with the dry of the previous year's growth. These spots, which had escaped the fire, often afforded but a scanty supply of provender for the animals.

In the afternoon of the following day the camp traveled about six miles. The hunters killed a buffalo cow and five calves. A good sized calf was also captured alive with the intention of making a camp pet of it. About 4 p. m. the company came to a column of fire which crossed their path, extending from the river as far as the eye could see to the north. They wisely concluded that it was safest to encamp on the burnt prairie. Some small patches of grass which the fire had spared, afforded a scanty supply of food for animals.

About 4 o'clock on the morning of the 6th there was a timely shower of rain, and the company passed safely to the west side of the line of fire and smoke. The country abounded in buffalo, antelope, elk and wolves. During the day immense herds of buffalo were in sight on both sides of the Platte river. Many hundreds were feeding within a short distance of the road, but manifested no alarm at the approach of the company. Professor O. Pratt in his journal says :

"During the time of our halts we had to watch our teams to keep them from mingling with the buffalo. I think I may safely say that I have seen ten thousand buffalo during the day. Some few antelope, which came near our wagons, we killed for food, their meat being very excellent, but we did not allow ourselves to kill any game only as we wanted for food. * * * Young buffalo calves frequently came in our way and we had to carry them away from the camp to prevent their following us."

About this time, between the buffalo and the prairie fires, the animals of the camp were nearly famished. The buffalo became very numerous. It was impracticable to give an approximate estimate of their numbers, say one hundred thousand or more. They were poor in flesh and no more were killed than the necessities of the camp required. At one time a herd of several miles in extent was seen. "The prairie was literally a dense, black mass of moving animals." Mr. Thomas Bullock says: "Our camp had to stop two or three times while the droves went around us. As soon as they had passed many would stop and look at us, as if amazed at such a sight.

We caught several calves alive. Remember, catching a buffalo calf and a domesticated one, are two different things. A swift horse is sometimes pushed to catch up with him. They are as swift as horses, and although the old animals are the ugliest racers of any brutes, they get over the ground very fast, and an inexperienced rider is soon left to admire their beauty in the distance." The bones and carcasses of buffalo were more or less abundant on the prairie, after the company passed the Loupe Fork. Among them were frequently found human bones, probably those of Indians. Several human skulls were found in a state of good preservation.

A considerable distance along the Platte, for want of better fuel, the pioneers often made their fires of the excrement of the buffalo. The emigration who have followed them for two hundred miles along the Platte, have been compelled to use the same material. It burns something like dry turf, and makes quite a good fire when dry, but is useless when wet.

Of May 10th, Apostle O. Pratt says in his journal: "Before we left this morning we wrote a letter addressed to the officers of our next camp, which will follow our track, in about six or eight weeks. The letter was carefully secured from the weather by sawing five or six inches into a board parallel to its surface. The board was about six inches wide and eighteen long. The letter was deposited in the track made by the saw and three cletes were respectively nailed upon the top and two sides, and after writing on the board necessary directions, it was nailed to the end of a pole, four to five inches in diameter and about fifteen feet in length. This pole was firmly set about five feet in the ground near our road." While traveling a bay horse made its appearance. It seemed quite wild. Some of the company gave chase with the hope of capturing it but without success. Feed for the teams continued scarce on account of having been eaten out by the buffalo.

Mr. William Clayton, clerk of the company, and others began to discuss the subject of attaching some machinery to a wagon to indicate the number of miles traveled each day. President Young requested Mr. Pratt to give the matter some attention. In a day or two, by the assistance of Mr. Harmon, a mechanic, a machine was made and attached to a wagon wheel which automatically measured the distance traveled whenever the wagon moved.

The 11th of May a human skull was found. The teeth were perfectly sound and well set in the jaw. Perhaps it had belonged to an Indian warrior who had fallen in one of the late battles between the Pawnees and Sioux, in which the latter were victorious. Some small scars on the bone indicated that the scalp had been removed. About this time there were indications that large parties of Indians had lately been in the vicinity. Also buffalo were scarce, evidently having been driven from the locality. The company encamped near a clear stream of water, about fifteen feet wide, in which a number of small fish called dace, were caught with a hook. Feed was scarce, Indian horses and the buffalo having left but little grass. From the Elk Horn until the South Pass was reached, a distance of seven hundred miles, it might be said every mile of travel increased the altitude and proportionately with that increase the air became cooler and more rarefied. This will account for the fact that on the morning of the 14th of May the animals suffered considerably with the cold.

Approaching Laramie the country became more broken, and, from hills near the road, the prospect was

often very extensive and beautiful.   Here and there
small herds of buffalo were grazing upon the hills and
in the valleys.   It was a new experience, even in the

A PRAIRIE DOG VILLAGE.

wonderfully varied lives of the pioneers.   There was a
wild, weird romance about the country, like some dream,
some imaginary scene materialized.   During the evenings
the sound of music in different parts of the camp seemed

strangely harmonious with the almost death-like solitude
of these uninhabited regions.

There were indications that Indians had discovered
the camp and were lurking around for the purpose of
stealing horses. During the night one was seen by the
guard creeping towards the camp on his hands and knees.
He was fired upon and immediately rose to his feet and
ran away. During the following day fresh tracks of
these nomadic robbers were seen in the sand. They
would sometimes follow emigrants hundreds of miles,
keeping secreted during the day and watching for opportunities to steal at night. The pioneers corraled their
wagons in a circle, with the tongues outside, and the forward wheel of one wagon locked into the hind wheel of
another. In the interior of this temporary fortification the
animals were secured, while the whole camp was strongly
guarded. When the animals were grazing during the
day, about fourteen men usually encircled them on all
sides to prevent them from straying, or being suddenly
frightened away by a dash from Indians, accompanied
with horrid yells for the purpose of scattering the animals
of emigrants out of their reach. If the Indians succeeded they could hunt up the animals at leisure after
the owners had gone on. Sometimes if small parties of
two or three men ventured in search of their lost animals,
they were robbed of their clothing, and of their horses,
if so fortunate as to have any. If permitted to escape
with their lives they returned to camp in a destitute, forlorn condition. At this time game was plentiful. Out
of the abundance of buffalo, deer, antelope, geese and
ducks, the hunters were able to supply the camp with
what meat they required. No fuel for several days except floodwood and buffalo excrement. The 16th of May,
the camp rested in the afternoon and the people met for

public worship.   Two days after they crossed a rapid
stream which they named Rattlesnake creek, from the
circumstance of finding a rattlesnake near it.

————————•—————————

CHAPTER XII.

ASH HOLLOW AND ITS REMINISCENCES—RATTLESNAKES—
VISIT OF INDIANS—CHIMNEY ROCK—ROMANTIC SCENERY
—A LUNAR RAINBOW—THE BLACK HILLS—FORT LARA-
MIE — CALIFORNIA EMIGRATION — LARAMIE PEAK—
MAKING ROADS—FERRY ACROSS THE PLATTE.

THE 20th of May Ash Hollow on the south side of
the Platte was passed.   It was so named from some
ash timber growing there.   It afterwards became a
noted way-mark in traveling up the Platte.   Rumor
located many a deadly fight here between hostile bands
of Indians, and also between them and white men. Near
here was a lone cedar tree in which had been deposited
the remains of an Indian child with the necessary accom-
paniments, according to their traditions, for its future
enjoyment and welfare.   The following day there was
found on the prairie a large petrified bone, once a part
of the frame-work of an animal of enormous size.   It
was a leg bone from the knee downwards, was seventeen
and one-half inches in length, eleven inches wide, six
inches thick, and its weight twenty-seven pounds.   It
was a curious specimen of ancient zoology.   Towards
evening the camp was visited by two or three Indians.
They appeared friendly and gave the men to understand

that a large number of their people were encamped near by.

May 22nd, the company crossed a stream which they called Crab creek. With glasses Chimney Rock was seen forty-two miles distant. The following day was Sunday. As was the general custom on that day the teams rested. By a barometrical measurement of Professor Pratt's, the height of a neighboring peak was 235 feet above the Platte river, and 3,590 feet above sea level. Rattlesnakes were numerous. Nathaniel Fairbanks was bitten by a large yellow one. Although remedies were applied he suffered considerably during the day. The people assembled for worship and were addressed by Brigham Young and others.

About 7 o'clock p. m. the wind blew a violent gale from the north, with rain and hail from a cold quarter. This made people and animals very uncomfortable. The morning of the 24th a few flakes of snow fell. From a real or fancied resemblance of the surrounding hills and rocks to ruined cities and towers, this region was named Bluff Ruins. At the noon halt the camp was visited by two Indians. By signs they made the company understand that their tribe was a short distance on the south side of the Platte. Food was given them and they returned to their camp, fording the river on foot. They notified their people of the approach of the pioneers, and, in the evening, thirty-five of their number, including squaws and boys, come to camp on horseback. They were much better dressed than the Indians on the Missouri river. Many of them had broadcloth clothes, blankets and fur caps, adorned with abundance of beads and other finery. They were armed with bows, steel-pointed arrows and a few firearms. They were of the Dacotah tribe, which interpreted means "cut throat,"

but generally known to the whites as Sioux. Their
chief's name was Owastate-cha. Soon after dark he
sent his men away to encamp, but he requested the
privilege of remaining with the pioneers over night.
This, doubtless, was a precautionary measure on his
part, as his people would disturb nothing belonging to
the camp while their chief was enjoying its hospitality.
A tent was spread for his accommodation. In the morning there was a hard frost. To a supper for the Indians
the previous evening the pioneers added a breakfast.

The 26th of May the pioneers passed Chimney
Rock, but about three miles north of it. At this point
the valley of the Platte was about 3,790 feet above sea
level. Prickly pears continued to grow more numerous.
This indicated that they were getting into a country of
not much rainfall during summer. They were still on
that section of the route where there was no timber on
the north side of the Platte and, consequently, no fuel
for camp use except flood wood, which was very scarce,
and "buffalo chips." The latter diminished in quantity
as the company traveled west. No buffalo had been
seen for several days, but antelopes were plentiful.

May 27th, the company passed the meridian of the
highest peak of Scott's Bluffs, which was near the river
on the south side. With indications of a shower in the
afternoon the company encamped for the night. The
showers along the Platte had been accompanied with
high winds, rushing in fitful, violent gusts, but of short
duration. The burned prairies were now mantled with
the beautiful verdure of spring, and the river bottoms,
refreshingly green, afforded luxurious herbage for the
camp animals.

"The bluffs on the opposite side of the river exhibited a great variety of forms, presenting scenes remark-

6

ably picturesque and interesting in their appearance.
There can be seen towers of various forms and heights.
Perpendicular walls, some of whose outlines are circular,
others rectilineal. Deep notches, both semi-circular and
rectangular, seemed to be excavated in their summits.
Many of these scenes closely resemble the artificial
works of man thrown partially into disorder and confusion by some great convulsion of nature."

May 30th, being Sunday, was another day of rest
for the teams. It was appointed a day for fasting and
prayer. A prayer meeting in the morning was followed
by preaching and exhortation in the afternoon. Towards
evening there was a thunder shower, and later, another
light one from the east. "The moon shone brightly in
the east, being about half an hour above the horizon. By
refraction of its mild rays through the falling drops it
produced a beautiful lunar rainbow in the west, but little
inferior in brightness to a solar one. Chimney Rock,
though forty miles distant, can be seen from the bluffs,
while the lowering peaks of the Black Hills, west of Laramie, present themselves like blue clouds stationary in
the horizon."

The 1st of June the pioneers encamped near Fort
Laramie, situated on the left bank of Laramie Fork,
about one and a half miles from its confluence with the
North Fork. Its walls were of adobe and about fifteen feet
high. Ranges of houses were built in the interior adjoining the walls, leaving a central yard of about one hundred feet square. It belonged to the American Fur
Company, was in charge of a Mr. Boudeau and was occupied by about eighteen men and their families.

In the evening the camp was visited by some Saints,
Mr. Crow and family, who left the southern states the
season before under the counsel of elders from the head-

·quarters of the Church, who had advised them of the contemplated move of the Saints to the Rocky Mountains and approved of the idea of attempting to intersect their trail up the Platte river.   This party of. fourteen persons had wintered at Pueblo with a detachment of the Mormon Battalion and a considerable company of Saints from the south, and had reached Laramie a few days in advance.

The 2nd of June a party of the pioneers crossed

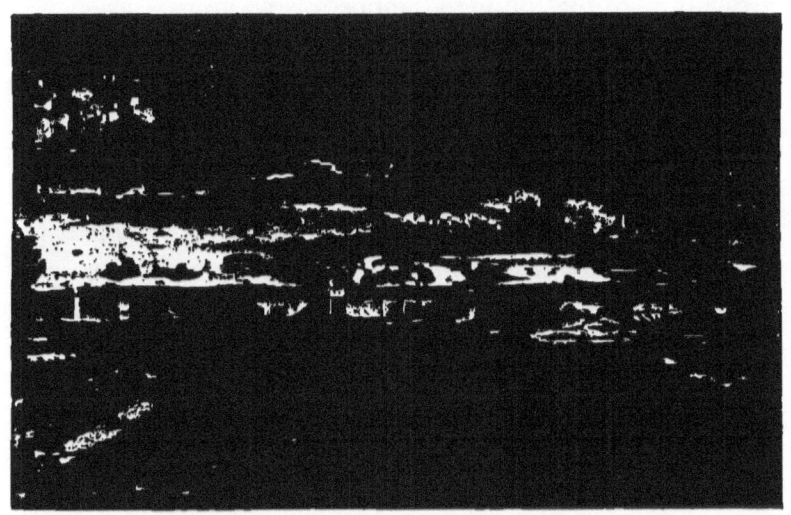

FORT LARAMIE.

the river in a boat of sole-leather. It had been the property of Mr. Ira Eldredge, and it carried his family outfit across the Mississippi and Missouri rivers; was utilized by the pioneers and had been brought by them from Winter Quarters as a wagon box.   The party crossed the river and walked up to Fort Laramie. They were kindly received and seated in a neat, comfortable apartment.   After a sociable, cheerful chat with Mr. Boudeau and others, they walked down to see his flatboat.   This

was engaged at the reasonable figure of fifteen dollars·
to ferry the company across the North Fork, as further
travel up its left bank would be attended with considerable difficulty. Indian aggressions and the severe droughts
to which the country was subject, had caused agriculture
to be entirely neglected. The whites, like the Indians,
depended on the flesh of wild animals for their principal
food. Whatever they had of the products of the earth
and other luxuries were hauled from the Missouri river,
a distance of five hundred miles, on wagons.

Early in the morning of the 3rd of June, the pioneers commenced ferrying across the North Fork of the
Platte, averaging about four wagons per hour. The
afternoon of the previous day they saw with their glasses
three or four white men coming in on horseback on the
opposite side of the Platte. While ferrying they learned
these men were from the states and had made the journey in seventeen days. They reported having passed
about two thousand wagons in detached companies on
their way to Oregon. One small company was expected
to arrive at Laramie on the 4th, a larger one the following day, and a still larger one on the 6th. These emigrants were principally from Missouri, Illinois and Iowa.
Emigration to the Pacific slope seemed to be greatly on
the increase.

The pioneers having safely crossed the North Fork,
resumed their journey about noon of the 4th. They followed the Oregon road near that stream. It was a great
change from the long levels of the Platte bottoms to a
broken, mountain road. From Laramie to Salt Lake
there was no lack of fuel for camp purposes, pine and
cedar on the hills, cottonwood and box elder along the
streams, with sagebrush abundant almost everywhere,
sometimes growing ten feet high.

The 7th of June three companies of Oregon emigrants came up with the pioneers. Under this date Mr. Pratt says in his journal: "This forenoon gained in elevation very fast. Laramie Peak, twelve or fifteen miles to the south-west, shows from this position to good advantage. Its top is whitened with snow that acts as a condenser upon the vapor of the atmosphere which comes within its vicinity, generating clouds, which are precipitated in showers upon the surrounding country. This peak has been visible to our camp for eight or ten days, and I believe that almost every afternoon since, we have been visited with thunder showers which seem to originate in the vicinity of the peak."

The night of the 7th of June the pioneers encamped on Horse Shoe creek. Next day they saw a solitary buffalo, the first one seen for upwards of two hundred miles. They traveled fifteen miles and encamped on Big Timber creek. About a mile from them were encamped a few wagons from Fort Bridger, on the west side of the mountains, loaded with furs and peltries, on their way to Fort Laramie.

The 9th of June the company crossed a stream about twenty feet wide which they called Little Timber. The banks being rather steep they were much improved by the use of spades and picks. It was a daily labor to repair the roads and leave them in a passable condition for the companies that were expected to follow. There was a daily detail of ten or twelve men who went in advance of the company, with the necessary tools to work the road. Distances were also measured with the machine before mentioned and boards set up every ten miles, conveying the intelligence to the traveler of the distance he was west of Laramie. The pioneers encamped on a stream called "A La Parele." Just

above camp it ran through a mountain forming a natural
bridge over the stream.   Three men with fifteen horses,
most of them carrying packs, passed the company.
They were from Santa Fe, New Mexico, and on their
way to San Francisco, in upper California, *via* the Great
Salt Lake.

The evening of June 11th, a short distance above
their camp were two small companies of emigrants which
had passed them a few days before.   The previous day
their teams took fright from the running of a horse.
Two wagons were upset and one woman and two children considerably injured, but no bones were broken.
The following day the pioneers made the point where
the Oregon road crossed the Platte river, one hundred
and twenty-four miles from Laramie.   They found the
channel about one hundred feet wide and the water
fifteen feet deep.   Here they overtook one of the foremost companies of the Oregon emigrants.   Three days
previous to their arrival the pioneers had sent a small
detachment in advance to this place, where they arrived
about four hours ahead of any emigrants, with the boat
of sole leather before mentioned.   As this would carry
fifteen or eighteen hundred pounds of freight, they were
employed by the emigrants to ferry them over.   Goods
were crossed in the skiff and the empty wagons floated.
In the operation the latter were frequently hurled several
times over by the force of the current.

A few miles from this place the hunters of the company killed a few buffalo and three or four grizzly bears,
the latter being quite numerous on the Black Hills.   June
14th the pioneers commenced crossing the Platte.   Some
of the wagons were crossed on light rafts made of pine
poles lashed together, others were floated, but the current was found too rapid to do this without injuring

them, so they resorted wholly to the slow process of rafting. Twenty-four wagons were crossed during the day. They remained at this place until the morning of the 19th. In this time two large canoes were constructed of cottonwood timber. These were placed parallel to each other, a few feet apart, and firmly fastened together with cross timbers well pinned on; across these slabs were fastened, running lengthwise of the canoes. With a little iron work, rudder and oars were attached, and they had a boat of sufficient strength to carry over a loaded wagon of the emigrants. Captain Groves and nine men were left in charge of this rude boat, and with it a considerable business was done in crossing the Oregon emigrants daily arriving in small companies and very anxious to be crossed over without delay. Those in charge of the ferry were instructed to come on with the next company, who were expected to arrive there in a month or six weeks. They were urged to take every precautionary measure to protect themselves from Indians.

CHAPTER XIII.

LEAVING THE PLATTE—SALERATUS LAKE—DEVIL'S GATE—
VALLEY OF THE SWEETWATER—WINTER AND SUMMER
MINGLED TOGETHER—THE SOUTH PASS — INTERESTING
INTERVIEWS WITH MAJOR HARRIS AND COLONEL BRIDGER
—ARRIVAL OF SAMUEL BRANNAN FROM THE BAY OF
SAN FRANCISCO — THE PUEBLO DETACHMENT OF THE
MORMON BATTALION—MOUNTAIN FEVER.

AT THIS point the pioneers left the North Fork of
the Platte for the Sweetwater river, distant twenty-
seven and a half miles. Twenty miles of the distance
they traveled on the 21st of June. During the forenoon
drive of the 22nd they passed the noted saleratus lake.
They found large quantities of this useful article in the
family economy. The Mormon emigration afterwards
hauled yearly supplies of this into the valley to use instead of the better, but far more expensive commercial
article, on account of heavy freight charges across the
plains. Several bushels were gathered and taken along
by the pioneers. The morning drive of seven and a half
miles brought them to the right bank of the Sweetwater,
about one mile below Independence Rock, and within
one-fourth of a mile of the upper end of the Devil's Gate.

Early in the morning of the 22nd of June, Professor
Pratt ascended to the top of Devil's Gate rock. By
barometrical measurement he found the perpendicular
wall four hundred feet above the river which here runs
through a chasm nine hundred or one thousand feet in
length, and one hundred and thirty feet in breadth. In
this chasm the water tumbles and foams with the noise
of a cataract over massive fragments of rock which have

fallen from above.   They found the valley of the Sweetwater from five to ten miles in breadth, bounded on the
north and south by mountain ridges, isolated hills and
rugged summits of massive granite, varying from twelve
hundred to two thousand feet in height.   In the afternoon
the first glimpse was caught of the Wind River mountains north of the road, but the air was too smoky to
discover more than a faint, blue outline.   They crossed
two or three small streams and, after making twenty and

INDEPENDENCE ROCK.

three-fourth miles over a sandy road, encamped on the
Sweetwater with good grass and wild sage for fuel.   Two
companies of emigrants encamped a short distance above
the pioneers.   We let Professor Pratt describe this
strange country where in the latter part of June, winter
mingled with summer.   "The Wind River chain of mountains, in the distance, exhibit their towering peaks
whitened by perpetual snow, which glittering in the sunbeams, resemble white, fleecy clouds.

"June 24th: Traveled seventeen and three-fourth miles and again encamped on the Sweetwater. We passed in the forenoon Sulphur Springs, sometimes called Ice Springs. We took a spade and dug down about one foot and found the ground frozen and large quantities of ice. A few yards west of this we saw two or three small lakes or ponds. The water in them was very salt and of a bitterish taste. The soil is covered in many places with saline efflorescences of a considerable depth."

June, 25th: Traveled twenty and one-fourth miles and encamped upon a tributary of the Sweetwater, the water clear and cold. Frequent banks of snow were upon the hills in their vicinity. Just below was quite a large and beautiful grove of aspen or poplar. The evening was cold rendering overcoats quite a necessary appendage. The perpetual snows which completely covered the Wind River chain gives the scenery a cold, wintry aspect.

June 26th: The grass was whitened with frost, and the sudden change from the high temperature of the sandy valleys below was most severely felt by man and beast. Resumed the journey during the forenoon and traveled eleven miles, crossing the main branches of the Sweetwater which were quite high, the result of the melting snows accumulated upon its banks, and in the mountains. At the largest and last of the main branches of the Sweetwater, the company halted for noon. Only in high altitudes was such a scene possible, abundance of good grass mingled with various plants and flowers upon the bottoms of the stream and a few yards distant, large banks of snow several feet in depth. We quote again from Professor Pratt. "This is eight miles east of the South Pass. Myself and several others came on in advance of the camp, and it was with great difficulty that we could determine the dividing point of land which separates the waters flowing into the Atlantic from those flowing into the Pacific. This country called the South Pass, for some fifteen or twenty miles in length and breadth is a gently undulating plain or prairie, thickly covered with wild sage from one to two feet in height. On the highest part of this plain, over which our road passes, and which separates the waters of the two oceans, is a small dry basin of fifteen or twenty acres, destitute of wild sage but containing good grass. From this basin about half a mile both to the east and to the west, the road gently rises about forty or fifty feet, either of which elevations may be considered as the highest on our road in the Pass."

On the western elevation the barmometer gave the altitude above the sea 7,085 feet. The distance of this Pass from Fort Laramie, as measured by our mile machine, is two hundred and seventy-five and a half miles. Four miles west of the Pass, at Pacific or Muddy Spring. were encamped a small company of men from Oregon on their way to the states. They were performing the journey on horseback and had left the settlements in Oregon on the 5th of May. Major Harris, a trapper and hunter, had resided in different parts of the country twenty or twenty-five years. He had acquired an extensive and intimate knowledge of it in all its main features. The pioneers obtained much information from him in relation to the interior basin of the Salt Lake, the country of their destination. His report, like that of Colonel Fremont's, was rather unfavorable to the founding of a colony in this basin, principally on account of the scarcity of timber. He said he had traveled the whole circumference of the lake and there was no outlet to it.

On the 28th of June the pioneers came to the forks

of the Oregon road and took the southern one. They halted at noon at the ford of Little Sandy. In the afternoon they met Col. James Bridger who encamped with them that evening. He was going on business to Laramie with a small company. Being a man extensively acquainted with the country, many inquiries were also made of him in relation to the Great Basin, and the country south. His information was rather more favorable for colonizing than that of Major Harris. While partaking of breakfast with Mr. Young, Col. Bridger remarked, "There is more bread on the table than I have before seen for years." "But, Mr. Bridger, how do you live?" inquired Mr. Young. He replied, "We live entirely on meat. We dry our deer and buffalo to eat, and also cook fresh when we can obtain it. We usually have our coffee, for that is easily obtained."

June 30th, the company arrived at the crossing of Green river. The water was very high, from twelve to fifteen feet deep and one hundred and eighty yards wide, with a very rapid current. Two rafts were made and each was rigged with a rudder and oars. The wagons were safely crossed without taking out any of their contents. The animals were made to swim over.

Towards sundown Mr. Samuel Brannan arrived in camp from the bay of San Francisco. As before stated he had been appointed to take charge of a company of two hundred and fourteen Saints who sailed out of New York harbor on the ship *Brooklyn*, on the 6th of Feb., 1846, for the Pacific coast. The 31st of July, the same year, the vessel entered the bay of San Francisco. The colony were located on the San Joaquin river. Mr. Brannan had left the bay of San Francisco on the 4th of April, 1847, ten days earlier than the pioneers left their place of rendezvous on the Elk Horn river, expressly to

meet the latter on their long anticipated journey to the
Rocky Mountains. He was accompanied by two men,
having left one at Fort Hall. He left California at a
season of the year when. it was considered unsafe to
attempt to cross the Sierra Nevada mountains, on
account of deep snows. He had not only braved this
danger, but as well that from the savage bands of Indians
that roamed over the desert regions through which he
traveled.

He also, in crossing the Sierra Nevada mountains,
passed directly over the camping ground where forty or
fifty California emigrants had perished and been eaten
up by their fellow-sufferers, only a few days before.
Their skulls and carcasses lay strewn in every direction.
He also met the last of these unfortunates making his
way into the settlements. He was a German, and had
lived upon human flesh for several weeks. The following
letter of Mr. Brannan's to a friend, L. N. Scovil, gives
further insight into the character of this hazardous trip:

"FORT HALL, June 18th, 1847.

"*Brother Newell:*

* * "I left Captain Sutter's post in California on
the 26th of April last, and arrived here on the 9th inst.
I am on my way to meet our emigration. I am now
one thousand miles on my road, and I think I shall meet
them in a couple of weeks. I shall start on my journey
again in the morning with two of my men and part of my
animals, and leave one man here and the rest of the
horses to recruit until my return, and then it is my intention to reach California in twenty days from this post.

"We crossed the snowy mountains of California, a
distance of forty miles with eleven head of horses and
mules in one day and two hours ; a thing that has never
been done before in less than three days. We traveled
on foot and drove our animals before us, the snow from
twenty to one hundred feet deep. When we arrived

through, it was difficult for any of us to stand on our feet. The people of California told us we could not cross there under two months, there being more snow on the mountains than had ever been known before, but God knows best and was kind enough to prepare the way before us. About a week before we entered the mountains, the weather was extremely warm. This caused the snow to settle more firmly together. The weather then turned cold and there fell about eighteen inches more of light snow. This kept the old snow from melting during the heat of the day, and made the traveling for our horses much better.

"During our journey we have endured many hardships and much fatigue in swimming rivers and climbing mountains, not being able to travel the regular route owing to the high waters.   *   *   *   *   We passed the cabins of those people who perished in the mountains which by this time you have heard of. It was a heart-rending picture."   *   *   *   *   *

The evening of the 3rd of July the people were called together. There were men in the company who expected their families to follow them in the companies that would leave Winter Quarters some time in June, and which were supposed to be four or five hundred miles on the road. They were given the privilege of returning to meet them. Five men volunteered on this errand. They started on the morning of the 4th, taking with them instructions to the Saints whom they expected to meet, also a short synopsis from the records of the camp containing distances from one notable point to another good camping place, etc. Should they meet the detachment of the Mormon Battalion under Captain Brown, if desired to do so, one was counseled to remain with it as a guide.

The anniversary of the declaration of American Independence coming on Sunday, the camp met for public

worship under the presidency of the Bishops, some of the
Twelve having started back for the ferry on the Platte,
with the brethren who returned to meet their families.
In the afternoon thirteen soldiers all belonging to the
Church came into the camp, accompanied by those who
went back to the ferry.   These thirteen men had been
detached by Captain Brown to go in advance of the main
body to regain possession of horses that had been stolen
from them at Pueblo.   They had learned that the thieves
were at Bridger's trading post, on Muddy Fork, a few
miles south-west of the camp.   These brethren were
greeted with three hearty cheers.   They were the first
representatives of the Battalion in the pioneer camp.

The following day the company traveled along the
right bank of Green river, three and a half miles then
made a short halt to water their animals.   Leaving the
river they gradually ascended the bluff skirting the river
bottoms, and traveled over a gently undulating sandy
plain, destitute of grass and water, for sixteen and a half
miles, then descended to the left bank of Black's Fork
and encamped for the night.   For a few days some
persons in camp had been slightly afflicted with fever.
Several causes tended to produce this.   There was a
great and somewhat sudden change in climatic conditions.   In fact the general environment of the people
was changed.   In traveling they were often enveloped
in clouds of suffocating dust which injuriously affected
the lungs and head.   The changes of temperature were
sudden and extreme.   The summer sun made the day
extremely warm, and the snowy mountains surrounding
the company on all sides, rendered the air cold and uncomfortable in its absence.   A number of salmon trout
were caught in the streams west of the South pass, but this
fine species of fish was not found east of the dividing ridge.

CHAPTER XIV.

DESCRIPTION OF FORT BRIDGER—START FOR SALT LAKE—AS
EXPECTED, MANY DIFFICULTIES WERE ENCOUNTERED—
RED MINERAL SPRING, TAR AND SULPHUR SPRINGS—
SICKNESS OF PRESIDENT YOUNG—O. PRATT WITH A DE-
TACHMENT, PIONEERS THE ROAD—FROSTY NIGHTS—
BEARS ON WEBER'S FORK—EAST CANYON CREEK—THE
LABORS OF CAMP HUNTERS—FIRST VIEW OF GREAT SALT
LAKE VALLEY—THE ADVANCE CAMP IN EMIGRATION
CANYON.

JULY 7th the pioneers encamped on the right bank of Black's Fork, in the vicinity of Fort Bridger. Within a few rods were nine Indian lodges, occupied by families of white trappers and hunters who had taken wives from surrounding tribes of Indians. Half-breed children were playing about these lodges. Bridger's trading post was a half mile west of the camp on an island, with no other road to it than a footpath. Black's Fork is here broken up into a number of rapid streams, forming several islands containing in all seven or eight hundred acres of excellent grass with considerable timber.

The fort consisted of two adjoining log houses with dirt roofs and a small fort enclosed with log pickets set in the ground, and about eight feet high. These houses and lodges were the home of fifty or sixty men, women and half-breed children. The altitude of the place was ascertained to be 6,665 feet, 420 feet lower than the South Pass from which it was distant 109½ miles by road measurement. Notwithstanding the cold nights mosquitoes were numerous and troublesome.

The morning of the 8th of July the thermometer stood at 66°. Ice had formed during the night, but it soon disappeared under the warmth of the rising sun. A brisk wind was blowing from the south-west. Several fine speckled trout were caught with the hook. It was a busy day with the blacksmiths, setting wagon tires, shoeing horses and making general preparations for a rough mountain road in a south-west direction towards Salt Lake.

With a two days' rest for the teams in this paradise for mountaineers and a general preparation for rough roads, travel was resumed on the 9th of July. Mr. S. Brannan, with a few others, returned towards the South Pass to meet the main detachment of the Battalion. The pioneers took Mr. Hastings' new route to the bay of San Francisco. The trail was scarcely discernible, as only a few wagons passed over it the previous year. They traveled thirteen miles in close proximity to some snow banks, and camped on a branch of Muddy Fork.

July 10th they passed a small spring which they named "Red Mineral spring," from the redness of the soil out of which it issued. The water had a very disagreeable taste and was supposed to contain alum in solution, also a large per cent. of copperas, which would make it poisonous. Five miles from this spring the company attained the summit of a ridge between two branches of Muddy Fork, the barometrical height of which was 7,315 feet, 230 feet higher than the South Pass. Nine miles further they reached the summit of the dividing ridge between the waters which flow into the Gulf of California and those that flow into the Great Salt Lake, or the branches of Muddy Fork on the east and of Bear river on the west. Where the road passed over, the altitude was 7,700 feet, or 615 feet higher than

7

the South Pass. This was the highest point over which the trail of the pioneers passed between the Missouri river and Great Salt Lake valley. The company traveled eighteen miles and encamped five miles from the summit of this high ridge. Professor Pratt, wandering in the hills, discovered smoke about two miles distant. When he returned to camp some horsemen rode over to it. They found it came from the fire of a small party from the bay of San Francisco on their way to the states.

The morning of July 11th was clear, calm and pleasant, although considerable ice had formed during the night. One and a half miles south of camp a mineral tar spring was discovered, and a few rods north-east some sulphur springs. At this point the road forked. A few wagon tracks bore to the south, and a few others took down a small stream, on which the company were encamped. The next morning the company took the right hand road down the creek. One and three-fourth miles brought them to the ford of Bear river. Barometrical measurement indicated this ford to be 6,836 feet in height. There the road again forked, and the right hand track, bearing a few degrees south of west, was taken. Antelope, which had been rather scarce, began to appear again in great numbers. Ten or twelve were brought in by the hunters during the day. The road was very difficult to find, except in places where the storms had not defaced nor the grass obscured it.

At the midday halt Mr. Young, being sick, concluded to stop a few hours and rest. Several wagons remained with him; by request the remainder of the company moved on. In the evening they encamped near a cave. It was explored about thirty feet, when the passage becoming quite small no one seemed disposed to go further. It was called Reddin's Cave, as that was

the name of one of the first of the company who explored it. Mr. Young, being still behind, on the morning of the 13th of July two messengers were sent back
to meet him. Unwilling to move on without their leader,
the camp waited. The messengers returned, accompanied by Mr. H. C. Kimball. They reported that Mr.
Young was getting better but did not think of moving
that day. The Twelve, who were present, directed Professor Pratt to take twenty-three wagons and forty-two
men, proceed on the journey and endeavor to find Mr.
Reid's route across the mountains, as the company had
been informed it would be impracticable to pass through
the canyon on account of the depth and rapidity of the
water. Mr. Pratt's detachment started at three o'clock
p. m. and traveled down Red Fork eight and three-fourth
miles and encamped. Altitude 6,070 feet.

The 14th of July Mr. Pratt's company traveled thirteen miles to the junction of Red and Weber Forks. He
says in his journal: "Our journey down Red Fork has truly
been very interesting and exceedingly picturesque. We
have been shut up in a narrow valley from ten to twenty
rods wide, while on each side the hills rise very abruptly
from eight to twelve hundred feet. The most of the
distance we have been walled in by vertical and overhanging precipices of red pudding stone. These rocks
are worked into curious shapes, probably by rains."

On the 15th two parties went in search of Mr. Reid's
trail across the mountains to the south-eastern shore of
Salt Lake. It was soon discovered, although so dimly
seen it could only occasionally be found. The grass had
grown up leaving scarcely a trace of the few wagons that
had passed there the previous year. Messrs. Pratt and
Brown followed this track about six miles up a ravine to
where it reached a dividing ridge leading down in a

southerly direction to another, and returned to camp. Cottonwood trees and thick clusters of willows fringed the banks of Weber's Fork making very close thickets for bears. The many tracks seen, and the large holes they had made in digging roots, indicated that they were very numerous. For several days showers had been frequent, and one occurred that morning, but too light to lay the dust.

Mr. Rockwell was sent back to report to those of the company in the rear, that the new route had been discovered. The journey was resumed up a small stream on Reid's route. A detachment of ten or twelve men was sent in advance of the wagons with necessary tools to make the road passable. This required considerable labor. The detachment traveled about six miles, and crossing the ridge began to descend another ravine. They descended two and a half miles in about four hours and encamped for the night. Mr. Newman and Professor Pratt walked down the ravine to examine the road. They found Mr. Reid's company had spent several hours in labor and then concluded to take a more available route up the ravine at the mouth of which the pioneers had encamped, going a circuitous course over the hills. They had evidently crossed the Weber without mentioning it.

July 17th we copy from O. Pratt's journal:

"A severe frost during the night. Early this morn-I started out alone, and on foot, to examine the country back, to see if there was not a more practicable route for the companies in the rear than the one we had come. I was soon satisfied we had taken the best and only practicable route. I returned to camp and counseled the company not to go any further until they had spent several hours' labor on the road we passed over yester-

day afternoon. All who were able to work labored
about two-thirds of the day upon it. Leaving orders for
the camp to move on towards night, Mr. Brown and
myself rode forward to explore. About three and a half
miles brought us down upon the right bank of a creek
with a swift current and supposed to be about twenty
feet wide. This creek (East Canyon creek) passes
through a canyon about forty rods below, where, for a few
rods it is shut up by perpendicular and overhanging walls,
being a break in the mountains which rises several
hundred feet upon each side. The creek plunges under-
neath a large rock which lies in its bed near the foot of
the canyon, blockading the same and making it wholly
impassable for wagons or teams. We followed the dimly
traced wagon tracks, up this stream for miles, crossing
the same thirteen times.

"The bottoms along the creek are thickly covered
with willows from five to fifteen rods wide, making an
immense labor in cutting a road through for the California emigrants last season. We still found the road
almost impassable and requiring much labor. The
mountains on each side rise abruptly from six hundred
to three thousand feet above the bed of the stream.
Leaving our horses we ascended to the summit of one
which appeared about two thousand feet high. We had
a prospect, limited in most directions by still higher peaks.
The country exhibited a broken succession of hills piled
on hills, and mountains on mountains in every direction.
We returned and met our camp about four and three-
quarter miles from where they were encamped in the
morning. They were about two miles above the canyon
on the left bank of Canyon creek. At this place is a
small rivulet which runs down from the mountains, the
water clear and cold."

The pioneers were now fairly among the deep gorges and towering peaks of the Wasatch mountains east of Great Salt Lake valley. It was on Canyon creek that the following circumstance occurred, illustrating the excessive toil endured by the camp hunters in providing

GLEN IN THE WASATCH.

food. There was no meat in camp and Joseph Hancock left it early one morning to make an effort to supply the want. He felt impressed that on the top of a high ridge which loomed up in the distance, in the clear mountain air, he would be successful. Arriving there, for the first time he saw a portion of Salt Lake valley, and realized

his anticipations of the morning by killing a large elk.
Making it lighter by leaving the offal he got the carcass

on his back and started in the direction of the camp.
He traveled well into the night without finding it.
Attempting to cross a creek on a beaver dam, he broke

through and found himself astride a large log with his extremities in the water below.   He was relieved of his burden as it lay on the log at his back.   Excessively weary he felt content to rest.   Unconsciously his. head dropped back on to the elk and he was sleeping as only the weary can sleep.   The first sound that greeted his senses was the crowing of a cock.   This was assurance that he was not far from friends, and a little reflection showed him that he had been thus detained by a kindly Providence, instead of making fruitless exertions in the darkness to find the object of his toil.   As day was breaking he dragged the elk across the dam and again resumed his burden.   By this time he was discovered by some of the men who were stirring early in the camp.

July 18th was Sunday.   The morning was cold and the ground whitened with frost.   The men remained in camp and attended meeting in the forenoon.   The morning of the 19th was also cold and frosty.   There was a great change in the temperature from night to mid-day when the air was warmed by the summer sun.   Messrs. Pratt and Brown started, soon after sunrise, to examine the road and country ahead.   They continued along the road they had traveled over the day before, and ascertained that it left Canyon creek near where they had turned back, and run along in a ravine to the west. They ascended this ravine four miles and found themselves on the top of a dividing ridge.   There they secured their horses and ascended a mountain on their right, several hundred feet.   From the ridge where the road crossed, and from this mountain peak, they could see over a great extent of country.   On the south-west they discovered an extensive, level prairie, a few miles distant which they thought must be near the lake.   This was their first view of any part of Great Salt Lake valley.

They returned to their horses and rode on down the south-west side of the ridge. This has since been known as the "Big Mountain" to distinguish it from the one just west of it, over which the road crosses, known as the "Little Mountain." At first the descent was very rapid. Several miles down, the small stream they were traveling along passed through a very high mountain, and it appeared impossible for wagons to pass in that direction. Looking around they found that the wagon trail ascended quite abruptly about a mile and a half, passed over a mountain and down into another narrow valley. This is Little Mountain before mentioned, and the narrow valley has since been known as Emigration canyon. Satisfied with their explorations, they returned on their trail and met the company six and one-fourth miles from their encampment the evening before. The men had performed a great amount of labor. Mr. Rockwell had returned bringing word that most of the pioneer wagons in the rear were within a few miles of the advance camp. The fresh track of a buffalo was discovered in the ravine. He had left some hair on the brush in his path, and was, evidently, a lonely wanderer and probably the only one of his kind within hundreds of miles.

July 20th Professor Pratt's detachment moved six miles and did much labor to improve the road. The altitude of the Big Mountain was 7,245 feet, one hundred and sixty feet higher than the South Pass. In the morning of July 21st there was no frost but a heavy dew. The leading division of the pioneers passed over the Little Mountain and halted for noon in the head of Emigration canyon. They called the swift running creek on which they halted "Last creek."

CHAPTER XV.

THE ADVANCE OF THE PIONEERS ENTERS GREAT SALT LAKE
VALLEY—DESCRIPTION OF THIS RESTING PLACE FOR
THE PILGRIMS—ARRIVAL OF PRESIDENT YOUNG—THE
CRICKETS AND CRICKET EATERS OF THE DESERT —
THIEVING PROPENSITIES OF THE INDIANS ILLUSTRATED.

ELDER ERASTUS SNOW came from the wagons
in the rear and reported them only a few miles back.
He went with Professor Pratt in advance of the wagons
down Last creek, four and one-half miles, to where it
issues into the broad, open valley below. To avoid a
narrow gorge near this point, the wagons traveling the
route the season before passed over an exceedingly steep
and dangerous hill. Destined to be the first of their
people to arrive at the object of their long and tedious
journey, these two men ascended this hill from the top
of which a broad, open valley, twenty or thirty miles long
lay stretched out before them. To the north-west the
waters of the Great Salt Lake glimmered in the bright,
noonday sunbeams, and from them rose high mountainous islands twenty to thirty miles in extent. Before them
was a vast wilderness in which the genius of solitude
reigned. That profound silence was the assurance of
room and rest for the wanderers who were about to take
possession of this unoccupied desert.

Professor Pratt says: "After issuing from the mountains among which we had been shut up for many days
and beholding, in a moment, such an extensive scenery
open before us, we could not refrain from a shout of joy,
which almost involuntarily escaped from our lips, the

moment the grand and lovely scenery was within our
view.   We immediately very gradually descended into
the lower parts of the valley, and although we had but
one horse between us, yet we traveled a circuit of about
twelve miles before we left the valley to return to our
camp, which we found one and a half miles up the ravine
from the valley, and three miles in advance of the noon
halt.   It was about nine o'clock in the evening when we
arrived.   The main body of the pioneers were encamped
about a mile and a half above the advance while the sick
were still farther in the rear."

With what exhilaration of spirits, with what nerve
and energy this advance camp of the pioneers must have
arisen on the morning of the 22nd of July!   The life's
blood must have flowed with increased velocity through
their veins in anticipation of that day, realizing the object
of their toils and hopes.   Apostles O. Pratt and George
A. Smith, accompanied by seven others, rode into the
valley to explore.   They left the camp to follow on and
work the road which here required considerable labor to
make it passable.   They discovered that by cutting out
the thick timber and under brush, and by some digging,
a much better road could be made through the canyon
than the old route over the steep hill before mentioned.
They left a written notice to that effect and passed on.

We will let Professor Pratt describe this day's explorations of Great Salt Lake valley:

"After going down into the valley about five miles,
we turned our course to the north down towards the
Salt Lake.   For three or four miles we found the soil of
most excellent quality.   Streams from the mountains and
springs were very abundant, the waters excellent and
generally with gravel bottoms.   A great variety of green
grass, and very luxuriant, covered the bottoms for miles

where the soil was sufficiently damp, but in other places although the soil was good, yet the grass had nearly dried up for want of moisture. We found the drier places swarming with very large crickets, about the size of a man's thumb.

"This valley is surrounded with mountains, except on the north, the tops of some of the highest being covered with snow. Every one or two miles the streams were emptying into it from the mountains on the east, many of which were sufficiently large to carry mills and other machinery. As we proceeded towards the Salt Lake the soil began to assume a more sterile appearance being, probably, at some seasons of the year overflowed with water. We found, as we proceeded on, great numbers of hot springs issuing from near the base of the mountains. These springs were highly impregnated with salt and sulphur. The temperature of some was nearly raised to the boiling point. We traveled about fifteen miles down after coming into the valley. The latter part of the distance the soil being unfit for agricultural purposes. We returned and found our wagons encamped in the valley five and one-fourth miles from where they left the canyon.

"The morning of the 23rd of July, two messengers were sent to President Young, and those who were with him, informing them of the discoveries and explorations of the advance party. The camp removed its position two miles to the north and encamped near the bank of a beautiful creek of pure, cold water. This stream is sufficiently large for mills and other machinery. Here we called the camp together and it fell to my lot to offer prayer and thanksgiving in behalf of our company, all of whom had been preserved from the Missouri river to this point, and, after dedicating ourselves and the land unto the Lord, and imploring His blessing upon our labors, we appointed various committees to attend to different branches of business, preparatory to putting in crops.   In about two hours after our arrival we began to plow, and the same afternoon built a dam to irrigate the soil, which at the place where we were plowing was exceedingly dry.   *   *   *   *   *   *   *

"Our two messengers returned bringing us word that the remainder of the wagons were only a few miles distant and would arrive the next day.   At three o'clock the thermometer stood at 96°."

The 24th of July has been celebrated as the anniversary of the arrival of the pioneers in the valley of the Great Salt Lake from the circumstance that on that day, 1847, Brigham Young, who had been detained by sickness, and those who had remained with him, first emerged from the defile in the Wasatch mountains and followed the track of the main body who preceded them. It was the culmination of a long series of efforts to find a place of rest, where the Saints could enjoy immunity from the pursuit of enemies.

There is a slight elevation of table land a short distance in front of Emigration canyon.   This hides the valley from the traveler until the top of it is reached. From this point Brigham Young and those who were with him, among whom were his brother L. D. Young, Apostles Wilford Woodruff and Heber C. Kimball, had their first view of the object of their toils, the valley of the Great Salt Lake. It requires no stretch of the imagination to comprehend that a feeling of joy, of exhilaration and thanksgiving filled to overflowing the hearts of these weary pilgrims. The faith that had sustained them through years of suffering and hope enabled them to discern in the near future the attainment of the object of

their sacrifices.   They experienced the same impulse to
shout for joy of those who had preceded them.

President Young, still feeble from the effects of his

THE FIRST VIEW OF THE VALLEY.

late illness, was riding under the cover of Elder Woodruff's carriage.   As the teams halted he came to the
front, took a general view of the country before him,
then uncovered his head, swung his hat and shouted with

all the energy his feeble condition permitted, "Hurrah! Hurrah!! Hurrah!!!" Then turning to Heber C. Kimball who was near, he exclaimed, "Brother Heber, *this is the place.*" The circumstances emphasized the expression with a world of meaning. "This is the place" that has been prophesied of from the days of Kirtland, where the Saints are to be gathered from the nations of the earth and acquire strength to further contend for the right. Here is the place where we will build temples to the Lord our God and make greater preparations than we have been able to do, surrounded by enemies, for the redemption of our race.

President Young's party found the main body encamped by some cottonwood trees on the bank of a branch of City Creek, about six miles from the mouth of Emigration canyon. They had had their first sight of the waters of the lake shimmering in the brilliant sunshine of an almost cloudless sky, also of Black Rock, which has since become a familiar landmark to many thousands of people. Not a cloud floated above them, and the heavens had that peculiar blue seldom seen except in a very rarefied atmosphere. Dark spots, indicating forests, were visible in the distant, inaccessible mountain tops, but the timber to be utilized by the colony was mostly hidden from sight in the deep gorges which debouched into the valley. The foothills which skirted the valley afforded no timber except scattering scrub cedar and pines. There were a few cottonwoods and a clump or two of willows along City Creek. The valley afforded no cooling forest shade, no green savannahs relieved the monotony of desolation. The most prominent varieties of vegetation were wild sunflowers with large, yellow blossoms and a species of dwarf thistle peculiar to the uplands. These grew thick on the dry benches, contending with the wild sage for the scanty nourishment afforded by the arid soil.

These plants were loaded with hideous crickets, their black and brown bodies forming anything but a pleasing contrast with the yellow tint of the sunflower blossoms. As these ugly, ogling-eyed insects fed and fattened on the juice of these plants, they were in a withered condition. Being the prominent vegetation on the bench lands at that season of the year, the appearance of the landscape begat an indescribable feeling of desolation. The air was almost painfully clear and the ground dry and parched. There was none of the haziness of lower altitudes to modify the sun's rays, and there was no shelter from them except under tents and wagon covers; still the heat was not so exhausting as in lower regions.

The most prominent animals of this desert were the howling and almost ever present wolf, the jack rabbit, or American hare, and an occasional mountain lion. The scattered specimens of humanity that wandered about in this region were almost on a level with the sneaking, thieving wolf. They were not only root diggers but cricket eaters. These ill-starred insects may be very palatable to the cultivated tastes of the Indian in the days when his existence depended on anything that would sustain life, but the writer believes that the sight of them would tend at least to modify the appetite of a starving white man.

The Indian bands of these valleys at that time utilized these crickets for food, in large quantities. The cricket harvest commenced soon after the arrival of the pioneers. It was after they had attained their full growth, were in fine condition, and when their live weight was about one ounce each. At such times they were very clumsy and easily handled. The squaws and pappooses would inclose a small piece of ground with stalks of sunflowers, leaving an opening on one side for the admittance of the game. They then surrounded a piece of ground, drove the crickets on it together, and forced them into the pen, in much the same manner that a flock of sheep are corraled. In this pen they would often be several inches thick. The entrance was closed, the fence fired, while some one in the pen frightened the crickets into the blaze. It would scorch their wings and legs and generally kill them. They were gathered up, usually dried in the sun on skins and if these were not available the ground was utilized for that purpose. When properly prepared they were packed in skin sacks and usually cached or buried in the ground for winter food. The process completed, the wings and legs, the only part considered offal, would be pretty well cleaned off. The fact that they were a staple article of food, evidences they were quite palatable and nourishing to the cultivated taste of the Indian.

The following circumstance, illustrating the thieving propensities of these aboriginal Americans indicates that the Saints did not much improve their Indian associations in changing their location from the vicinity of the thieving Pawnees and Omahas to the midst of the cricket eaters of the desert. Towards evening after the arrival of President Young, the Indian chief, Wanship, to whose people the surrounding country belonged, came into camp. He was soon followed by twelve or fifteen braves. Probably few of them had before seen a white man, except mountaineers who more or less assimilated with the barbarian in their habits. They had a human curiosity to gratify, and a natural right to know something of their new neighbors. A few ideas were exchanged by signs and a little bread was distributed by the pioneers. While

8

engaged in these friendly preliminaries to a better acquaintance one of Wanship's sons went out of camp to where the visiting Indians had left their horses. Suddenly he gave a tremendous yell. This appeared to have a peculiar significance, for every Indian in camp sprang to his feet.

As was afterwards ascertained, Little Chief, brother of Wanship, at that time lived with his band at the foot of Utah Lake, and his sons were on a visit to their uncle Wanship and their cousins. All went to the pioneer camp together. While Wanship's boys were gratifying their curiosity in the camp their three cousins mounted two of their horses, two on one and one on the other, and rode off. When young Wanship discovered the theft the yell he gave signified to his friends that something was wrong. The band was soon mounted and in hot pursuit, the fastest horses leading out at full speed. In about an hour they returned to camp with one of their stolen ponies. They overtook and killed the two Indians on one horse, three or four miles from camp going south. The other thief was pursued but escaped. These incidents gave the pioneers some comprehension of the character of their new neighbors.

The 25th of July Lorenzo D. Young went up City Creek to a scrubby oak tree, near where the bridge now crosses the creek at the north-east corner of the temple block. It seemed a more desirable camp ground than the one then occupied. He returned to camp and, by permission, moved his wagons on to the ground. President Young and others soon after came along, and being also pleased with the spot, directed the company to move on to it. The season was far advanced, and those having seeds lost no time in putting them into the ground.

The pioneers, from the first, did not expect to raise

a crop that season, but took seeds with them to plant that they might learn, as soon as possible, something of the character of the soil and climate of their new location. It would be great satisfaction to know that food plants would grow. There was also a chance of producing some germs of plants for the ensuing year. Men, well acquainted with the country, had spoken discouragingly of the chances for successful colonization. Col. James Bridger had expressed doubts whether the food plants used by man in temperate climates would grow at all. This will explain the anxiety of the pioneers to experiment in that direction.

CHAPTER XVI.

THE INITIAL POINT FOR THE SURVEY OF THE COUNTRY—FIRST LESSONS IN IRRIGATION—ARRIVAL OF THE PUEBLO DETACHMENT OF THE MORMON BATTALION ACCOMPANIED BY A COMPANY OF SAINTS FROM THE SOUTHERN STATES—HOW THESE COMPANIES CAME TO CONNECT WITH THE PIONEERS—NARRATIVE OF ELDER THOMAS BULLOCK—SALT LAKE VALLEY MEXICAN DOMAIN—PREPARATIONS FOR DEFENCE AND SHELTER—BRIGHAM YOUNG RETURNS TO WINTER QUARTERS TO ORGANIZE THE GATHERING—WHAT THE PIONEERS ACCOMPLISHED IN ONE MONTH.

A THOROUGH examination of the country was necessary for the colonists to fit themselves into their new environment to advantage. Its features and characteristics were strange and novel. If it contained the elements of wealth it also required different methods of developing that wealth to those they had been accustomed to on the rich bottom lands and rolling prairies of Illinois and Iowa.

In the forepart of the day, July 25th, Brigham Young and others walked to the top of Ensign Peak, now north of Salt Lake City. From there they had an excellent view of the country west and south. Its apparent facilities were freely discussed from that standpoint. They then descended to camp where a team was brought into service, driven by L. D. Young. With this they visited various other points to obtain a more extended idea of their surroundings. Then on foot they more particularly examined the ground now known as the temple block. At the south-east corner of this piece of ground President Young made a mark with his cane and said, "We will make this the initial point for the survey of the country."

They were in the desert to found a state. Their being there was the result of circumstances forced upon them and the outgrowth of an all-absorbing religious faith. The ruling idea was manifest in partitioning the soil. Ten acres of land were first appropriated to sacred purposes, the erection of buildings for religious worship, and eventually a magnificent temple in which the higher ordinances of their religion could be observed.

While the pioneers were engaged in plowing the new soil, putting in seeds, taking their first lessons in irrigation, and examining their surroundings, on the 27th of July, three days after their arrival, the detachment of the Mormon Battalion, under Captain James Brown, accompanied by a company of Saints from the Southern States, entered the valley. Following so closely on the heels of the company from Winter Quarters they might, very appropriately, be considered the rear division of the first pioneers to the great basin.

To understand how a part of the Mormon Battalion and a considerable company of Saints came to follow the first pioneers so closely, it will be necessary to go back to the march of the Battalion to the Pacific coast. The previous year, when that notable body of men arrived at the town of Santa Fe, New Mexico, on the 15th of October, their commander, Colonel Cooke, ordered the men unfit for active service and the women with the Battalion back to Pueblo on the Arkansas river to winter. He considerately detailed the husbands of the women as a guard to the invalids and women. This detachment left Santa Fe on the 18th of October. Owing to the feeble condition of many of the men and the weakness of teams, there was much suffering on this march.

The 17th of November, 1846, the detachment arrived at Pueblo. There they found a company of Saints from the state of Mississippi who were expecting to find the Church on its way to the mountains, for thus had they been advised by Elders who had ministered among them before leaving their homes; huts were built and considering the circumstances, the winter was spent quite comfortably.

The 18th of May, 1847, the detachment received orders to march *via* Salt Lake to California. The 24th of May it commenced its march by crossing the Arkansas river. Owing to high water and other difficulties the journey was a very fatiguing one. The 5th of June it crossed the south fork of the Platte river. There it was met by a party from the pioneers, who were only a few days ahead of the detachment, on their way to Great Salt Lake valley. The pioneers had received information of the detachment, and of the Saints accompanying it, from a Mr. Crow whom they found at Laramie on their arrival there, as we have before stated.   There seems a special providence that the general government should have ordered these Mormon soldiers in the right direction to so easily gather with their people.   Apostle Amasa Lyman, one of the party sent by President Young, remained with the detachment.   On the 16th of June it encamped near Laramie.   The pioneers had left there about twelve days before.   As these soldiers were now on the trail of their migrating people, the long march from Great Salt Lake valley to California, for the purpose of being discharged, appeared no longer necessary. They were at the crossing of Green river the day their term of service expired.   Thus by a chain of singular providences this detachment, and the company of Saints from Mississippi, became early pioneers of Utah.   The military were disbanded by Captain Brown and at once commenced their labors to make a home in the desert.

The following extract from a letter written by President B. Young, dated January 6th, 1848, and addressed to Elders Hyde, Pratt and Taylor in Europe, explains how the detachment of the Battalion and the Saints who wintered with them became fully posted as to the intended movements of the Church in the spring of 1847, and thus prepared to intercept the pioneers on their journey to the mountains.   President Young states in this letter that on or about the 19th of October, 1846, John D. Lee, Howard Egan and Lieutenant Pace left the Battalion at Santa Fe to return to Winter Quarters.   "On the route Brother Lee met Elders Brown and Crosby of Mississippi, on their return from the Arkansas river where they had been with the camp this season, and not finding us, as they had anticipated, had located their company on that river for the winter, and were on their return for a reinforcement to join them in the spring, hoping to fall in with us and pass over the mountains together. They had a joyful meeting and we have written them how and when to unite their camps with ours at the foot of the mountains next spring."

As John D. Lee and party left Santa Fe about the same time as did the detachment for Pueblo, there is no doubt he informed Messrs. Brown and Crosby of their march for that place.

The Twelve, and several others went out on the road to meet the men of the Battalion, numbering about one hundred and fifty, and the emigrants from the state of Mississippi. About the time the two parties met there was a thunder shower, with sufficient rain to raise the mountain streams very rapidly. After their arrival, the camp on City Creek numbered between three and four hundred souls.

The following extract from a letter of Mr. Thomas Bullock will give a still better understanding of the impressions made on the pioneers by their new surroundings :

"After passing Fort Bridger, a delightful camping place, you can camp almost anywhere. The grass will sustain your animals anytime in the year. When the muskett grass is dry it answers for corn, hay and grass at the same time. Between Fort Bridger and the valley the mountains are very high. The road winds through the valleys, some of which are narrow, not more than ten rods wide, while the rocks in places overhang the road. The dividing ridge that we have to go over is about 7,300 feet above the level of the sea. From this ridge you will see the Twin Peaks covered with eternal snow. Those peaks run into the valley and when you see them you will sing out, 'I shall soon be at home now.'

"There is no fear of your traveling far out of the way, for you are hemmed in by mountains on each side. After crossing a small creek twenty-one times in five miles, and between mountains a mile high, on making a sudden bend in the road, you come into full view of the Great Salt Lake and of a valley about twenty by thirty miles. Although there is very little timber to be seen, you will be sure to say, 'Thank God I am home at last.' On this spot I am now talking to you about, the pioneers arrived on the 24th of July last, at 5 p. m. The next morning they removed to the spot where the city will be built; at noon consecrated and dedicated the place to the Lord. The same afternoon four plows were turning up the ground. Next day the brethren had planted five acres of potatoes, and irrigated all the land at night.

"The following Sunday was a day of rest, a day of rejoicing before the Lord. His spirit was poured out, and peace dwelt in the valleys of the mountains. The first Sabbath in the valley where a city is to be built unto the Lord, by a holy people, will be long remembered by that little band of pioneers who cried, Hosanna to the Lamb of God!"

The following stanzas from a poem by W. W. Phelps, chime in beautifully with the sentiment of the above:

> A life in the desert plains,
>   A home in the mountain's breast,
> Where the Indian rudely reigns
>   And the hell is farther west ;
> Where the storm king sorely rides,
>   In his flying, cloudy car,
> With his nimble windy guides,
>   O'er the snow-capped mountains far.
>
> Behold, how the valley smiles!
>   The sky like a mirror's seen ;

And the spotted mountain wilds
Are a world of evergreen,
Where the hairy nations leap,
　And the feathered gentry soar,
In the clear, blue upper deep
As the rushing waters roar.

*　　*　　*　　*　　*　　*　　*

When the pioneers arrived in Great Salt Lake valley it was Mexican domain, held by right of conquest, awaiting the fortunes of a war then pending between the United States and Mexico. At the close of the war a large tract of country, including what is now Utah Territory, was ceded to the former. The Mormon Battalion assisted in its conquest, and the Mormon people were the first to colonize it.

There seemed no limit to the difficulties to be overcome by these colonizers of the desert. Circumstances were constantly changing and unavoidable issues as constantly arising. To successfully grapple with them, required experience and an enlightened judgment in the leaders of the people, and in the people themselves, an abiding faith in their God and those leaders.

The Saints were locating among the wild tribes of the desert, a thousand miles from a civilization that cast them out, and from which they could expect neither sympathy nor assistance in emergencies. They must organize from the surrounding elements the means of subsistence or perish. With policy or force, or both, they must defend themselves from the aggressions of the wild tribes by which they were surrounded or suffer extinction at their hands. Wisdom dictated that they should assume the best possible position for defence. For this purpose ten acres of ground were surveyed one mile south-west of the temple block, on which to build their houses in fort form. This was inclosed with an adobe wall eight feet high and three feet thick at the bottom, slanting gradually to the top. Inside of this wall the houses were built, the fort wall forming one side of the rooms. Rapid progress was made by these pioneers in preparing shelter for their families. They had been so much under tents and wagon covers, that any house that would protect them from the elements was a luxury. Besides, winter was approaching and bitter experience had taught them the wisdom of making the best possible preparation for it.

Under the great pressure of the season's operations, one short month was all the time President Young could spare to personally direct the infant colony. The much desired haven of rest had been found and a beginning made, but the great mass of the Saints expelled from Illinois, were in a scattered condition at Winter Quarters and east of the Missouri river. The gathering which had now been inaugurated was yet to be thoroughly systematized.

The order and rapidity with which this grand exodus had so far been conducted, and with which it was completed, has historically marked the great executive abilities of the quorum of Twelve Apostles, with Brigham Young as a central directing power. The 25th of August, 1847, accompanied by H. C. Kimball and forty others, among whom was Elder Thomas Bullock, he left Salt Lake valley, for Winter Quarters.

The following statements from a letter written by Mr. Thomas Bullock to his friend, F. D. Richards, gives us a general description of what the pioneers accomplished in one month. They plowed and planted eighty-four acres with corn, beans, potatoes, buckwheat, turnips and a variety of garden vegetables. They irrigated all the

land, surveyed and laid out a city with streets running east and west, north and south, into blocks of ten acres, subdivided into eight lots of one and a quarter acres each. The streets eight rods wide designed for a walk on each side twenty feet wide, to be ornamented with shade trees. All the houses to be built twenty feet back from the street fence, with flower gardens in front. One block , was reserved for a temple and three for public grounds; the latter designed for promenades, with fountains of the purest water, and each square, ornamented with every-thing delightful.   *   *   *   *   *   *   *
They also built twenty-seven log houses, laid off a ten acre lot for a fort, where one hundred and sixty families could winter until they built on their own inheritances. They manufactured one hundred and twenty-five bushels of beautiful salt. We continue the description in Elder Bullock's words.

"The water is so strong that I can walk in it without touching bottom, I can float on it, yet in fresh water I cannot swim a yard. It is most delightful to bathe in, as is also the warm spring, a mile and a half north of the city. Every person, who was sick, that bathed in this spring recovered. My fingers rooted out the stones, and a couple of brethren afterwards assisted me with spades to dig out a place about sixteen feet square to bathe in. Seven or eight persons often bathe in it at a time. Those who once go there want to go again. The water is 109° Fahr. with strong sulphur and salt taste. Two miles further north is a hot spring with water heated to 126°. The water rushes out of a large rock, and I could not hold my fingers in it while I could count eleven.   *   *   *   There are altogether about fifty springs in three miles.   *   *   *   *
These springs, like the Pool of Siloam, heal all who

bathe, no matter what their complaints.   The air is very salubrious and with these warm springs I can truly say, we have found a healthy country."

The pioneers seemed early to comprehend many of the advantages of their new location; immunity from the oppression of mobs, air in which there was no ague and fever, abundance of good land and water in the valley, and of timber in the mountains, the latter out of their way but available when needed, an inland sea affording delightful bathing, an abundance of fine salt with but little labor to obtain it, and a "Pool of Siloam" in which they could wash and be clean from diseases engendered in the miasmatical atmosphere of Illinois and Iowa; all free as the invigorating air they breathed, was, indeed a marvelous change of conditions.

CHAPTER XVII.

THE IMMIGRATION OF 1847—ORGANIZATION AND METHOD OF TRAVEL—SUBLIME FAITH OF THESE SAINTS—MAIL FACILITIES—FIRST LESSON IN STAMPEDES—WRITING ON A BUFFALO SKULL—STAMPEDE AND LOSS OF TWENTY YOKE OF OXEN—P. H. YOUNG BRINGS NEWS FROM THE PIONEERS—SICKNESS AND DEATH—THE ALKALI LANDS—MEET RETURNING SOLDIERS AND PIONEERS— EXCITING STAMPEDE—DEATH OF SISTER GRANT— ARRIVAL IN THE VALLEY.

WE WILL now leave the pioneers; those in the valley to pursue their urgent labors, and those return-ing to Winter Quarters to continue their wearisome journey under difficulties, and go back and bring up the emigration who were expected in a short time, to follow the trail of the pioneers. The wagons to make up these companies began to gather on the west side of the Elk Horn river about the 12th of June, 1847. On the 15th about three hundred wagons having collected, a meeting was called around a liberty pole erected to designate a place for public gathering. Orson Spencer's company was the first organized. It moved off the ground on the 18th of June. The 19th, Captain J. M. Grant's hundred traveled fifteen miles and encamped in sight of Captain Spencer's. The order of encampment was for the wagons to form a circle with their front ends outside. At one point a sufficient space was left between two wagons to drive the cattle in and out. This space was partially closed by passing chains to the wagons on either side of the passage. In this way a convenient corral was formed in which to secure the cattle at night. Experience proved this method to be better adapted to companies in which all the wagons were built for heavy loads of freight, strong and heavy enough to resist the pressure of the cattle in the rush of a stampede. In time other expedients were adopted in which there was not so much danger to wagons and their occupants.

The writer has not been able to obtain very satisfactory returns of the organization of this emigration, but the five hundred and sixty or five hundred and sixty-six wagons appeared to have been organized into five hundreds, respectively, under the direction of Orson Spencer, J. M. Grant, A. O. Smoot, John Taylor and P. P. Pratt. The following from the autobiography of Parley P. Pratt furnishes some information not found elsewhere. He says:

"Arriving at Elk Horn river with a small company we made a ferry of a raft of dry cottonwood timber and rafted over our own company of about fifty wagons. We then organized for herding and grazing purposes, and continued to aid others in crossing and organizing until five hundred and sixty-six wagons were finally crossed and organized ready for a march. In the final organization of this vast company Father Isaac Morley and Bishop Whitney assisted, or rather took the oversight — being a committee appointed for that purpose by the Presidency before they left. As Brother Taylor and myself were present, we were appointed and invited to take a general superintendency of this emigration.

"The organization consisted of companies of tens, fifties and hundreds, with a captain over each, and the whole presided over by a president and two counselors, a marshal, etc. President John Young was called to preside, having been nominated by the Presidency before their departure. John Van Cott was appointed marshal.

"Thus organized, this large company moved on up the Platte about the 4th of July. * * * Arriving at the north fork of the Platte river, we continued up it quite a distance above the trail the pioneers had made, as we could not ford the river in their track. We at length found a ford, and, with some difficulty on account of quicksand, forded the river, and made our way over to the main Platte, re-entering the pioneer trail. As we passed up the Platte on this trail the companies in front had frequently to halt and build bridges, etc. * * * * After journeying for several hundred miles up the Platte, we at length met two messengers from the pioneers under President Young, from Salt Lake valley. These were O. P. Rockwell and E. T. Benson, who had been sent out to find us and report our progress and circumstances. Having visited all the camps, they returned to the valley, or rather to where they met the President and pioneers on their way back to Winter Quarters on the Missouri. I accompanied them back nearly one day's ride on the way, and then bade them God speed and returned to my own camp. Soon after this our fifty met the President and company of pioneers and camped with them one day."

Having given Parley P. Pratt's outlining of a part of the journey, we will go back and fill it up with other interesting items, many of them from Miss E. R. Snow's journal.

On the 23rd the companies traveled two wagons abreast. That night four organizations of hundreds, respectively, under the command of captains John Taylor, P. P. Pratt, J. M. Grant and A. O. Smoot camped on the road within a distance of six miles. All who expected to follow the pioneers this season were now fairly on the way.

In this move was one of the grandest exhibitions on record of the faith of a people in the divine inspiration of their leaders. When ancient Israel followed their Moses out of Egypt it was with doubts and complaints. A more fitting parallel to the case of these Latter-day Saints is found in that of the Jaredites. With no other assurance of their safety than the assertion of their leaders, that the Lord would guide them across "the great waters" to the goodly land which they and their children should inherit, they embarked on vessels without sails, compass or rudder to float out on, to them a limitless ocean at the mercy of winds and ocean currents. Their faith in God and their leaders was evidently boundless.

These two thousand Saints set their faces towards the setting sun, with their wives and their little ones with no other guide in the vast and almost unexplored wilderness than the trail left by their leaders, who at the time of their starting, had been gone over two months and were then buried in the profound silence of the desert, without the slightest intimation of their fate, of their success or failure. They expected to find their leaders somewhere in the great expanse of desert, plain, and mountain peaks and valleys, lying between the Missouri river and the Pacific Ocean, two thousand miles distant. In 1846, they planted a colony on the western ocean ; about the same time in 1847, they planted another in the heart of the continent. From the first colonizing of the Atlantic coast the western frontier had been an imaginary line, constantly moving westward, with the log cabins of the white man, until it reached the Mississippi and Missouri rivers. With the march of the emigrating Saints in 1847 the "Western Frontier" vanished and became historical.

When the emigrating camps were getting under way the pioneers were along by Independence Rock and Devil's Gate. The wagons of the emigrating companies were generally drawn by from four to eight oxen each, and the rate of travel was from ten to fifteen miles per day. The animals were sustained, solely by the grass the country produced. On the 1st of July, they crossed Loupe Fork of the Platte. "They sometimes traveled two, sometimes four, and sometimes six wagons abreast, on roads and without roads. A Mr. Russell found a bucket which he recognized as one he had given to H. C. Kimball. The 5th of July the companies camped on Grand Island where a board was found on which the pioneers had written comforting words, marked the distance two hundred and seventeen miles from Winter Quarters." These way tokens indicating the welfare of their leaders, and the great anxiety of those leaders for their people who were to follow, were very cheering to these emigrating camps.

In the morning of the 14th of July the camps received their first lesson in stampedes on the plains. They learned the terrible pressure of a mass of frightened cattle upon the wagons of a corral which encloses them.

The account of it is from the journal of Miss E. R. Snow.

"This morning a fearful circumstance occurred. Some one was shaking a buffalo robe at the back of a wagon from which some of the cattle in the corral took fright and started on the run ; those frightened others ; they commenced bellowing ; and all in a huddle, ran for the gateway of the enclosure, which being altogether too narrow for the egress of the rushing multitude that thronged into the passage, they piled one on top of another until the top ones were above the tops of the adjacent wagons, moving them from their stations while the inmates at this early hour, being so suddenly and unceremoniously aroused from their morning sleep, and not knowing the cause of this terrible uproar and confusion, were some of them almost paralyzed with fear. At length those that could, broke from the enclosure, the bellowing subsided and quiet was restored ; but the sad effect of the fright caused much suffering to some whose nerves were not sufficient for the trying scene. In the encounter two wagon wheels were crushed, Captain K's only cow was killed, and several oxen had horns knocked off."

Captain Grant brought a buffalo skull into camp on which the pioneers had written, "All well—feed bad—are only three hundred miles from Winter Quarters," etc. The writing was dated May 9th. Up to that point the pioneers had made three hundred miles in twenty-six days, and the emigrating companies had not done much better. A large bear was killed and divided among J. M. Grant's hundred. The cattle of Captain Smoot's division broke out of the corral and in the morning twenty yoke were gone. This was a serious loss and on the 21st, after much deliberation, several hunters were sent after the lost cattle.

9

July 23rd the cannon was fired in the first company. The occasion was a visit from one hundred Sioux Indians. The following day those sent in search of the lost cattle returned with only four head.

The 25th of July Phineas H. Young and nine others of the pioneers met the companies. A meeting was called and a letter read from President Young, and one from Willard Richards. This interesting circumstance took place the 25th of July, the day after the pioneers arrived in the valley.

As before stated, after the pioneers had crossed Green river, five men were sent back on their trail on the 4th of July to meet the advancing companies of Saints and assist them as guides through the Black Hills. Those selected were Phineas H. Young, Aaron Farr, Rodney Badger, William Walker and Jonathan Pugmire. At the old Platte ferry, one hundred and twenty miles west of Laramie, they were joined by five more of the pioneers. They expected to meet the companies near the Black Hills but, instead, found them about three hundred miles west of Winter Quarters. This unexpectedly long distance to travel, with the increase of numbers at the ferry, nearly caused the starvation of the whole company of guides. They had plenty of food to Laramie, from there until they met the companies they were almost destitute and suffered greatly. For five days and nights, they had but two prairie dogs and a skunk to divide among ten men.

They found no game. Of the armies of buffalo met by the pioneers not one was to be seen, for the Indians had driven them off and they had gone into the hills.

It was not only a great relief to the guides when they met the companies opposite Ash Hollow but, as well, of the emigrating camps who were following cautiously in the track of the pioneer band. The news brought of the successful journey of the pioneers as far as Green river; the certainty that they had already reached the valleys of the Rocky Mountains, with the presence of the guides sent to pilot the companies through the Black Hills, gave great comfort and assurance to the emigrating Saints, who could not but feel some anxiety as to the result of the season's operations.

The 26th of July many Indians passed the companies with tents and baggage fastened to mules and horses, and on drays formed of tent poles drawn by horses, mules and dogs. Covers for little ones were made by fastening skins over bows which were attached to the upper side of the drays.

On the morning of August 4th the people were cheered by the arrival of fourteen Mormon soldiers of the Battalion, who were an escort to General Kearney on his way to Fort Leavenworth. There they expected to get their discharge. They were husbands and sons of women in the companies. To them more especially it was a joyful meeting.

"Death," says Sister Snow, "made occasional inroads among us. Nursing the sick in tents and wagons was a laborious service ; but the patient faithfulness with which it was performed is, no doubt, registered in the archives above, as an unfailing memento of brotherly and sisterly love. The burial of the dead by the wayside was a sad office. For husbands, wives and children to consign the cherished remains of loved ones to a lone, desert grave, was enough to try the firmest heart-strings. Today a Sister Ewing who had passed away after a sickness of two weeks, was buried. The burial was attended with all the propriety the circumstances would

permit.   After the customary dressing the body was
wrapped in a quilt and consigned to its narrow house.
It truly seemed sad and we sorrowed deeply as we turned
from the lonely grave." The 9th of August the companies were fairly in the Black Hills.   On the 12th, Mrs.
Mary Noble gave birth to a daughter in her wagon.
The same day charcoal was burned for the camp blacksmiths, and five gallons of tar was made by one of the
companies.

On the 19th a Sister Love was run over by a wagon
loaded with sixteen hundred pounds.   One wheel ran
over her breast.   She was administered to and was
around again in a day or two.

August 25th.   This was the day the pioneers left
the valley for Winter Quarters.   The emigrating camps
passed the board marked one hundred and twenty miles
from Fort Laramie.   When the herd was brought in on
the 28th, half the animals were missing.   Those who had
their teams went on.   Three horsemen and three foot-
men went back on the road for the lost cattle.   However
they had taken the other direction, and were found by
the teams that had gone on.   The party returning them
were met by boys sent in that direction from the wagons
that remained in camp.

August 30th the companies passed the ferryboat,
used by the pioneers in crossing the Sweetwater below
Independence Rock.   The road along here passes
through the alkali lands.   As this was the first experience of our emigration passing through this district, so
fatal to cattle, the losses were heavy.   Their carcasses
were numerous along the wayside.   The second fifty was
almost disabled.

These misfortunes developed the communistic character of the Saints.   The 1st of September a meeting

was called to take into consideration the best means of modifying the difficulties of the situation. An effort was made to equalize the strength of the companies. "It was motioned that the captains be authorized to act for the companies and yoke whatever in their judgment was proper to be put to service, cows, heifers, calves, etc. Some thought this motion oppressive, but it was carried by a majority."

Of the meeting of soldiers and pioneers from the valley Miss Snow writes, September 2nd: "Last eve we had the pleasure of hearing from the valley and of tasting salt from the Great Salt Lake by a small party of soldiers and pioneers with three wagons, and on the 3rd met a larger party with perhaps eighteen wagons. On the 4th of September J. C. Little, a returning pioneer, took tea with us with mutual satisfaction. The pioneers call our present encampment three hundred miles from the valley.

"September 7th: Yesterday, we passed the two hundred and forty mile board—snow-storm last night and it continued to fall at intervals today. September 8th: This morning as we were starting, Harvey Pierce, and others, came up and informed us that the pioneers were only eighteen miles distant, and would soon be with us. It was decided to go two miles further to a good camping place. The road went over a slough, the bridge over which was so much out of repair that it was thought impossible for wagons to cross, and a halt was called to repair the crossing. The slough was at the foot of a long gentle slope, and the teams two and three abreast, were standing from the top nearly down to the place where the men were commencing to fix the bridge.

"At this time when many of the teamsters were lounging at ease, two of our young men, riding at full speed with blankets flying and whips in hand, rode up, and in passing the teams in the rear, so frightened them that they started down the hill, and as they went they started others until almost in a moment nearly all were in motion, increasing their rapidity until the scene was fearfully alarming. Many of them crossed the slough in different directions, and where the best of teamsters would not dare to drive, not one team crossing on the bridge. Many lives were exposed, but through the great blessing of our Heavenly Father no one was much hurt.

"The writer of this sketch happened to be sitting on the back seat of a two-seated carriage, holding a pair of high strung horses with all the strength I could exert. I prayed with all the fervency of my spirit. I knew full well that if they once started nothing could stop them. Sister Pierce and her daughter, with whom I was traveling, after making ineffectual efforts to stop one of their teams, came to the horses I was holding and took them by the bits. So frightened were they, that although they made no attempt to move, their flesh shook with a tremor from head to foot. My arms were lame for several days. We arrived at our encampment and spent the day with the pioneers. President Young, H. C. Kimball and A. Lyman took supper with us."

Of this joyful occasion Elder John Taylor writes in a letter to the Saints in England, dated Great Salt Lake City, December 7th, 1847. "Four hundred miles from this place we received by express from the pioneers, the pleasing intelligence of their arrival at this place which they had selected for the Saints. On our arrival at the South Pass of the Rocky Mountains, the hundred that I was with met the pioneers on the return to Winter Quarters, in company with a number of the Battalion who had been engaged in the service of the United States. We felt as though it was a time to rejoice. Our hearts were gladdened and we prepared a feast for them, and spread a table in the wilderness, on the tops of the mountains, at which one hundred and thirty of them sat down to partake. We mutually felt edified and rejoiced. We praised the Lord and blessed one another, and in the morning we separated; they to pursue their weary course and we to come to our present location."

The people of Captain Grant's company and the pioneers were so delighted with the visit, and there was such a sense of security, that the stock were left unguarded; as a result, forty horses and mules were stolen. On the 9th an armed company was sent on their trail. Late in the evening one of the party returned with two horses. In the evening there was preaching by the pioneers and the pioneer song was sung. The 10th of September the company sent in pursuit of the stolen animals returned with only three horses.

The pioneers and Captain Grant's company parted, each going their ways with pleasant reminiscences of the interview. President Young had advised the leaders of the companies to keep them together until they arrived at Green river. From there they might be permitted to brake up into tens, as in this shape they could travel better through the gorges and defiles of the Wasatch mountains. On the 14th Captain Grant's company was given leave to so break up. About this time Capt. Grant's wife died. She had been failing sometime. Sister Snow writes; "I was with her much, previous to her death, which occurred so near Salt Lake valley, that by forced drives night and day, her remains were brought through for interment. Not so, however, with her beautiful babe of eight or ten months, whose death preceded her's about two weeks; it was buried in the desert."

The 29th of September Sister Snow first saw the part of the valley visible from the Big mountain. For the incidents of the last two days of the ten with which she traveled, we copy from her journal. As the companies were traveling in tens it will give a fair idea of the experience of others:

"October 1st. This day we traveled through brush and timber, but what was still worse, through black dust with which we all were so densely covered that our identities might me questioned. When up the mount to Bellow's Peak we met Brother John Taylor, who, having reached the valley, was returning to meet that portion of his company now in the rear. Riding on horseback, through the interminable dust, his face was covered with a black mask, and in his happy, jocular way, lest I should compliment him, he hastened to ask me if I had lately seen my face. Our appearance was truly ludicrous. It mattered little to us as we went slash, mash, down the mount, over stumps, trees, roots, ruts, etc., where no one dared to ride who could walk.

"October 2nd. Captain Pierce and most of his ten arrived in the valley a little after ourselves. The general order of travel having been discontinued for a few days past as we neared the valley, small detachments arrived according to circumstances. Many were in before us, and perhaps as many after."

In the following from the letter of John Taylor of the 7th of December before referred to, he doubtless refers to the arrival of all the emigrating Saints:

"We arrived here on the 5th of October, generally enjoying good health. I have never in all my experience known so little sickness and so few deaths among so many people in the same space of time. There have been from six to seven deaths. Two or three were infants and the remainder were mostly, if not all, severely indisposed before they started."

The first few days of October closed the season's operations on the plains. The moving of families and their effects one thousand miles under surrounding conditions was a great experiment, but it was as eminently successful as it first appeared venturesome.

CHAPTER XVIII.

ADVANTAGES OF THE NEW GATHERING PLACE—ORGANIZA-
TION OF A FIRST PRESIDENCY—THE FIRST GENERAL
EPISTLE TO THE SAINTS ORGANIZING THE GATHERING.

PRESIDENT YOUNG and company duly reached Winter Quarters. Owing to the heavy loss of animals the men performed much of the journey on foot, while they subsisted on the flesh of wild animals which they killed by the way.

Of necessity, the Nauvoo exodus suspended the work of gathering until a new location could be found. Considering the world as the field from which the wheat was to be gathered, Great Salt Lake valley was mnch more a central point than any before occupied by the Saints. About one thousand miles of desert, land travel intervened between it and the Pacific Ocean, and between it and the large navigable rivers flowing into the Gulf of Mexico. The point was about equally protected on all sides from the incursion of outside enemies, until the colony should have time to grow and be better able to struggle with antagonisms.

On the return of President Young to Winter Quarters the Apostles appear to have at once taken up the labor of organizing the First Presidency, and of systematizing the gathering. The better location of the Saints made this practicable on a more comprehensive scale than ever before. Their labors culminated in a general epistle to the Saints throughout the earth, dated Winter Quarters, December 23rd, 1847. This contained general instructions to meet the conditions of the Saints everywhere. It may be considered the great trumpet call to the hosts of Israel throughout the world to gather together to the place the Lord had appointed.

The epistle opens with a review of the condition of the Church, the necessity of united effort under general counsel, and a few items connected with the movement from Nauvoo; the difficulties encountered in crossing Iowa, a distance of about three hundred miles, at a very inclement season of the year; the arrival of many of the Saints near Council Bluffs; their locating on the lands of the Pottowatomie Indians, afterwards vacated in favor of the United States; the raising of the Mormon Battalion and consequent weakening of the strength of the "camps of Israel" and then says:

"When the strength of our camps had taken its departure in the Battalion the aged, the infirm, the widow and the fatherless that remained, full of hope and buoyant with faith, determined to prosecute their journey, a small portion of which went as far west as the Pawnee Mission, where, finding it too late to pass the mountains, they turned aside to winter on the banks of the Missouri, at the mouth of Running Water, about two hundred and fifty miles north-west of the Missouri settlements; while the far more extensive and feeble numbers located at this place, called by us Winter Quarters, where upwards of seven hundred houses were built in the short time of about three months, while the great majority located on Pottowatomie lands." * * * *

Mention is made of the journey of the pioneers to Great Salt Lake valley. A general description is given of the country, which from that time was looked upon as a haven of rest and peace by the Saints.

"After tarrying four or five weeks, many of the pioneers commenced their return, nearly destitute of provisions, accompanied by a part of the Battalion, who were quite destitute except a very small quantity of beef, which was soon exhausted. The company had to depend for their subsistence on wild beasts, such as buffalo, deer, antelope, etc., which most of the way were very scarce and many obtained were exceedingly poor and unwholesome. Between the Green and Sweetwater rivers we met five hundred and sixty-six wagons of the emigrating Saints on their way to the valley, at our last encampment with whom we had fifty horses and mules stolen by the Indians, and a few days after we were attacked by a large body of Sioux who drove off many of our horses, but most of these were recovered.

"Our route was by Fort Bridger, the South Pass, Fort John (Laramie), and from thence on the north bank of the Platte to Winter Quarters, where we arrived on the 31st of October, all well, having performed the long and tedious journey with ox as well as horse teams, and with little food except wild flesh, without losing a single man, although many were sick when they left in the spring, insomuch that they were unable to walk until we had traveled more than one-half of the outward distance.

"On the 11th inst. (December) fifteen of the Battalion arrived from California with a pilot from the valley, having suffered much on their return from cold and hunger, with no provisions part of their way but a little horse flesh of the worst kind."

This company of Battalion men left a party of about thirty men of the Battalion on the Sweetwater searching for buffalo. They arrived at Winter Quarters on the 18th of December in a very destitute condition. They also had suffered much from cold and hunger, having subsisted on their worn-out horses and mules.

The following expresses the universal desire of the Saints to find shelter from their enemies and the demon of persecution: "The Saints in this vicinity are bearing their privations in meekness and patience, and making all their exertions tend to their removal westward. Their hearts and all their labors are toward the setting sun, for they desire to be so far removed from those who have been their oppressors that there shall be an everlasting barrier between them and future persecution. * * *

"In compliance with the wishes of the sub-agents we expect to vacate the Omaha lands in the spring.

"Thus, brethren, we have given you a brief idea of what has transpired among us since we left Nauvoo, the present situation of the Saints in this vicinity, and of our feelings and views in general, as preparatory to the reply which we are about to give to the cry, What shall we do?"

The answer to this all-absorbing question to the watching, expectant Saints throughout the world we only give so far as it is applicable to those scattered in the United States and the Canadas.

"Gather yourselves together speedily near to this place, on the east side of the Missouri river, and, if possible, be ready to start from hence by the 1st of May next, or as soon as grass is sufficiently grown, and go to the Great Salt Lake City, with bread sufficient to sustain you until you can raise grain the following season.

"Let the Saints who have been driven and scattered from Nauvoo, and all others in the western states, gather immediately to the east bank of the river, bringing with them all the young stock of various kinds they possibly can; and let all the Saints in the United States and Canada gather to the same place by the first spring navigation, or as soon as they can, bringing their money, goods and effects with them; and so far as they can consistently, gather young stock by the way which is much needed here and will be ready sale; and when here let all who can, go directly over the mountains, and those who cannot, let them go immediately to work at making improvements, raising grain and stock on the lands recently vacated by the Pottowatomie Indians and owned by the United States, and by industry they can soon gather sufficient means to prosecute their journey. In a year or two their young cattle will grow into teams; by interchange of labor they can raise their own grain and provisions, and build their own wagons, and by sale of their improvements to citizens who will gladly come and occupy, they can replenish their clothing, and thus speedily and comfortably procure an outfit. All Saints who are coming on this route will do well to furnish themselves with woollen or winter, instead of summer clothing, generally, as they will be exposed to many chilling blasts before they pass the mountain heights.

"We have before named the Pottowatomie lands as the best place for the brethren to assemble on the route, because the journey is so very long that they must have a stopping place, and this is the nearest point to their final destination which makes it not only desirable but necessary; and as it is a wilderness country, it will not infringe on the rights and privileges of any one; and yet it is so

near western Missouri that a few days travel will give
them an opportunity of trade, if necessity requires, and
this is the best general rendezvous that now presents
without intruding on the rights of others.

"The brethren must recollect that from this point
they pass through a savage country, and their safety
depends on good firearms and plenty of ammunition, and
then they may have their teams run off in open daylight,
as we have had, unless they shall watch closely and con-
tinuously.

"The Saints in western California, who choose are at
liberty to remain ; and all who may hereafter arrive on
the western coast, may exercise their privilege of tarrying
in the vicinity or of coming to head quarters."

Apostle Orson Hyde was left in charge of affairs on
the Missouri during the absence of the pioneers in 1847.
At a feast and grand council held at his house on the 5th
of December, 1847, a First Presidency was chosen by the
Apostles. It consisted of Brigham Young as chief and
H. C. Kimball and Willard Richards as his counselors.
The choice of the Apostles was accepted by the people
at a conference in the log tabernacle in Kanesville, the
24th of December. Orson Hyde was installed, as
President of the Quorum of Twelve Apostles. From
that time until the culmination of the Nauvoo Exodus,
he held the important position of general manager of
affairs at the eastern end of the Mormon emigration
route to the mountains. The Church was now fully
organized according to the pattern given by the Prophet
Joseph, and during the winter of 1847-8 plans were well
matured for the important operations of the coming season.

CHAPTER XIX.

THE MORMON BATTALION AFTER THEIR DISCHARGE AT LOS
ANGELES—INCIDENTS OF THEIR TRAVEL TO SALT LAKE
VALLEY—ABOUT FIFTY OF THEM CONTINUE THEIR
TRAVELS TO WINTER QUARTERS—A WONDERFUL MARCH
OF FOUR THOUSAND MILES UNDER DIFFICULTIES IN
SEVENTEEN MONTHS.

A FITTING close of this season's operations is a sketch of the travels of a part of the Mormon Battalion after their discharge, which took place at Los Angeles, California, on the 16th of July, 1847. So isolated had these men been in the wilds of the Rocky Mountains and in an enemy's country, that they had received no news from their families, or of the movements of their people since the arrival in their camp at Santa Fe of John D. Lee and Howard Egan, in October, the previous year.

When discharged the men had very indefinite ideas of the country along the Pacific coast, and the sources of reliable information were very limited. The idea was prevalent among them that their people would emigrate to the neighborhood of Bear Lake. They had some conception of its location and it was the objective point of their intended travels. The officers of the Battalion met together and leaders were appointed to take companies by different routes. Lieutenant Lorenzo Clark was to take a company *via* Cajon Pass and the Muddy; Captain Jefferson Hunt one up the coast; other leaders in other directions. Owing to dissatisfactions these arrangments were not carried out, and all took their way according to chance or inclination. Captain Hunt took a party up the coast. Lieutenant L. Clark, from whom we have obtained the following incidents of its travels, was one of this party. With this company of fifteen or twenty men were also Philemon C. Merrill and James Ferguson, respectively lieutenant and adjutant of the Battalion.

The law in California at that time permitted a traveler to kill beef for food, but required him to take the brand with him, either cut out of the hide or its form on a piece of paper. If overtaken by the owner with evidence of ownership by being in possession of the same brand, he was expected to pay the customary value of the animal. This party killed four beeves, for two of which they paid four dollars each. To this staple article of food was added some bread as there were opportunities to buy, and also fruit obtained at Spanish missions along the route.

Many of the Battalion men not having means for travel, scattered through the country for employment. Near San Francisco was a hotel kept by a Mr. Skinner. There the company rested three or four days. At the same time a party of marines from a vessel lying in the bay of San Francisco were there on a pleasure excursion. They had heard much of the Mormon Battalion and seemed pleased to make the acquaintance of men who had belonged to it. The officers invited them to dinner aboard their vessel. The invitation was declined, as its acceptance would cause too much delay. Means were too limited to purchase more in San Francisco than a small supply of provisions. This party continued on to Sutter's Fort, near where the city of Sacramento now stands. There they connected with a party led by Captain Andrew Lytle, who had traveled a route near the

western base of the Rocky Mountains.   From Los
Angeles to Salt Lake valley, Elisha Averett, ex-musician
of the Battalion, led a company of ten men as pioneers.
As such they pioneered the way of Captain Lytle's company to Sutter's Fort, and from there took the lead of
the much larger company that continued their journey
to Salt Lake valley.

Most of the following incidents in the journey of
Captain Lytle's command from Los Angeles to Winter
Quarters are from the *History of the Mormon Bat-
talion.*

On the 20th of July, 1847, the majority of those who
did not re-enlist were organized for traveling with
Andrew Lytle and James Pace captains of hundreds ;
Wm. Hyde, Daniel Tyler and Redick N. Allred captains
of fifties ; Elisha Averett captain of ten pioneers.

On the 21st the pioneers advanced not knowing
whither they went, only they had been informed that by
traveling northward under the base of the mountains,
Sutter's Fort might be reached in about 600 miles.

The second day's travel wàs over a high rugged
mountain, where two pack-animals lost their footing and
rolled down twenty or thirty feet before they could regain it.   They reached Francisco's ranch and remained
there four days awaiting the arrival of the other two
fifties who had tarried behind to complete their outfit.
If the fifties were full the entire company numbered one
hundred and sixty men, but Mr. Tyler who accompanied
the party furnishes no definite statement of the number.

At Francisco's ranch beef cattle were purchased for
all of the men who intended to return to their families
that year.   The 27th, the rear companies joined the
advance.   The company experienced some loss and
trouble from Californians, who sold them stolen animals,

10

probably with the connivance of the owners, who would afterwards replevy them.

A portion of the next three days of travel was over very high, rugged mountains, in which they lost fifteen of their beef cattle. They then concluded to rest, butcher their beeves and dry the meat. The first of August they encamped in a beautiful valley where they found cut in the bark of a tree the name of Peter Lebeck, who was killed by a grizzly bear on the 17th of October, 1837. The bones of the bear, which was killed by Lebeck's comrade, were lying on the ground near by.

A ride of fifteen miles the following day brought them to Tulare river. They traveled up this stream some twenty-three miles to find a ford, and finally crossed a part of their goods on a raft while some of the men forded it with their baggage on their heads. The night of the 5th they were all night watering their animals out of a few holes dug in damp places. The 9th of August they found a large stream of water in a beautiful valley, over which they rafted themselves and baggage and swam their animals. On the 11th they crossed a dry plain. In the afternoon the weather was excessively warm, there was but little air stirring, and that little was hot and suffocating. Two men gave out and others made little progress. For a time it almost seemed that all would perish. Those first in camp drank, filled their canteens and hurried back to relieve their thirsting comrades. All finally reached camp. The party agreed it was the hottest day they ever experienced in any country.

The 12th and 13th the pioneers made an effort to find Walker's Pass over the mountains to the east. The effort was fruitless, and the company soon after decided to follow, as near as practicable, Fremont's trail to Sutter's Fort, then a lone military post in the wilderness. The

15th of August they encamped on what was supposed to
be the San Joaquin river.   On the 20th they arrived at
the Sacramento river, where were several small farms
cultivated by Indians.   On the 22nd they crossed a
beautiful valley and encamped on a fine mountain stream.
From there three men were sent ahead to Sutter's Fort
to engage a supply of provisions.   The following day
they passed some Indian wigwams.   The men being
absent the women and children fled and hid in the brush.
A few of the males visited the camp at night.

On the 24th of July the company were overjoyed to
find a colony of Americans, the first they had seen since
leaving Fort Leavenworth the previous year.   The best
of all was news brought by a man named Smith, who
said he had accompanied Samuel Brannan on his trip to
meet the pioneers.   He informed them that the Saints
were settling in Great Salt Lake valley, and that five
hundred wagons were on their way there.   This was the
first intelligence received by the Battalion of the movements of the Church since the news brought by J. D.
Lee and party the previous October.   Their objective
point was now well defined.   The following day was one
of rest with a meeting in the evening.   Some men having
a poor outfit wished to remain until spring, as wages
were good.   The fact that there was a settlement of
Saints who had sailed from New York in the ship *Brooklyn* within a few miles made the situation seem less
isolated.

At Sutter's Fort there appears to have been a fusion
of the men of the different companies who wished to
travel on to Great Salt Lake.   Tender-footed animals
were shod and unbolted flour, the kind manufactured at
that time in California, bought for the journey.   The
27th of August Captain Averett with his pioneers and

about thirty other men started out, while the main body
remained to complete preparations.   About eighteen
miles from Sutter's Fort the route changed from a northern to an eastern course.

On the 28th the company arrived at Captain Johnson's mill on Bear Creek.   It was said he was one of
Fremont's battalion, and his wife one of the survivors of
the ill-fated company who were snowed in at the foot of
the Sierras.   Her mother, Mrs. Murray, was among the
number who perished.   The company crossed the plains
in the summer of 1846.· They passed through Great
Salt Lake valley around the south end of the lake. They
split up into factions, each party taking its own course.
The few who remained with the persevering Captain
Hastings pushed through to California; the others were
caught in the snows of the Sierra Nevada Mountains.
Mrs. Murray was with the party immediately in the rear of
the captain, and consequently nearest the source of relief.
After several had died with hunger and others were sub-
sisting upon their flesh, a few of them, one of whom was
Mrs. Murray's eldest daughter, afterwards Mrs. Johnson,
resolved to attempt to cross the mountains for relief.
Fitting themselves out with snow-shoes they proceeded
some distance and were met by Captain Hastings and ·a
relief party from Sacramento valley with provisions.

At the camp the relief party found Mrs. Murray
dead and others ravenous from hunger.   Children were
crying for the flesh of their parents while it was being
cooked.   There were suspicions that Mrs. Murray had
been foully dealt with, as she was in good health when her
daughter left her and not likely to have perished from
hunger during the brief period of her absence.

Leaving Johnson's mill the company followed General Kearney's trail.   He had preceded them for the

states with an escort of Battalion men.   In Bear valley
were three wagons and a blacksmith's forge, abandoned
by the unfortunate emigrants.   There the company had
a fine treat of huckleberries.   The 3rd of September
they passed other wagons where General Kearney's
party had buried the remains of some of the emigrants.
At night they reached the spot where the rear wagons of
the unfortunate Hastings' company were blocked by the
snow.   There a terrible scene was presented.   A skull
still covered with hair lay here, a mangled arm or leg
yonder, with bones broken to obtain the marrow they

A SCENE OF HORROR.

contained.   A whole body covered with a blanket occupied another place, and portions of other bodies were
scattered around.   It had evidently been a scene of
intense human suffering and of some of the most fiendish
acts that man, frantic with the cravings of hunger, could
perpetrate.

Leaving this scene of horrors on the morning of the
6th of September, in a short time the company met
Samuel Brannan returning from his trip to meet the
Saints.   He informed them that the pioneers had reached
Salt Lake valley in safety, but his description of the
facilities of the place were not favorable for colonization.

He considered it no place for an agricultural people, and expressed his confidence that the Saints would emigrate to California the next spring. On being asked if he had given his views to President Brigham Young, he answered that he had. On further inquiry as to how his views were received, he said, in substance, that he laughed and made some rather insignificant remark; "but," said Brannan, "when he has fairly tried it, he will find that I was right and he was wrong, and will come to California."

The company camped with Mr. Brannan. After he left the following morning Captain James Brown of the Pueblo detachment arrived from Salt Lake valley. Nearly every soldier received one or more letters from family and friends. Some received cheering news, others were saddened with the loss of a parent, wife or child. Captain Brown also brought an epistle from the Twelve Apostles counseling those who had not the means of subsistence to remain, labor in California and bring their earnings with them in the spring. One half or more of the company returned to California in accordance with this counsel.

There, also, the advance of the company was overtaken by those left at Sutter's Fort, and by a few others who had traveled slowly with Brother Henry Hoyt who was sick. He had gradually failed but to his death, which occurred on the 3rd of September, 1847, he manifested a stern resolution to go on. Just before his death he was asked if he did not wish to stop and rest; his answer "No; go on," were the last words he spoke. He was buried as well as circumstances permitted. In the absence of tools with which to dig his grave it was rather shallow, but timbers and brush were piled upon it to protect his remains from the wolves.

The 16th of October the company arrived in Salt Lake valley, overjoyed to meet friends and relatives. Many of the men were very destitute of clothing. Their necessities were partially relieved by some of the influential brethren, among whom were Apostle John Taylor and Bishop Edward Hunter, taking up a collection among the settlers of such articles of clothing as they could spare for the benefit of the "Battalion boys." The men in some instances presented almost a ludicrous appearance after donning the additions to their wardrobes, but with them comfort was a first consideration, and they were thankful to get anything that would promote it. The Battalion men benefitted the colony by bringing in a variety of garden and fruit tree seeds, also seed grain, of which there were scanty supplies. Captain J. Hunt packed through two bushels of seed wheat. James Pace introduced the club-head wheat and Daniel Tyler the California pea, now the general field pea of Utah. We may as well add here the soldiers who wintered at Pueblo brought with them the taos wheat now so common in Utah.

A few of the Battalion found their families in the valley and had no farther to go; others were so worn down with fatigue and sickness that they were unable to go farther at that time; and still others preferred to remain until the following spring and endeavor to prepare a home for their families. Thirty-two of the number, however, determined to make an effort to spend the winter with their wives and children in Winter Quarters, and nerved with this hope were prepared to take the chances of the cold and storms of approaching winter in the mountains and on the plains.

CHAPTER XX.

CAPTAIN P. C. MERRILL'S COMPANY LEAVES SALT LAKE
FOR WINTER QUARTERS — EXCESSIVE COLD — DIFFI-
CULTIES IN CROSSING LOUPE FORK—SUFFERING FOR
FOOD—MISFORTUNE OF ALPHEUS HAWS—HORSE BEEF—
PAWNEE INDIANS — DIVIDING FOOD UNDER DIFFI-
CULTIES—A TURKEY FOR SUPPER—PROVIDENTIAL SUP-
PLY OF FOOD—ARRIVAL IN WINTER QUARTERS—CAPT.
LYTLE'S COMPANY LIVE MOSTLY ON WILD MEAT—DIF-
FICULTIES AT LOUPE FORK—SUPPER ON A DONKEY'S
BRAINS—ANOTHER ON THE CONTENTS OF A MULE'S
HEAD—A FEAST ON RAWHIDE SADDLE BAGS—MULE
BEEF FOR TEN DAYS—ARRIVAL AT WINTER QUARTERS.

SOON after the arrival of the Battalion men in Salt
Lake City a company of fifteen men started for
Winter Quarters, led by P. C. Merrill who was accom-
panied by a nephew.   In addition the company was made
up as follows: Lorenzo Clark, who has furnished the
items of this sketch, John Thompson, Wm. Hyde,
Philander Colton and son, Wm. Robinson, Geo. P.
Dykes, Alpheus P. Haws, Luther T. Tuttle, Samuel
Clark, Geo. W. Oman, Sterling Davis, and Ira Miles
acting as guide, but not a Battalion man.

From the understanding these men had obtained of
the route, they expected to cross the plains in about
thirty days, whereas, they were sixty.   An extension of
time which greatly increased difficulties and prolonged
suffering.   In places Indians had burned the grass. This
weakened animals and compelled slow traveling.   The
weather became very cold.   They encamped at Fort
Bridger over night where Captain Lytle's company

overtook them. This circumstance would indicate that Captain Merrill's company may have left Salt Lake the day before Captain Lytle's. Captain Merrill's company went ahead in the morning and saw no more of the other until its arrival in Winter Quarters.

The weather was very cold to Laramie, with occasional snow. The company crossed the Platte on the ice, then for seventy miles had no other fuel than "buffalo chips" found under about a foot of snow. There being but little grass they were obliged to hunt feed for the animals on islands in the river. So severe was the cold one night, that the mules' ears were frozen half way down to the head and afterwards dropped off. The weather moderated some a few days before reaching Laramie. They had killed buffalo along as needed, and one day decided to lay by the following day and kill and dry a supply of meat, but when the morrow came they found themselves suddenly off the buffalo range. This neglect or miscalculation caused much suffering for food afterwards.

Arriving at the Loupe Fork they found ice running in the current, but solid some distance from each bank. The quicksand bottom changed so rapidly that when they had crossed an animal or two in one place they were obliged to hunt up another. In making these changes and contending with difficulties, they traveled eight miles up the river and were eight days in getting across. The last day Alpheus Haws lost the last animal of five with which he left California, and with it a part of his outfit. He involuntarily left his only shoes in the quicksand and, standing on the ice barefooted, saw about all he had rolling down stream in the turbulent waters.

A poor, sore-backed horse mired in the quicksand standing up. The ensuing night the ice froze firmly

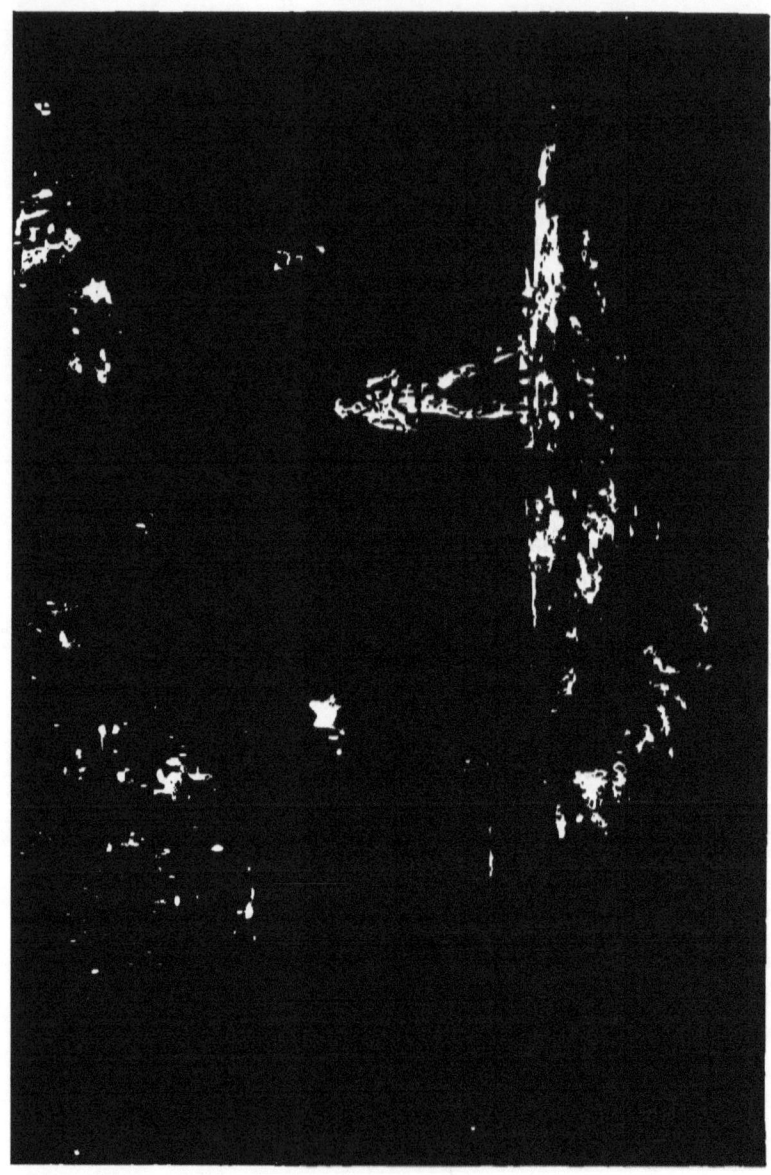

around him. In the morning he was cut out, dragged ashore, dressed and the meat jerked for future use.

They might have fared worse without the horse beef. It helped to keep soul and body together.

The day after these events the company arrived at what was known as the "Pawnee Station," where they found an old cornfield. The pioneers had gleaned it, but these starving men gleaned it a little closer; found a few nubbins from which they ate the corn raw and pronounced it delicious. Continuing their journey, the next day they were met by about 200 Pawnee Indians. At first they appeared hostile. As Sterling Davis was leading his mule an Indian seized it by the bit. He raised a stick he carried in his hand to strike the Indian, but Captain Merrill perceived the motion in time to check it, telling him it would be the signal for the massacre of the company, as the Indians had surrounded them with bows drawn. Mr. Haws had sufficient knowledge of their language to make them understand. He informed them who the company were. The men had on white blankets tied around their necks and bodies the same as they were often worn by Indians, and the Pawnees claimed they thought them a band of Sioux who had come to prevent them from killing buffalo. When told some of them recollected the circumstance of the Battalion being mustered at Council Point the previous year. As the Indians became satisfied with the identity of the men, they at once began to manifest a friendly disposition. They invited Mr. Haws and three or four others to their camp, unsaddled their animals, gave the men food, principally dried beaver and venison, and by them sent food to last the party a day or more. When that was exhausted the company halted a day to rest animals and hunt for food. Wm. Robinson killed a small deer in the forenoon and brought it to the camp where it was eaten for dinner.

The company had agreed in the morning that a part should take care of the animals and share with the hunters in the anticipated food supply. Mr. D. wished to hunt. He went out an hour or two returned to camp where he lay around for the rest of the day. The sun about half an hour high Mr. Lorenzo Clark killed a doe. It was the custom in camp, when food was scarce, to divide as equally as possible a parcel to each man. Then one of the company stood with his back to the parcels while another man touched each parcel in succession asking, "Who shall have this?" When it was handed to the one named. That evening Mr. D. was left out as he would neither "fish nor cut bait." It was believed he went sufficiently hungry to feast on a deer skin that he had used under his saddle.

The following day the party traveled without food except a little some may have saved by shortening their supper. Towards evening a single turkey was killed and divided as was customary. The entrails fell to the lot of Mr. Lorenzo Clark. He threw them on to the coals as he received them and, when sufficiently roasted, devoured them for supper.

At this camp a council was called. The guide had made some error, and thought the company was further from their destination than events afterwards proved. It was proposed that a man take the best animal in the company, go ahead and have some provisions sent out; but Wm. Hyde suggested that they were soldiers and thought they had better remain together, trust in God and not send in. After traveling a short distance the following morning, the men were much surprised to find the Liberty pole which had been erected on the bank of the Platte river. They had been informed in Salt Lake that this was only twelve miles from the crossing of the Elk Horn river. There was a shout of joy at the sight of this waymark, that gave them the assurance they were near their destination. The snow was about a foot deep, and it continued to fall during the day. That evening their camp fire near the crossing of the Elk Horn, was hardly kindled before a drove of turkeys came along from which five were killed. These made supper and breakfast and a little to take along. The next day, nerved up with the expectation of reaching home, they traveled the thirty miles to Winter Quarters with daylight. There they found what they sadly needed friends, food and rest.

The Salt Lake colony, with a reasonable prospect of semi-starvation before them, could not furnish flour to the Battalion men, but they were informed that flour was for sale at Fort Bridger, one hundred and fifteen miles on their journey. With this expectation the largest party of the Battalion men, about thirty, left Salt Lake valley the 18th of October, 1847, probably the day after that under Captain Merrill. They arrived at Fort Bridger in the first severe snow-storm of the season, and there learned that the flour on sale had all been disposed of to Oregon and California emigrants. Captain Bridger thought they would find what they wanted at Laramie on reasonable terms. They left Salt Lake with ten pounds of flour per man and were not yet entirely without. A little beef was purchased to last them until they could find game and they pushed on.

At the upper crossing of the Platte river, one hundred miles west of Laramie, they baked their last cake, the ten pounds of flour per man having been eked out for sixteen days. Between Bridger and Laramie they killed two buffalo bulls, an elk and some small game. In fact, the Battalion men in their travels from Sutter's Fort to Winter Quarters depended principally on their guns for subsistence.   They reached Fort Laramie about the 10th of November and were again disappointed in getting flour.   Captain Andrew Lytle bought one pound of crackers for 25 cents, the only breadstuff purchased. There was a little dried buffalo meat for sale, and those who had money purchased what meat they could afford and divided with the company.   Twelve miles below Laramie a few ·men crossed to the south side of the Platte river and purchased of a trader one hundred pounds of flour for $25.   There being about three pounds per man and five hundred miles to travel without any hope of a further supply, it was decided to use it only for making gravy or thickening soup.

The trader warned them that if they killed buffalo they might have trouble with the Indians.   Sixty or seventy miles below Laramie their supply of meat was exhausted and around them were a few scattering buffalo. The gnawings of hunger will force men to run some risks to obtain food.   They killed a bull and calf. While dressing them a smoke and some Indians were discovered on the south side of the river.   The hunters with their buffalo beef reached camp sometime after dark unmolested.   Awaking one morning about one hundred and fifty miles below Laramie the men found themselves under about a foot of snow.   From there to Winter Quarters, three hundred and fifty miles, they broke their trail through snow from one to two feet in depth.

Just before crossing the Loupe Fork the company lost a few animals, supposed to have been stolen by the Pawnee Indians.   Near the crossing of this stream was found the head of a donkey which Captain Merrill's company had killed for beef.   Captain Allred opened the skull and with his messmates made a supper of the brains.

About the same time Martin Ewell opened the skull of a mule killed for food the day before by Captain Pace's company and feasted on the contents. The day of their arrival at Loupe Fork the company divided and ate the last of their food, which consisted chiefly of rawhide "saddle bags," which had been used from California for carrying provisions. This feast was partaken of during a cold storm which lasted several days. The next food was a young mule of Captain Lytle's, which was too much exhausted to go further. This was the first domestic animal killed for food by this company since leaving California. The company had many times looked wistfully upon a small female dog belonging to Mr. Joseph Thorne, who with his wife and children had accompanied it from Bridger. The temptation was soon removed by Mr. Thorne trading the canine to the Pawnee Indians for a small piece of dried buffalo meat.

Owing to floating ice they were unable to cross the Loupe Fork for five days. During this time they traveled a few miles down the river and found Captain Pace's company just in time to save them from the danger of being robbed by Pawnee Indians. The two parties afterwards traveled together. Captain Pace and seven other men got in a hurry soon after passing Laramie and pushed on. The event proved they had overrated their ability to travel faster than the main company. They were overtaken near the Loupe Fork and soon after concluded to remain with their former companions.

On the opposite side of the river was an Indian farm. With the hope of obtaining a little corn a few men ventured to ford the stream. The field had been twice gleaned before by other travelers, and these gleaners were rewarded with only a few decaying ears. It was probably the same field gleaned by the pioneers in the spring and a few days before by P. C. Merrill's company. Captain Pace and William Maxwell visited an Indian camp to purchase food, but failed to get any as the Indians had none to spare. They, however, remained over night, were furnished a good supper and breakfast, and otherwise treated kindly.

The night of the fifth day after their arrival on its banks the cold was intense and the river froze over, so that on the morning of the sixth day the company began to cross on the ice, which bent and cracked. Holes were made in it, but with perseverance everything was safely deposited on the other bank. As the rising sun warmed the atmosphere, thus weakening the ice, the last few trips were extremely dangerous. Soon after the ice broke up and the stream was covered with floating fragments. Truly a kindly providence had favored them. From the killing of Captain Lytle's mule to their arrival in Winter Quarters, about ten days' travel, this company subsisted on mule meat alone, without salt.

On the Elk Horn river, thirty miles from Winter Quarters, they found a ferry boat with ropes stretched across the stream, ready to step into and pull over. The company understood this boat was built by the pioneers and first used by them. It served the companies who followed their trail, then the pioneers, then Captain Merrill's company on their return to Winter Quarters, and Captain Lytle's company were fortunate to find it available to them. They crossed the stream the 17th of December, 1847. Hoping the next day to end their excessive toils and sufferings, the men arose early in the morning and were soon on the march for the goal that they had been long struggling for.

The foremost men arrived in Winter Quarters about sundown, those in the rear a little after dark. The com-

pany was just two months journeying from Salt Lake to
the Missouri river.   We may in part imagine the joy of
families and friends, but to sense the fruition of long-
cherished hopes and the pleasing satisfaction of these
men, one would need to pass through a similar bitter
experience.   No doubt, however, the joys of some were
tinged with sadness as they found vacant places never
to be filled in this life in their circle of loved ones.   All
the soldiers, although generally highly respectable, were
unavoidably dirty and ragged, but they found only warm
hearts to receive them, from President Young to the
least child who knew what the words "Mormon Battalion" meant.   They knew that that valiant corps had
been offered a living sacrifice for the Church and the
nation.

CHAPTER XXI.

CONDITION OF THE PEOPLE ON THE SHORES OF THE GREAT
SALT LAKE—GREAT SCARCITY OF FOOD—THE SITUA-
TION AS SHOWN BY L. D. YOUNG'S NARRATIVE.

BEFORE commencing the history of the emigrating
Saints in 1848, it will be interesting to look in upon
the colony in the wilderness and see how they were far-
ing for food—the one essential to existence.   When man
has the opportunity and skill to construct shelter and to
gather from the elements food to sustain him, his preservation is reasonably sure.   While the Saints in the valley
lacked no inherent qualifications for making homes in

11

the desert, from unavoidable conditions there was often a serious want of food.

The Saints who crossed the plains in 1847, designed to take breadstuff to sustain them until they could harvest the ensuing year, but they were not prepared for emergencies that might arise from unforseen circumstances. Probably about two hundred Battalion men were in the valley during the winter of 1847-48. They were men who had been forced by circumstances into many very straitened conditions. Their energies and endurance had been taxed to the utmost for two years. These fiery trials developed in them the noblest attributes of manhood—faith in God and a sublime fortitude. Only a community of interest and feeling saved many of these men, and others, from death by starvation during the first year after the arrival of the pioneers on the shore of the Great Salt Lake. By way of illustration let Lorenzo D. Young who sacrificed and suffered tell the story of his experience; he says:

"Oliver G. Workman, a Battalion man, without family, came to Salt Lake with others from California in the autumn of 1847, and there he met his brother Jacob and family and assisted in providing food. The following spring, flour became so scarce that it was very difficult for the needy to obtain even a moiety. Mr. Workman came to me twice and stated that he had tried to get a little and could not. I told him I had none to sell at any price, but I let him have a few pounds each time.

"In a few days he came to me the third time and stated that he had tried to get a little flour until he was discouraged. He expressed his regret at being under the necessity of coming again but, said he, 'What can I do? My brother's wife is famishing!' I remarked that

I had only a little flour left and I stepped into another
room where Mrs. Young lay on the bed sick. I stated
the case to her and asked, 'What shall we do?' The question was quite as important to us as to Mr. Workman; but
she replied, 'We cannot see anyone starve. Divide to
the last pound.' I weighed what I thought we might
spare. It was seven pounds. As I handed the sack
containing it to Mr. Workman he put his hand into his
pocket, and, without counting handed out a handful of
gold. I again told him I had no flour to sell; that I
would not exchange him a pound of flour for a pound of
gold. He returned the gold to his pocket, and, as he
turned to go away he was overpowered by his feelings
and shed tears.

"Soon after this occurrence myself and family were
entirely out of food. It had been necessary to work my
oxen very hard through the winter, and all my cattle
were too poor for food. I heard of a man on Mill Creek
who had a three-year-old steer which he was keeping
for beef, with the design of going to California in the
spring. I succeeded in trading him a pair of large oxen
by agreeing to give him one quarter of the animal after
it was dressed. I drove the steer home, butchered it
and hung the hide on the fence with the flesh side out.
This furnished a feast for the magpies as they picked off
what little meat remained on it. My share of the beef,
with what little food could be gathered from other
sources, kept us along for several weeks. During that
time I made every possible exertion to obtain more food,
but without success.

"Circumstances again seemed desperate. I took
the hide off the fence and put it to soak in City creek.
When it became soft and pliable I cut it into strips for
convenience in handling. I labored on it about two days,

scraping the flesh side clean and getting the hair off the other. After I became satisfied with its condition, I turned it over to Mrs. Young. To prepare a meal, a piece of raw-hide was boiled until it became a glue soup, when salt was added to season. This being a native product was abundant while other condiments were as scarce as the food they were intended to season.

"From the wreck of affairs in Nauvoo Mrs. Young saved a favorite set of china. I never knew more need of an inviting looking table than in those days of glue soup. Mrs. Young decked it out in the most inviting manner possible; the center piece, a pan of glue soup, with a ladle for dipping and conveying it to our plates. The Lord was always asked to bless the scanty fare. We satisfied our appetites as best we could, with a thankful feeling that we had that much to sustain life. Mrs. Young's health was generally poor, and on that diet she daily grew weaker. I felt that something must be done or she would die for want of nourishment. I went to a man that I understood had considerable flour and offered him a horse for a few pounds. He was one of a few Saints who had but little faith that we could remain in the country, and he designed going to California when spring was sufficiently advanced. His fears that he might be short prevented him from letting me have any flour. I met Bishop E. Hunter and made known my situation. Said he, 'I have but little flour, but Sister Young must not die for want of some.' He let me have seven pounds. Mrs. Young ever after believed that the kindness of Brother Hunter saved her life. On her dying bed, and about an hour and a half before she expired, she spoke of the circumstance and blessed him.

"On the bottom lands along the river Jordan, this-

tles grew in abundance. The roots of these afforded considerable nourishment.   As the large, dry top usually
remained attached to the root until a new growth in the
spring, they could be found and dug in the winter. They
were a great help to the Saints in times of scarcity.   In
the spring of 1848 many acres of bottom land had been
dug over.   I, at times, as well as others, was compelled
to avail myself of this means of sustaining life.   As vegetation grew in the spring, other roots and herbs were
used for food.   Segoes for a time were in considerable
demand, but several persons were poisoned by eating
the wrong variety.   Three persons died in as many
weeks from this cause.   After the sad occurrence they
were not much used as edibles.

"One morning I met Brother Welcome Chapman
with a basket of cowslips.   As I had been accustomed
to these for early spring greens in my youth, to me at
that time they seemed a great luxury.   That they grew
in this mountain region surprised me.   Only those who
have longed for something palatable and refreshing can
appreciate the feelings that caused me to exclaim with
considerable enthusiasm, 'Brother Chapman, where on
earth did you get them?'   He replied, 'I have found a
little spot up the canyon where they grow, and I go and
get a basket of them in the morning to last us during
the day.'   I asked him if the supply was sufficient to let
me have some.   He thought so, and gave me what
he then had.   When cooked we enjoyed them very much.
They were a change, a variety.   Brother Chapman continued to furnish a few greens, from which we realized
much benefit.   In those times faith was an important
factor in our lives.   The prayer that the Lord would
bless our food that it might strengthen us, was made up
of no idle words.   It came from the heart, and in return

the blessing was often realized.   With the meager fare I
was able to accomplish considerable labor."

Elder Young's experience, with some variation, was
that of hundreds of the early colonizers of Salt Lake
valley.   Strangers who now visit the country cannot
properly sense its primitive barrenness, and the privations endured from being a thousand miles from outside
resources.   The youth born in the country can never
realize, without a similar experience, the toil and privation with which was laid the foundation for the comfort
and luxury they enjoy.

CHAPTER XXII.

THE EMIGRATION OF 1848—ORGANIZATION OF THE COM-
PANIES GOING WITH PRESIDENT YOUNG—GOOD NEWS
FROM THE VALLEY—THE LAST COMPANIES UNDER
ELDERS RICHARDS AND LYMAN—SPECIAL EPISTLE FROM
PRESIDENT YOUNG ; HIS ARRIVAL IN THE VALLEY—
ARRIVAL OF THE LAST COMPANIES—REMARKABLE PROPH-
ECY—LETTER OF P. P. PRATT, A REIGN OF PEACE—WHAT
OTHERS THOUGHT OF THE MORMONS IN GREAT SALT
LAKE VALLEY.

THE LAST day of May 1848, President B. Young
commenced organizing the people into hundreds,
fifties and tens, and appointing the officers necessary for
managing so large a body of people.   We are indebted
to Elder Thos. Bullock for the census of the companies
organized under his suspervision.   Wagons, 623 ; souls,
1891 ; horses, 131 ; mules, 44 ; oxen, 2012 ; cows, 983 ;

loose cattle, 334 ; sheep, 654 ; pigs, 237 ; chickens, 904 ; cats, 54 ; dogs, 134 ; goats, 3 ; geese, 10 ; beehives, 5 ; doves, 11 ; squirrels, 1 ; ducks, 5.

"On the 1st of June, Lorenze Snow's company moved off the ground to the Liberty Pole on the Platte, to make room for other waggons that came pouring in from Winter Quarters.   *   *   *   *   *

"The 2nd 'of June Zera Pulsipher's camp followed on the trail, and we received a visit from Elders Hyde, Woodruff, Benson and others, by whom we learned that the Pawnee and Otoe Indians had a fight in rear of Winter Quarters, in which several were killed."

The third of June W. G. Perkin's company left the place of rendezvous, and President Young's company on the 5th. Lucy, wife of Elisha H. Grove's was run over by her wagon which broke her leg. The company traveled twelve miles. June 6th, after a travel of thirteen and a quarter miles, the company encamped on the Platte river. The organization of the camp was perfected, and a night and day guard arranged. The 29th of June the company first came in sight of buffalo. The 12th of July, it was on Crab creek, a little over four hundred and nine miles from Winter Quarters. It rested ten days, travelled twenty-seven days, averaging fifteen miles per day.

Between ten and eleven o'clock in the evening of the 12th of July, John Y. Green, Isaac Dunham, Joseph W. Young and Rufus Allen, arrived from the valley bringing news up to the 18th of May, the day of starting. Soon after another mail arrived with a few letters with dates up to the 9th of June. News from the valley was of deep interest to these traveling camps. Prosperity there meant future sustenance and comfort to them. Thos. Bullock the clerk of the camps, summed up the news as follows :

The health of the people was good. A large amount of spring crops had been put in. They were planting until within a few days of the starting of the mail, when the crickets had done considerable damage to the wheat and corn, but the gulls came and swept away the plague. From the arrival of the pioneers to the departure of this mail, there had been but fifteen interments. To balance these deaths, in one row of eight houses adjoining each other, in one week there were seven births, and it was thought there had been one hundred and twenty births during the residence of the people in the valley. Several saw and grist-mills were in operation, and in process of erection. Twelve miles of fence inclosing a large field for farming purposes, was nearly complete.

With President Young and company well on their way to the valley, we will return to Winter Quarters. About the 25th of June, Elders Willard Richards and Amasa Lyman left the Elk Horn with about three hundred wagons, making a little more than nine hundred, comprising the season's emigration. As was intended, Winter Quarters was evacuated. The first companies averaged about three persons to the wagon. At this rate about two thousand eight hundred people went from the Missouri river to the Mountains in 1848.

The first general epistle of the Presidency of the Church, from Great Salt Lake valley, furnishes some further information concerning the emigration of this year. During the winter and spring of 1848, efforts were made for the removal of the Church from Winter Quarters to Salt Lake valley. The effort was finally facilitated by a loan of teams, by the brethren on the Pottowatomie lands and friends in an about camp.

Young and Kimball left Winter Quarters in May and
Brother Richards in July.   *   *   *   At the Elk Horn
a portion of Brother Kimball's camp was fired on by a
band of Otoes and Omahas.   Three men were wounded
of which two were maimed for life."   No other serious
losses of lives and property are reported of this season's
emigration.

A special epistle signed by Brigham Young, dated
Great Salt Salt Lake City, October 9th, 1848, and
addressed to the presiding authorities and Saints in
Pottowatomie county and adjacent regions, explains
under what circumstances the teams loaned the emigration, by their friends on the Missouri river, were returned,
and also contains other items of interest.

The document opens with warm expressions of
gratitude for deliverance from enemies, their arrival at
the haven of rest for the Saints, and says, "On the 28th
of August last, we wrote you an epistle from the Sweetwater, from which place we returned those wagons and
teams that the brethren in Iowa had kindly loaned us to
assist us on our journey, considering it wisdom that they
should have an early start, make the best of their way
while the weather and feed were in tolerable condition,
so that they may reach their destination before the
severity of the weather would be likely to set in upon
them—while we remained at Sweetwater with our goods
and families on the ground, exposed to the keen, frosty
nights and storms that are so prevalent in that country.
On the 30th of August we were glad to meet with a
number of brethren from the valley, with forty-seven
wagons and one hundred and twenty-four yoke of oxen,
being three yoke of cattle over and above replacing the
wagons and teams that we had previously sent back to
the Saints in Iowa, towards filling the vacancy of the

great number of cattle that had unfortunately died on our hands, and been left by the wayside. * * * *

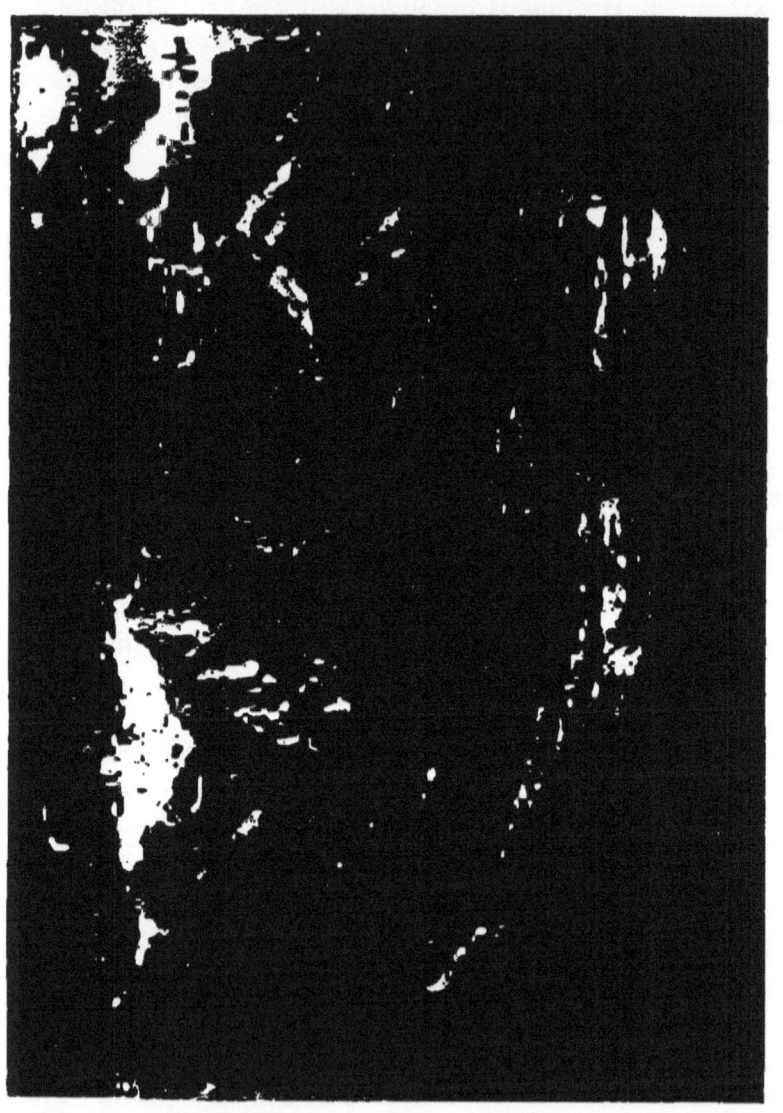

CLIFFS OF THE WASATCH.

"Our hearts fainted not; but, relying on the arm of Jehovah, we reloaded our wagons and continued our

journey.   On the 1st of September, we went through
the South Pass to the waters that flow into the Pacific,
and had a miserable evening's journey of it.   The next
day we had a mizzling rain, and only removed about a
mile in order to find feed to sustain our cattle.   At night
a snowstorm passed over us and on Sunday, the 3rd of
September, the entire Wind river chain of mountains
was covered with snow.   The weather was then severe,
but afterwards cleared up with pleasant days and frosty
nights, which continued with us nearly the whole of our
journey, with the exception of showers which were of
frequent occurrence, but never so heavy as in the states,
and we considered ourselves the highly favored of the
Lord.   We were under the necessity of traveling from
this place in small companies on account of the many
narrow canyons, crossings of creeks and scanty feed, so
as to expedite our journey."

President Young arrived in the valley on Saturday,
the 20th of September.   He was escorted into the city
by Bishop Edward Hunter and others, who guided them
through the grain fields to the west side of the fort.
President Kimball arrived in the afternoon of Sunday
the 21st.   The usual Sabbath meeting was adjourned
two hours to give him, and company, an opportunity of
being present.   Many of the people went out to welcome
him into the valley.   At the meeting in the Bowery, a
beautiful hymn of welcome, composed by Miss Eliza R.
Snow, was sung by the choir.

On the arrival of the Presidency in the valley, they
found the people living in four forts, composed mostly of
houses.   These inclosed about forty-seven acres of land.
The companies of Willard Richards and Amasa Lyman
arrived in the valley the 18th and 20th of October.   With
the season's emigration of 1848, the people on the shores

of Salt Lake numbered about five thousand souls. Considering the recent losses of the Saints by persecution,
the distance of the colony from the Missouri river and
the great difficulties encountered on the route, this was
an immense immigration within eighteen months after
the pioneers left Winter Quarters. This was the year in
which the growing crops of the people on the shores of
Salt Lake were saved from destruction by crickets by
immense flocks of white gulls. Mr. Alma Eldredge,
then a mere youth, thus speaks of this kindly providence:

"The crickets, in immense swarms, appeared to be
sweeping away all hopes of bread for the coming year.
As the people were in a state of semi-starvation, their
anxiety to save their growing crops was intense. They
had fought the crickets on a warm summer day until
weary and discouraged and had started for their homes
to rest, but before arriving there they saw immense
flocks of gulls settling down on their fields. It was a
query whether they were friends or enemies, but they
were left undisturbed. In the morning a committee was
sent to the field to see what the birds had done. To
their great joy they found the crickets mostly destroyed
and their crops saved."

Although the Saints had to contend with many difficulties incident to settling a new and desert country,
among the most prominent of which were frosts,
crickets and drought, yet sufficient was accomplished to
give them an assurance of future success. On the return
of a portion of the Mormon Battalion, through the northern part of western California, they discovered an extensive gold mine which enabled them, by a few days delay, to
bring sufficient of the dust to make money plentiful for all
ordinary purposes in Salt Lake valley. In exchange, the
dust was deposited with the Presidency who issued bills

or a paper currency, and the "Kirtland Safety Fund" bills re-signed was on a par with gold.   It was significant of great changes that the obsolete bills of the Kirtland bank should find a circulation on the shores of Salt Lake.

It was after the arrival of this season's emigration in the valley that Heber C. Kimball, in view of the great destitution of his people for clothing and many other necessaries of life, declared to them, that States goods would be sold in the streets of Salt Lake City as cheap as in New York, and the people be abundantly provided with clothing.   Nothing in the changing routine of human life could have appeared to that isolated people more improbable.   After the spirit of prophecy had left him, his remarks to his friends indicated that he, himself, had but little faith in its fulfillment.

The reader will recollect that Parley P. Pratt entered the valley with the companies that followed the pioneers in 1847.   After residing there nearly a year he wrote a letter, expressing his sentiments and views to his brother, O. Pratt and the Saints in England.   It is a beautiful pen picture of the reign of peace in the valley, and a witness that the Saints had found the haven of rest they had been seeking.

"September 5th, 1848.

"DEAR BROTHER ORSON :—   *   *   *   *   "I have now resided almost a year in this lone retreat, where civilized man has not made his home for the last thousand years, and where the ripening harvest has not been enjoyed for ages until the present season.   During all this period the sound of war, the rise and fall of empires, the revolution of States and kingdoms—the news of any kind has scarcely reached my ears.

"It is but a few days since we heard of the revolutions and convulsions which are agitating Europe.   No elections, no police reports, no murders, no wars, in our

little world. How quiet, how still, how peaceful, how
happy.   How lonesome, how free from excitement we
live.   The legislation of our High Council, the decision
of some judge or court of the Church, a meeting, a dance,
a visit or exploring tour, an arrival of a party of trappers
and traders, a Mexican caravan, a party arrived from the
Pacific, from the States, from Fort Hall or Fort Bridger,
a visit of Indians or perhaps a mail from the distant world
once or twice a year is all that breaks upon the monotony
of our peaceful and busy life.

"Our old firelocks have not been brushed up, or our
swords unsheathed because of any alarm. No police-
men or watchmen, of any kind, have been on duty to
guard us from external or internal danger. The drum
has beat to be sure, but it was mingled with merry-making, or its martial sound was rather to remind us that
war had once been known among the nations, than to
arouse us to tread the martial and measured step of those
who muster for war, or march to the battle field. Oh
what a life we live! It is the dream of the poets actually
fulfilled in real life. Here we can cultivate the mind,
renew the spirits, invigorate the body, cheer the heart,
and ennoble the soul of man. Here we can cultivate
every science and every art calculated to enlarge the
the mind, accommodate the body, or polish and advance
our race. And here we can receive and extend that
pure intelligence which is unmingled with the jargon o
mystic Babylon, and which will fit a man after a long life
of health and usefulness, to enjoy the mansions of bliss
and the society of those who are purified in the blood of
the Lamb."

"How beautiful upon the mountains are the feet
of him that bringeth glad tidings," is beautifully in
harmony with the sentiments and spirit of the fore-
going.

About this time the following excerpts appeared in
eastern papers. This wonderful move of a religious
body of people whose singular and powerful doctrines and

organization had, in the short space of sixteen years, greatly weakened the orthodox religion of the highest civilization of the continent, was already attracting marked attention.   When its enemies supposed it in the very throes of dissolution it suddenly developed wonderful vitality and power.

"THE MORMON SETTLEMENTS IN THE GREAT SALT LAKE VALLEY.

"We wish to call the readers attention to the new and most extraordinary condition of the Mormons. Several thousands of them have found a resting place in the most remarkable spot on the North American continent.   Since the children of Israel wandered through the wilderness, or the crusaders rushed on Palestine, there has been nothing so historically singular, as the emigration and recent settlement of the Mormons.   Thousands of them came from the Manchesters and Sheffields of England, to join other thousands congregated from Western New York and New York and New England— boasted descendants of the pilgrim fathers—together to follow after a New Jerusalem in the west.

"Having a temple amid the churches and schools of Lake County, Ohio, and driven from it by popular opinion, they built the Nauvoo of Illinois.   It becomes a great town.   Twenty thousand people flock to it.   They are again assaulted by popular persecution, their prophet murdered, their town depopulated, and finally their temple burned !   Does all this persecution to which they have been subjected, destroy them ?   Not at all. Seven thousand are now settled, in flourishing circumstances, on the plateau summit of the North American continent.   Thousands more are about to join them from Iowa, and thousands more are coming from Wales.   The spectacle is most singular and this is one of the singular episodes of the great drama of the age.   The spot on which the Mormons are now settled is, geographically, one of the most interesting in the western world."—*Cincinnati Atlas.*

"The Mormon Saints after enduring all the sufferings of persecution in Missouri and Illinois, many of their leaders and Apostles having·been slain, and the whole body of the survivors having been hunted from place to place, have at last, found a New Jerusalem, or holy land, in the Great Salt Lake valley, situated between the Rocky Mountains and the Sierra Nevada which belongs to the Territory of California, and may be called Eastern California.   This is one of the most remarkable regions on the globe,   *   *   *   They are an industrious race, and are well qualified to develop the resources of the rich region in which they have located themselves.   This is, indeed, probably their New Jerusalem, where they will be able to build up a city with pillars of gold, slated with silver and paved with rubies and emeralds.   Who knows?   According to the observations of that region made by Fremont and Abert, and Kearney and others, some portions of that great country are really wonderful. It seems to be a sort of Holy Land on a large scale.   It has the Salt Sea in it, much larger than that of Palestine; and it has also a Jordan, a Mount Horeb, and almost all the great features of the ancient Holy Land, but on a tremendously large scale.

"Brigham Young seems to be the Moses of the whole concern.   This expedition of the Mormons has some analogy to that of the exodus of the Israelites from Egypt.   Illinois and Missouri and Iowa have been to the Mormons the land of bondage from which they have escaped, and in which their leaders and Saints were shot down in the way that we shot down the mob in Massacre place up town.   Now they promise to become a free, powerful and prosperous people."   *   *   *
—*New York Herald.*

CHAPTER XXIII.

CONDITION OF THE SALT LAKE COLONY IN THE WINTER OF
1848-49—THE FRONTIER GUARDIAN—A LOCAL GOV-
ERNMENT ORGANIZED — REVIEW—PRESIDENCY OF THE
CHURCH TRANSFERRED TO SALT LAKE—APOSTLES AND
ELDERS ON THE MISSOURI RIVER—THE EMIGRATION OF
1849—SPECIAL INSTRUCTIONS — ANXIETY AS TO THE
FATE OF THE SALT LAKE COLONY.

THE winter of 1848-49 was severe. The 5th of February the mercury fell to 33° below the freezing
point. The surrounding mountains were difficult of
access on account of deep snow. This, with the poor
condition of the working animals, from the scarcity of
feed and extreme cold, made it difficult at times to obtain
sufficient fuel for the comfort of the people. In the forepart of February the Bishops took an inventory of the
bread stuff in the valley. They reported a little more
than three-fourths of a pound per day for each person
until the 9th of the following July. Since harvest the
previous year, corn had been two dollars per bushel,
while some had sold for three. Wheat had ranged from
four to five dollars per bushel.

The first number of the *Frontier Guardian* was
published at Kanesville, Iowa, the 7th of February, 1849.
It was the first paper published by the Saints after their
evacuation of Nauvoo. The principal object of its publication was to spread information among the Saints and
defend their interests. With regard to education, the
editor says:

12

"It affords unmeasured pleasure to see the favorable results of some limited exertions, not long since made, in favor of education.   Two flourishing schools in our little town, of about eighty scholars each, conducted by a principal and an assistant to each one, with many others in various parts of the county that have sprung into being, may be continued with increased zeal and numbers, by giving to the subject of education that attention which we trust it may be in our power to bestow."

The paper was a semi-weekly and declared its purposes in a prospectus as follows:

"The *Guardian* is not intended to enter the field of political strife and contention.   Still it will reserve the right and privilege of recommending such men to the suffrages of the people as the editor may think will prove true and faithful guardians of the national peace and honor, and of the persons and property of her citizens. It will be devoted to the news of the day; to the signs of the times; to religion and prophecy, both ancient and modern; to literature and poetry; to the arts and sciences, together with all and singular whatever the spirit of the times may dictate.   It will strongly advocate the establishing of common schools along the frontier, and also in various settlements in the interior, and will try, by all lawful and honorable means, to accomplish so desirable an object."

The unredeemed character of the country is well illustrated by the results of a winter's hunt, of two rival parties of one hundred men each.   There were killed about seven hundred wolves and foxes, two wolverines, twenty minks and pole cats, five hundred hawks, owls and magpies and one thousand ravens in Salt Lake valley and vicinity.

The following, from the first general epistle of the First Presidency of the Church sent east from Salt Lake City, indicates the necessity of organizing a local government, and also gives assurance that, in the hearts of these persecuted colonizers of the desert, there was no lack of patriotism; that they had no conception of becoming independent of the general government.

"In consequence of Indian depredations on our horses, cattle and other property, and the wicked conduct of a few base fellows who have come among the Saints, the inhabitants of this valley, as is common in new countries generally, have organized a temporary government, to exist during its necessity, or until we can obtain a charter for a Territorial government, a petition for which is already in progress."

This petition was perfected and sent to Washington, D. C., per Dr. J. M. Bernhisel, agent for the people of Great Salt Lake valley. The following from the biographical sketch of Alma Eldredge in *Tullidge's History of Northern and Eastern Utah*, gives some idea of the suffering for food in the summer of 1849:

"The summer of 1849 told hard on the masses of the people. The land for miles around the settlements was literally dug over by persons in search of segoes and thistles, articles which were used for food to assist in keeping soul and body together. Weeds of various kinds were used in like manner, and all sorts of economy were practiced, to the fullest extent, to alleviate the pangs of hunger and modify the suffering condition of the wanderers. Finally harvest came and the exiles began to prosper. I saw mothers with infants at the breast which were nursing their life's blood, as it were, on account of the reduced condition which privation and hunger had brought them to. Their strength was so far exhausted that they would reel and tremble when attempting to walk, and often could proceed only by artificial means."

The Presidency of the Church was now transferred from the Missouri river to Great Salt Lake valley.

Between it and the people, still scattered in the United States, were the vast plains along the Platte river, and a wilderness of mountains with towering peaks and rugged defiles. The denizens of this wilderness of plains and mountains were wild beasts and the little less wild and savage Indian. The latter bore the white man but little good will, and was by heritage a wandering robber. The most rapid means of communication across this forbiding country was with horses and mules. To take along feed for animals was to overburden them and neutralize its benefits. They must subsist, as best they could, on the grasses that grew on the route. Under these conditions it was practicably impossible to make the journey between these points, with the same animals, in less than thirty days, and it usually required more than this time.

There was no government postal service, no telegraph line for rapid communication across the plains, hence the great necessity of that care and efficiency in fitting out the emigration which can only result from good, executive ability combined with experience.

Under these natural disadvantages great care was necessary on the part of the Presidency of the Church to select competent agents to carry out their general instructions in detail. The President of the Apostles, O. Hyde, was selected as the presiding genius at the east end of the emigration route. There was a large corps of experienced and capable elders to assist him when he needed. To aid him in the emigration of 1849 he had with him Apostles George A. Smith and E. T. Benson.

These leaders of a gathering dispensation, issued their instructions for the march of their people to the west, with that clearness and precision of detail which, in all important operations, is a token of success. They were published in the *Frontier Guardian* February 21st, 1849. The spirit of them foreshadows the general instructions from the valley the following spring.

"SALT LAKE EMIGRANTS.

"It is intended for companies to start from this point, to emigrate to the great valley of Salt Lake, so soon as grass is sufficiently grown to sustain cattle and teams. Whenever a company of fifty wagons have assembled at the camping ground, on this side of the river near this place, (the precise place will be designated in due time,) they will forthwith be organized and start on their journey. This number can travel with much more ease, comfort and speed than any greater number. Our experience has proven this to us. The men and boys that will naturally go with fifty wagons, will be quite sufficient to protect themselves on the journey against the Indians. Every man and boy capable of using a rifle or musket should, by all means have one and a good one. If any are deficient in this respect, we will furnish every company with what they may lack, provided the captain and principal men of each company will become responsible for the arms, and deliver them safely to the High Council in the valley, as there are quite a lot of arms here that belong there, and we wish to forward them on.

"The organization of companies will be strictly military, and every one should be amply provided with arms and ammunition adequate to any and every exigence. Our experience last year on the Elk Horn river with the Omaha Indians, abundantly shows the importance of a rigid observance of the above. The bill of particulars, embracing provisions, and other articles to be taken, will appear in the *Guardian* in due time.

"Every wagon, before starting, will be examined to see if it contains the requisite amount of provisions, utensils and means of defense. If they are delinquent in these they will not be allowed to cross the river to proceed with our companies. The severity of the winter here, awakens some fears that they have had a severe winter in the valley, and it will be, most likely, thought better to take a greater amount of provisions than was at first anticipated. A few extra barrels of flour will do no harm."

The following editorial appeared in the *Frontier Guardian* of May 16th, 1849:

"The valley of the Salt Lake is in north latitude 40° 30', and in longitude west from London 112°. The altitude of that place is 4,300 feet above the level of the sea. From the unfavorable accounts given from the regions west and south of the Salt Lake valley, the severely cold weather and very deep snows, we fear somewhat for the safety of our friends in the valley. * * * * We have received no mail from them, as yet, but are in daily expectation of one. We are very anxious to hear from that quarter, yet are almost afraid to hear lest the very severe winter has seriously affected that infant settlement. Yet we hope for the best."

This indicates the great anxiety of the Saints on the Missouri river to learn the situation of their friends in the valley. The long, tedious winter and almost the entire spring had passed without any news from the infant colony environed in the mountain snows, with no other resource, in case of misfortune, than the God in whom they trusted and their own exertions and powers of endurance.

Isolated among bands of savages, with a scanty supply of food, it is no wonder that to the anxious hearts of friends in the United States, vague rumors of disaster seemed to float around in the elements foreshadowing evil. With great expectancy the spring mail was waited for to give assurance of safety and peace.

The general epistle sent out in the spring arrived in Kanesville in time for publication, May 30, 1849, and it would seem none to soon for the guidance of those preparing to cross the plains that season. The council it contained concerning the emigration was almost entirely based on their present and prospective food supply in the valley. There was evident necessity for those already there making great efforts to raise food for those who were coming. President Young left the direction of affairs on the Missouri river entirely to his capable agents.

"For the future, it is not wisdom for the Saints to leave the states or California, for this place, unless they have teams and means sufficient to come through without any assistance from the valley, and that they should bring breadstuffs sufficient to last them a few months after their arrival, for the harvest will not be gathered nor the grain ready for grinding. The inhabitants of the valley will be altogether dependent on the crop of this season for their support, and will have no time to leave their tillage with their teams to bring in emigrating camps as they have hitherto done."

To meet the counsel given in the epistle the following instructions to the Saints appeared in the *Frontier Guardian* of May 13, 1849:

"Emigrants will eat about one pound of breadstuff per day on the road to Salt Lake besides, milk, butter, beans, dried fruit, bacon and various other little comforts if they can get them; say one hundred pounds of breadstuff for one person, old and young, on the road, and two hundred pounds to a person after he gets there to last six months, in all three hundred pounds of best breadstuff to start from here with, besides all the cows he can take, and as many little necessaries and comforts as he can procure and haul."

CHAPTER XXIV.

GREAT RUSH OF PEOPLE TO CALIFORNIA—SICKNESS AND
   DEATH ALONG THE PLATTE RIVER—CAPTAIN EGAN'S
   COMPANY—GREAT WASTE OF PROPERTY—THE LAST
   TRAIN—PEACE AND PROSPERITY ON THE SHORES OF
   SALT LAKE—KEY NOTE OF THE GATHERING FOR 1850
   —THIRTY THOUSAND DOLLARS TO HELP THE POOR—
   NEWS FROM THE CAMPS OF ISRAEL.

IN THE year 1849, there was a great rush of people
   to California. The gold fever was evidently increasing
in intensity. These people mostly traveled on the south
side of the Platte river. A few of the Saints, also,
unfortunately took that road. Many deaths occurred
principally from cholera but some from other causes.
While there was sickness on the pioneer route
north of the Platte, the mortality was quite limited compared with that on the south side of the river. Captain
Howard Egan took the latter route, with a company of
Saints, about the middle of May. It consisted of 57
souls, 22 wagons, 46 yoke of oxen, 21 cows, 6 horses, 5
mules, 3 head of young cattle, 21 fowls, 6 dogs and 1
cat. This return indicates that this third year of the
emigration, there was not quite as extensive a supply of
domestic animals taken as at first.

In a letter of June 19, 1849, to the *Frontier
Guardian*, Captain Egan gives some interesting facts
concerning the California emigration.

"May 21st., the company met three wagons on
their way back to Missouri. They reported having lost
a number of their company by measles. An old man

stated that one of his sons was then very sick in his wagon. They had left their company sixty-five miles west of the Missouri river. The same day Captain Egan passed a company from Missouri with five cases of cholera.

"May 27th. Ten miles west of the Pawnee village, we heard that a company from Pittsburg had quarreled and killed one man. They were heaving out sugar, coffee, tools of all kinds and breaking up into small companies.

"May 29th. Passed a company from Missouri who had lost a man with the measles. Yesterday met a lieutenant from Fort Kearney. He reports that many belonging to companies from Missouri had had the cholera, and that sixty had died between Independence and Grand Island.

"May 31st. Eight miles east of the head of Grand Island passed where the St. Joseph and Independence road intersects this road. There is one continual string of wagons as far as the eye can extend, before and behind us. All seem to be moving on peaceably and quiet. They reported a great deal of sickness in the companies for the first two or three weeks, but now mostly enjoying good health. In the evening there were twenty-nine camps in sight, numbering from fifteen to forty wagons each.

June 1st. Arrived at Fort Kearney. Ascertained that up to the last of May, 4,131 wagons had passed, headed for the west, and there are probably 2,000 behind us. It is reported there are 2,000 wagons at the crossing of the South Fork of the Platte, waiting, as the river is too high to cross. Some of the companies are selling their wagons and packing from this place. Wagons which cost one hundred and twenty-five dollars in the states sold for from ten to twenty dollars. Bacon has been sold for one cent per pound, flour from one to two dollars per hundred; other articles in proportion. It seems impossible for all the wagons which are on the road to get over the mountains this season."

The third season's effort to get off to the mountains

the victims of the Nauvoo persecutions, closed by the departure of the last company about the middle of July. The *Frontier Guardian*, of July 25, notices the event as follows:

"THE LAST TRAIN.

"On Saturday, the 14th, about noon, the last wagons left Winter Quarters and began to bend their way westward over the boundless plains that lie between us and the valley of the Great Salt Lake. Slowly and majestically they moved along, displaying a column of upwards of three hundred wagons, cattle, sheep, hogs, horses, mules, chickens, turkeys, geese, doves, goats, etc., etc., besides lots of men, women and children.

"In this company was the Yankee with his machinery, the Southerner with his colored attendant, the Englishman with all kinds of mechanic's tools, the farmer, the merchant, the doctor, the minister, and almost everything necessary for a settlement in a new country, provisioned for nine months from the time of starting. They were led by Messrs. George A. Smith and E. T. Benson. They have our best wishes for their prosperity and safety on their journey, and we hope they may be able to make for themselves comfortable homes in the distant and secluded valleys of our American Piedmont."

A short but lively picture of scenes in Salt Lake valley in the summer of 1849, is found in a letter of P. P. Pratt to his brother Orson, who was then in England. It is dated Great Salt Lake City, July 8th.

"Scores or hundreds of people now arrive here daily, and all stop to rest and refit. After crossing the great prairie wilderness for a thousand miles, where nothing is seen like civilization or cultivation, this spot suddenly bursts upon their astonished vision like a paradise in the midst of the desert. So great is the effect that many of them burst forth in an ecstacy of admiration on emerging from the canyon, and gaining a first view of our town and its fields and gardens. Some shed tears, some shout, some dance and skip for joy, and all, doubtless, feel the spirit of the place resting upon them, with its joyous and heavenly influence, bearing witness that here live the industrious, the free, the intelligent and the good.

"In truth our town presents a plateau of several square miles, dotted with houses, and every foot of it except the broad and pleasant streets, enclosed and under cultivation. Fields of yellow wheat are waving in the breeze; corn, oats, flax and garden vegetables fill the vacuum and extend every way as far as the eye can distinguish objects."

The following excerpt from an epistle of the First Presidency to the authorities of the Church in Pottowatomie county, Iowa, shows that the gathering of the poor of their people, who were still on the Missouri river, was a leading purpose in the minds of Brigham Young and his co-workers. It was a prelude to the great effort made the ensuing conference for the attainment of this object, which resulted in sending to the Missouri river Bishop Edward Hunter, as agent for gathering the poor, backed with the leverage of $30,000 in gold. This epistle was the keynote of the gathering in 1850.

"Great Salt Lake City,

"July 20th, 1849.

"* * * * * The brethren in Pottowatomie county, Iowa, in Missouri, Nauvoo and vicinities must remember, pause and reflect that we came to this valley when there was no house, nor fence, and no corn nor wheat, save what we brought with us; and that our every nerve and all our energies will be exerted to sustain ourselves, to build houses, fences, and raise grain, which from all appearances must command as high a price as from five to ten dollars per bushel for wheat, and from two to six dollars for corn, and other things in proportion.

"When these small matters of journeying more than a thousand miles over the sage plains, and settling and preparing to live, and sustain ourselves with the common necessaries of life are overcome, then the poor shall feel our helping hand to assist them to remove to this valley."

As the emigration is now fairly on the way, news from their moving camps in the form of letters to their friends will be of deep interest to the readers of the succeeding generation.

"CAMP OF ISRAEL, NEAR FORT CHILDS, TWO HUNDRED
AND EIGHT MILES FROM WINTER QUARTERS,

"Sunday, August 5th, 1849.

"BROTHER ORSON HYDE:

"While the bright and glorious luminary of day is mounting up from his eastern temple and the camps of Israel are corraled in the open prairie, with the canopy of heaven for their covering, except their canvas, and the herdsmen are guarding the cattle with their rifles in hand, and the camps are busy doing the duty devolving upon them, by our request our clerk has seated himself to write a hasty sketch to you for the *Guardian*, and to all others whom it may concern.

"We received with joy, on the morning of the 2nd inst., the letters you sent us by Captain Cane, and we wish you to embrace every opportunity of doing the like, and we will cheerfully return the compliment.

"We have had no serious accidents in our camps. All have enjoyed good health, with one or two exceptions. We have met with no losses of cattle. Indeed, in everything we have been blessed, for which we feel to raise our hearts in prayer, thanksgiving and gratitude to our Father in heaven.   Surely the angel of mercy has gone before us, and round about the camps of Israel. We had two or three stampedes before we adopted the plan of chaining and tying up our cattle.   Since then none have occurred in our camp, but our cattle rest in peace and quietness.   We corral our loose cattle, horses and sheep inside and tie our oxen outside, which we think the safest plan in case of fright or stampede, and we find it answers well.   *   *   *   *   *

"In Captain Richards' company a stampede took place last Sabbath evening, but without loss.   They corraled.   This company we expect is at Elm creek, thirteen miles ahead of us.   On our journey thus far we have passed seven graves.   Some of gold-diggers, others of Saints.   All but one, an infant, died of cholera, as the head-boards inform us.   Among others we see the name of A. Kellogg, at Prairie creek, one hundred and eighty-seven miles from Winter Quarters.   Died of cholera, 23rd of June last.   Also Samuel Gully, captain of a hundred in Brother O. Spencer's company of Saints, lies one hundred and eighty-five miles from Winter Quarters in the open prairie, his grave is neatly turfed over.   He died of cholera, July 5th, 1849, aged thirty-nine years. *   *   *   *   So you perceive the destroyer is on the vast plains as well as in the cities and towns.   *   *

"Since we wrote you concerning our organization at the Elk Horn, we have had a re-organization at the Platte liberty pole, which we deemed advisable.   The rules of the camps are the same as those adopted by President Young's company last year.   The camps are denominated G. A. Smith's, including the Welsh company, and E. T. Benson's, including the Norwegian company.   It was thought best to divide thus on account of numbers, and so separate the camps but keep close to each other.   Isaac Clark, president of both camps in G. A. Smith's company.   Elisha Everett, captain of hundred.   Charles Hopkins, captain of fifty in E. T. Benson's company.

"The reason we are anxious for all companies com

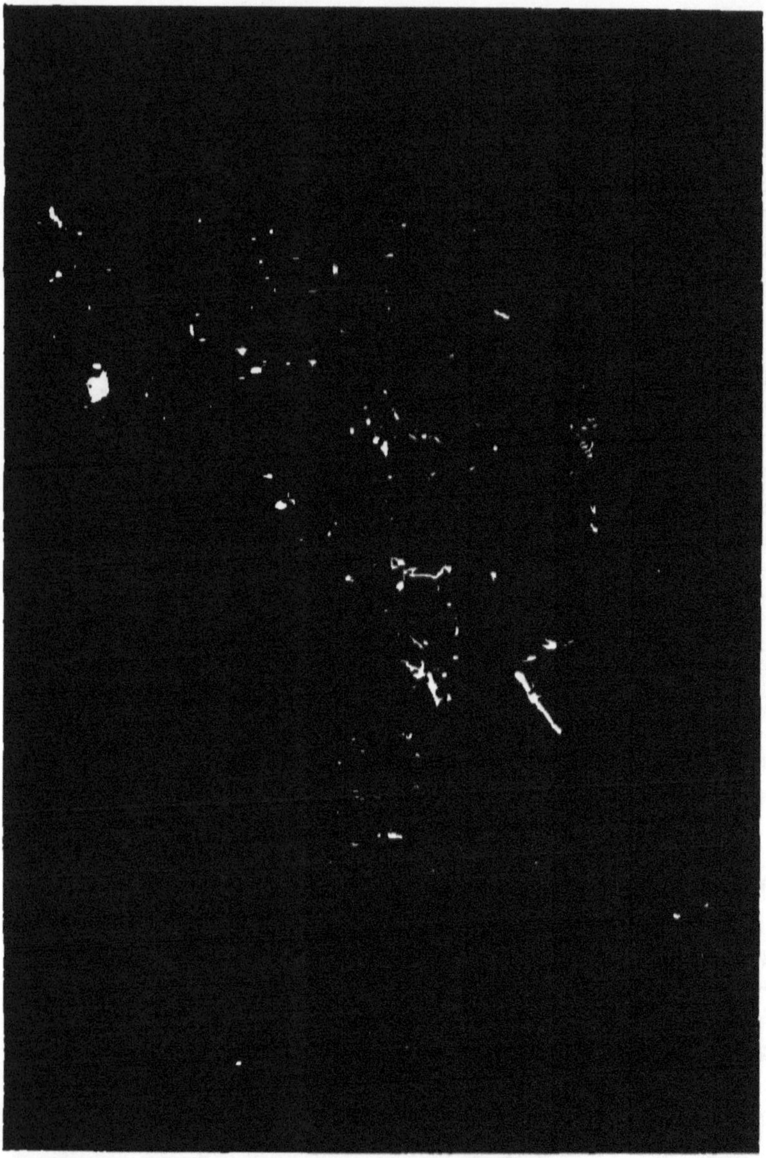

A STAMPEDE AMONG THE CATTLE.

ing this way to tie up their cattle is because of loss and danger. Indeed, there are few that can comprehend the terrors of a stampede. Picture to yourselves three or four hundred head of frightened oxen, steers, cows, etc., running, bellowing, roaring, foaming, mad and furious, the ground shaking beneath their feet like an earthquake; chains rattling, yokes cracking, horns flying and the cry of the guard, 'Every man turn out.' Horses mounted and, in the darkness of night, through high grass, sloughs, mud and mire, pursue the bellowing and furious herd, leaving the women and children frightened, with a few guards with rifles to guard the camp. After an hour or two, perhaps, the cattle will begin to get weary and quiet, and if luck and good fortune attend the horsemen they will head them and drive them back to camp, except those that sometimes swim rivers, etc. The terrors of a stampede are not soon forgotten. Good chains and ropes to tie up will prevent this.   *   *   *

     "Signed,   WILLIAM J. APPLEBY,
      " Clerk and Historian of the camps."

Another communication from Messrs. Smith and Benson to Elder Hyde followed the above, headed :

"CAMP OF ISRAEL, SPRING CREEK, THREE HUNDRED AND
    "FORTY-FIVE MILES FROM WINTER QUARTERS,

        "August 21st, 1849.

" BROTHER HYDE :

     "*   *   *   * Another opportunity favors us this morning of writing you by Brother Babbitt, who came into camp a few hours ago, twenty-six days from Salt Lake.

    *   ·   *   *   *   *   *   *   *

     "We have sustained no losses, no serious accidents of any kind. The destroyer has not laid any of us low; but, indeed, in everything we have been blessed and prospered, and the angel of peace and mercy, it appears, has been our shield and Joseph's God our protector, for which we feel truly thankful to Him whose we are and whom we desire to serve and obey. To be sure, we have had our trials in wet, muddy, miry roads, sand bluffs, sloughs, rivers, etc., also quite frequent and heavy showers of

rain, thunder, lightning, wind and great hail, but it has
caused where last year no grass grew and no water was
to be found, plenty of each for us the present year, and
the buffalo, antelope, ducks, etc., supply the camps with
meats which are excellent and plenty.

"So you will perceive we are happy and contented,
and blessed with the spirit of the Lord.   We surely
rejoice, and oft is the time the camps resound with the
songs of Zion, and fervent aspirations to heaven for the
mercies and blessings we enjoy, including protection
from the Indians.   They have not molested us.   Indeed,
we have not seen half a dozen Indians since we left
Winter Quarters.   The cholera, it appears, has
frightened them and they have deserted the path of the
white man.   Scores of them have already died with it
and been left on the prairie, covered over with a few
skins, and the wolves have come and devoured the flesh
from their bones.   *   *   *   *   *

"We have been visited with two or three severe
hail storms.   One took place last Friday evening.   A
description of it we copy from Elder Appleby's journal
of the camp.

"August 18th.   Last evening we experienced
another heavy shower.   It came on as the camps were
tying up their cattle.   A dark cloud had been observed
lying off south of the Platte, near which we were
encamped.   After sometime it appeared to separate;
one part passed east of us, the other, a short time
after came over us, and saturated our canvas well, and
made those who were tying up their cattle expedite the
business or else take the large, cold drops.   However,
it soon passed over and appeared to follow the one gone
east, as if to wage a battle, as both seemed prepared.

"After a little they appeared to meet and, united,
they bent their way to give the camp a round of their
artillery.   On they came, riding upon the wind with the
speed of the llama over the prairies, roaring and tumbling, charged with electricity, the lightning flashed its
vivid glare through the darkness of the night and storm.

Sometimes a shaft would descend to earth followed by rumbling peals of thunder that caused the earth to tremble. At length they reached the camp, and, as if to defeat us if we undertook to keep them at bay, they first gave us a fine drenching, perhaps to wet our ammunition. * * After a few minutes their batteries were opened indeed ; first canister, then grape, afterwards the half pounders, not hot shot, but cold and hard, was poured into our camp. The plains and distant hills reverberated with the sound of the artillery of heaven. The cattle being made fast withstood the storm without seeking for shelter, except some horses that broke loose, and loose cattle in the corral.

"The guard, in the midst of the battle, cried the hour as the hail fell upon them, sometimes striking them on the head nearly stunning them. * * * * However, after a while, appearing to have spent their fury they retired, leaving the camp master of the field, and a considerable quantity of their large shot behind lying in and around it. * * * The camp after their retreat reposed in sleep. The sentinels paced the dark, and in the morning all was well ; no one killed nor wounded; no cattle missing, and not an enemy lying on the battle field."

On the evening of September 3rd, 1849, Hon. A. W. Babbitt, bearing the above letter, arrived in Kanesville. He was thirty-six days on the road and water bound eight days of that time. He went safely through with one man, Oliver G. Workman, seven horses and a light wagon in whichhe took the mail.

13

CHAPTER XXV.

THE following is a synopsis of the news from Salt
Lake, furnished by Colonel Babbitt to the *Frontier
Guardian* of September 5th, 1849. The prophecy of
Heber C. Kimball, in the autumn of 1848, that goods
would be sold cheaper in the streets of Salt Lake City
than they could be purchased in the eastern cities, was
amply fulfilled in the summer of 1849. The valley had
been a place of general deposit for the surplus property
of the California emigrants. When they saw a few bags
and kegs of gold dust which had been brought from
California by returning Mormons, they became wild with
enthusiasm. Pack mules and horses, worth in ordinary
times, twenty-five or thirty dollars, readily brought two
hundred dollars in valuable property at low prices. Good
property was daily offered at auction in all parts of the
city.

Sometimes three or four heavy wagons, with a yoke
of oxen thrown in, would be offered for a light one-

horse wagon. Common domestic sheeting sold for from 5 to 10 cents per yard by the bolt; the best of spades and shovels for 50 cents each ; vests, that cost in St. Louis $1.50, for 37½ cents; full chests of joiner tools worth $150 in the east, sold for $25. Almost every article, except sugar and coffee, sold on an average, 50 per cent. below wholesale prices in the eastern cities.

"Through the alkali belt, east of the South Pass, their losses in cattle were enormous. Many of the men would pay no attention to the warning of the Saints, not to let their cattle drink water strongly impregnated with saleratus. They said it was all a 'Mormon humbug' about the alkali being strong enough to kill their cattle. As the result more than 2,000 carcasses of oxen lay strewn along the road in the alkali district, and the offensive smell made it almost impossible to travel in the vicinity."

The cholera had been very fatal among the Indians. Mr. Babbitt reported passing, in one place, ten deserted lodges with many dead Indians lying about, and the bodies torn and half eaten by wolves.

Livingston and Kinkead's company, and Captain William Miller, were met two hundred miles west of Laramie, at the time all well. Captain Howard Egan and company were met at the Weber river, about forty miles from the valley. Messrs. Hickman and Hatch west of the South Pass; Perkin's hundred, of Captain Allen Taylor's and Enoch Reese's fifties, still east of Laramie.

Apostles George A. Smith and E. T. Benson's companies were well but getting along slowly on account of constant rains and high water. But four of our people had died of cholera on the road. We copy the following *verbatim* from the *Frontier Guardian*:

"Mr. Babbitt certainly deserves our thanks for his perseverance in swimming rivers and towing over his wagon on rafts made with a hatchet and tied together with lariats.   It cannot be a very pleasant job to freight a rude sort of raft with a wagon, push off into a rapid current, pull out about one-fourth of the distance across, then take one end of a rope in your teeth, while the other end is attached to a raft and plunge into the stream, like a spaniel, and swim over with raft and cargo in tow, being swept down streams over snags and sawyers, for a quarter or half a mile, as Mr. B. informs us has been his lot in two or three instances.

"But, Oh! the sacrifice of property thrown out and left by the road side, by the Californians between Laramie and the valley, is beyond calculation. * * * * *

"Mr. B. thinks that Livingston and Kinkead will be broken merchants because of so many goods getting into the valley before theirs and having been sold for less than prime cost.   The market is glutted."

Mr. Babbitt's surmises that Salt Lake was overstocked with goods proved not to be well founded. Livingston and Kinkead soon disposed of their stock of merchandise ; sugar and coffee at 40 cents per pound, calico 25 cents per yard, and other goods at proportionately high prices.

The following papers not only give some items of historical interest but are as well a curiosity.   The writer evidently expected they would fall into the hands of Messrs. Smith and Benson but they forded the Loupe Fork lower down the stream.   They were found on the grave of a gold-digger and, through a Mr. Reed who was hunting with the Indians, they found their way into the hands of the editor of the *Frontier Guardian*.   As before stated Captain Gully died with the cholera and was buried by the wayside.

"UPPER CROSSING OF THE LOUPE,
"June 26th, 1849.

" *Bros. Geo. A Smith and E. T. Benson:*

"MY DEAR SIRS: We arrived here on the 22nd and 23rd, all in tolerable health. Soon after the arrival of Brother Wm. Miller's fifty, Brother Nelson McCarthy was attacked with cholera and is buried at this point. * * * We have waited here three days with but little prospects of crossing until today about twelve o'clock, when the Disposer of all good seems to have ordered a place for us to cross. * * * We have found the road very heavy. Yet our cattle have improved. * * * As yet I have not been able to send back the report of our numbers, but have them ready for the first opportunity. I leave them here hoping you may receive this. I do it short as I am in feeble health. Wagons, 120; souls, 352; oxen, 480; cows, 315; loose cattle, 17; horses, 29; mules, sheep, 102; pigs, 31; chickens, 62; cats 25; dogs, 25; geese, 2; ducks, 2; doves, 7; hives of bees, 1.

"Most respectfully your Friend and Servt.,
SAMUEL GULLY."

Considering this was the third season's emigration, this company was well fitted out with animal life for the benefit of the new colony.

With the wonderful changes of forty years, it seems like a dream of the past that the writer crossed the plains in 1849, with Enoch Reese's fifty, of Captain Perkins' hundred. At one time stampedes were so frequent and dangerous that there seemed but little room for choice between hostile Indians and stampeding cattle.

So subject to panic did the cattle become, that the leaders of the people thought it advisable for the companies to break up into tens long before reaching Laramie. The following morning, after this was done, the cattle of Captain Lorenzo Clark's ten to which the

writer belonged, stampeded with quite serious loss.   He
arrived in Great Salt Lake valley on the 16th of October.
He found a destitute but cheerful people, struggling with
the sterile elements for existence.   Nature had poorly
remunerated the labors of the husbandman ; the country
was nearly destitute of game available for subsistence,
and the scarcity of cattle rendered their preservation
necessary for the future prosperity of the increasing
population.   The people were a thousand miles from
outside resources, and necessity compelled the utmost
economy in the preservation of food, until time permitted
them to organize the means of subsistence from the
elements, and learn the invaluable lesson how to turn
deserts into gardens and desolate places into fruitful
fields.   Baptized in the fires of persecution, tempered to
bear oppression and wrong to the limit of human endurance, practically outlawed and expelled from the soil of
Missouri and Illinois by their fellow citizens for their religious belief, the principles of liberty and equality, embodied in the constitution of their country, had become
indelibly stamped on their hearts by the brand of affliction. Here in the fastnesses of the mountains they hoped
to be free from oppression, until they were able to
struggle successfully for the right.

There are few instances in modern history where a
people so few in number, so oppressed by enemies, so
crippled in resources had been of so much practical
benefit to their country, and fewer still who received so
little care and so many insults from their government.

Taught self relience by the necessity of self preservation ; accustomed to hardship and toil from the
force of circumstances ; indifferent alike to the attacks of
slander and to the sneers of contempt, through implicit
confidence in the divinity of their principles, they were,

at the time of which we speak, masters of the situation into which their enemies had forced them.

The second general epistle of the Presidency of the Church, from Great Salt Lake valley dated October 12th, 1849, was published in the *Frontier Guardian* of the ensuing 26th of December.   Of the emigration not yet arrived in the valley it says :—

"Elder Dan Jones, from Wales, is within a few days travel, accompanied by a portion of the Welsh brethren and the remainder are located on Pottowatomie lands. "Elders Geo. A. Smith and E. T. Benson are in the same vicinity, with Dan Jones, accompanied by their families and a large company of Saints, from whom we received an express five days since, which left them in universal health and prosperity.   They will probably be here in two weeks.   We have sent teams to help them on their journey.

"The direct emigration of the Saints to this place will be some five or six hundred wagons this season, besides many who came in search of gold have heard the gospel for the first time, and will go no further, having believed and been baptized "   *   *   *   *   *   *

The epistle states that the grain crops had been good, but late crops of corn, buckwheat, vegetables, etc., had been injured by the frosts, but it speaks very encouragingly of the food supply for the ensuing year.

"We have great occasion for thanksgiving to Him who giveth the increase, that He has blest our labors so that, with prudence, we shall have a comfortable supply for ourselves and our brethren on the way who may be in need, until another harvest ; but we feel the need of more laborers, for more efficient help, and multiplied means of farming and building at this place.   We want men ; brethren come from the States, from the nations, come ! and help us build and grow, until we can say enough ; the valleys of Ephraim are full."

We have seen by a letter from the Presidency to the authorities in Pottowatomie county, written on the 26th of the previous July, that a great effort for gathering the poor was then in contemplation. This epistle gives an account of that important organization the Perpetual Emigration Fund Company, and outlines its operations for the year 1850.

" About one month since we suggested the propriety of creating a perpetual fund for the purpose of helping the poor Saints to emigrate to this place, agreeably to our covenants in the temple that we would never cease our exertions, by all the means and influences within our reach, till all the Saints who were obliged to leave Nauvoo shall be located at some gathering place of the Saints. The Council approved the suggestion and a committee was immediately appointed to raise a fund by voluntary contribution to be forwarded east next mail.

" The October Conference sanctioned the doings of the committee, and appointed Brother Edward Hunter, a tried, faithful and approved Bishop, a general agent to bear the Perpetual Emigrating Funds to the States, to superintend the direction and appropriation thereof and return the same to this place, with such poor brethren as shall be wisdom to help.

"We wish all to understand that this fund is to be Perpetual, and is never to be diverted from the object of gathering the poor to Zion while there are Saints to be gathered, unless He whose right it is to rule shall otherwise command.   *   *   *   *   *

" This Perpetual Fund is to be under the direction of the Presidency at all times, and as soon as Bishop Hunter shall return with the same and his freight of

Saints to this place, the cattle and teams will be disposed of to the best advantage, and the avails with all we can add to it, will be sent forth immediately on another mission and we want you all prepared to meet it, and add to it, and so would we continue to increase it, from year to year, until when 'a nation is born in a day' they can be removed the next if the Lord will. Therefore ye poor and meek of the earth, lift up your hearts and rejoice in the Holy One of Israel, for your redemption draweth nigh : but in your rejoicings be patient, for though your turn to emigrate may not be the first year, or even the second, it will come, and its tarryings will be short, if all Saints who have been assisted will be as liberal as those in the valley."

This organization continued its beneficent operations in gathering many thousands of poor Saints from the nations, opening to them a way of temporal salvation from poverty and oppression, until it was throttled by congressional enactment in 1887.

The following is another interesting letter from the emigrating companies on the plains.

"CAMP OF ISRAEL, MUDDY FORK, 930 MILES FROM WIN-
TER QUARTERS,

"October 18th, 1849.

"*Elder O. Hyde*,

"DEAR BRETHREN :   *   *   *   *   The last we wrote you was at Fort Laramie, since then no opportunity of sending letters to the States has presented itself. After leaving Laramie we continued our journey slowly as heretofore, but making progress every day, keeping a vigilant eye to the welfare of our cattle. The first three hundred miles of our journey nearly was through mud and mire, after that heavy sand for a considerable distance, but pasture was first-rate. Our cattle withstood the journey well, and up to our arrival at Laramie, we believe, neither our camp nor Brother Benson's had lost a single head with the exception of one or two cows that got killed in the yoke.

"After we passed Laramie the feed became inferior, but we found a sufficient supply for our cattle. Indeed, we have found a plenty all the while, with the exception of two or three days in the neighborhood of the Willow Springs, where the alkali or poisonous springs abound. Through these wild plains lie ·the bones of hundreds of cattle that have died the past summer. No less than the bones of nine head were counted in one heap, belonging to the gold diggers bound for California. Through this desolate part of our journey we lost but a few head of our cattle, and those that died were chiefly worn down by the journey. When we arrived at the Sweetwater river, about six miles below Independence Rock, a recruit of some sixty yoke of cattle, together with several wagons and teamsters from the valley, met us. They had been sent by the President to our relief under the charge of Brothers David Fullmer and Joseph Young. This was a welcome meeting to us, as our cattle were much fatigued and needed respite.

"The cattle thus sent were divided between the three camps, viz.: E. T. Benson's, Captain Richard's and ours. This relieved us much, and the weather being pleasant we rolled along with ease. At Independence Rock some twenty-five or thirty head strayed away, but we recovered them all, except one cow, after following thirteen head about one hundred miles.

"We crossed over Rocky Ridge on the 2nd of this month, near the summit of the South Pass, with the Wind River chain of mountains on the north. Towards night it began to snow and blow quite hard and fast from the north-east. The weather increased in coldness, which obliged us to encamp the best way we could without corraling, on a branch of the Sweetwater. E. T. Benson's and Captain Richard's camps were ten or twelve miles ahead of us on Willow Creek.

"We turned our cattle loose and drove them into the willows near by to do the best they could and share their fate. Such a storm of wind and snow as we experienced, we think, was never exceeded in severity in Pottowatomie. For thirty-six hours it continued to howl around us, unceasingly blowing nearly a hurricane, drifting the snow in every direction. The snow froze to whatever it touched. Being unable to keep fires, except a few who had stoves in their wagons, we had to be content without them and do the best we could.

"Many were the mothers and infants who were obliged to be in bed under their frail coverings that sheltered them from the pitiless blast and kept them from perishing, with, perhaps, only a dry piece of bread or a few crackers to subsist upon.   *   *   *   The snow drifted around us in some places to the depth of three or four feet. Many were the reflections that passed through our minds in regard to our situation and the welfare of our cattle during the storm; but we felt resigned to our fate and Heaven's will.

"On the morning of the third day the storm abated. We turned out in the chilling blast from off the everlasting snow-capped mountains, ourselves at an altitude of 7,000 feet, to look for our famishing, perishing cattle. As we wended our way down the stream among the willows, it was, indeed, a sorrowful sight to behold our dead cattle, one after another, cold and stiff, lying in the snow banks, food for wolves, ravens, catamounts, magpies, etc., that inhabit these mountainous regions in countless numbers and live on prey.

"The greater part of our cattle had made their way during the storm about five miles off, to the Sweetwater, where they obtained pasture and fared quite well, not one being found dead, while those that tarried behind fell a prey to hunger and the merciless storm. Upwards of sixty head of cattle perished in the three camps. Those that survived the storm did not recover from its effects for several days, others died in consequence, and some show the effects yet, although they are improving

at present as we find plenty of mountain grass, and that
hearty and good. We are in tolerable good rolling
order, making from twelve to fifteen miles per day. We
hope, if we are prospered, to reach the valley in eight
or ten days from this time.   *   *   *   *

"Not a solitary death has occurred, of man, woman
or child, in our camp, although we have experienced
storms and endured cold weather. It was so cold during
the storm and after, that chickens, pigs, etc., froze to
death and men crossed over the Sweetwater on the ice.

"Many have been the graves we have passed on
our journey, some of friends near and dear, others of
strangers that have fallen by the shaft of the destroyer
while traveling over these boundless plains of sage and
mountains of rock, where the buffalo, elk, antelope,
bear, ravenous wolf, etc., range undisturbed, except by
the red man or the journeying emigrant. We have seen
many graves of gold-seekers whose bodies have been
disinterred by wolves, and the bones, pantaloons, hose
and other things strewed around, with the headboard
lying near, informing the traveler who had been buried,
where from, the day they died, age, disease, etc. But
we have not seen a solitary tomb of the Saints disturbed
by the wolves.

"Among the graves of those whose bones lie
around bleaching in the sun, their flesh consumed by
the ravenous wolves, we recognize the names of several
noted mobocrats from the states of Missouri and Illinois
who took an active, prominent part in persecuting, mob-
bing and driving the Saints from these states. Among
others we noticed at the South Pass of the Rocky
Mountains, the grave of E. Dodd, of Gallatin, Missouri,
died on the 19th of July last, of typhus fever. The
wolves had completely disinterred him. The clothes in
which he had been buried lay strewed around. His
under jaw bone lay in the grave with the teeth complete,
the only remains that were discernible of him. It is
believed he was the same Dodd who was a prominent
mobocrat and who took an active part in the murder of

the Saints at Haun's Mill, Missouri. 'If so, it is a right-
eous retribution. Our God will surely inflict punishment
upon the heads of our oppressors in His own due time
and way.   *   *   *   *

"As ever, we remain your brethren in Christ,

"GEORGE A. SMITH,

"W. I. APPLEBY."

CHAPTER XXVI.

BISHOP HUNTER AGENT FOR GATHERING THE POOR—CHAR-
ACTERISTIC ANECDOTES—INSTRUCTIONS FOR THE EMI-
GRATION OF 1850—THE CALL FOR THE GATHERING
OF THE CAMPS OF ISRAEL—DEARTH OF NEWS IN GREAT
SALT LAKE VALLEY—NEWS FROM PARTIES SNOWED IN
IN THE MOUNTAINS.

THE first company of Elders sent on foreign missions
from Utah left Great Salt Lake City on the 19th of
October and carried the last mail sent east in 1849. It
was under the leadership of Jedediah M. Grant.

With this company went Edward Hunter, Bishop of
the thirteenth ward of Great Salt Lake City. He was
sent by the chief authorities of the Church to the Missouri river as agent of the P. E. Fund Company, with
$30,000 in gold to gather up as many as possible of the
Saints remaining of the Nauvoo exodus and bring them
to Utah. His character peculiarly adapted him for the
work of gathering the poor.

Aside from his excellent business qualifications
nature had endowed him with humane and self-sacrific-

ing principles.   Under the unavoidable hardships of traveling, in that early period, he not only manifested a kindly regard for the comfort of others but, as well, ever carried his full share of the general burden.   What was said of the Prophet Joseph Smith was, as well, applicable to him, "He was always willing to carry his part of the burden, and to share in any suffering or deprivation inflicted upon his friends."

The following incidents, related by Charles F. Decker who traveled with him illustrate this trait of his character and also his detestation of "camp shirks."

He had a good natured way of making such characters ashamed rather than angry.   It was necessary to cross the Platte river.   The quicksand was bad and it was thought necessary for those in a condition to do so to wade the river and thus lighten the loads.   It was, no doubt, a chilling operation at that altitude in the month of November.   It appeared to require a general lively effort to insure the crossing of the teams in safety. Some persons in poor health, whom the strong brethren proposed should remain in the wagons, refused to do so, while others, in good health seriously objected to wetting their lower extremities.

The brethren began to roll at the wheels of a wagon, the team of which appeared to have more than it could contend with in the quicksand.   In the wagon was a Brother J. who, although enjoying very· good health, objected to getting out for fear of catching his death cold.   Bishop Hunter, having hold of one of the hind wheels, quietly remarked, "Brethren, I think this wagon will have to be tipped over before it will go out."   Suiting action to the idea he raised his side of the wagon until it appeared to be going over.   Mr. J., inside, anticipating such a catastrophe, cried out, with some energy

"Oh let me get out first!" and sprang into the water. The Bishop quietly remarked, "Well, well, brethren, I think the wagon will go along now, suppose we try it."

One cold evening the company encamped on the bank of the Platte river. Wood for camp purposes could only be obtained by crossing a considerable branch of the river on to an island. It was very unpleasant to ford the stream, but of two evils this seemed the least. The more ambitious of the men took their axes and started, at once, for the island. Mr. J. and another similar character remained on the bank to take wood from those who might bring it through the water. Bishop Hunter discovering the situation, as he came from camp passed between them, seized one with each arm and took both with him into the water, good naturedly remarking, "Come brethren, we are wet now, let us go and get some wood."

This company arrived in Kanesville December 11th, 1849. It carried the following letter of instructions concerning the emigration of 1850. It emphasizes the fact that the spirit of gathering the scattered Saints burned in the bosoms of the First Presidency of the Church and the Apostles, and that, by their teachings and examples they were spreading the fire until it was reaching the heart of every person, endowed with the spirit of the latter-day work in the United States.

"GREAT SALT LAKE CITY,

"October 16th, 1849.

"PRESIDENT ORSON HYDE:

"*Beloved Brother :* The Lord has been devising, or rather making manifest, ways and means to facilitate the gathering of His Saints in these last days, and we lose no time in cheering your heart with the intelligence, and

offering such suggestions as may be wisdom for you to
follow in helping to roll on this glorious work of gathering Israel.   *   *   *   *   *   *   *   *

"We write you more particularly at this time, concerning the gathering, and the mission of our general
agent for the Perpetual Emigration Fund for the coming
year, Bishop Edward Hunter, who will soon be with you,
bearing the funds already raised in this place, and we
will here state our instructions to Bishop Hunter, so that
you may the more fully comprehend our designs.

"In the first place this fund has been raised by
voluntary donations, and is to be continued by the same
process, and by so managing as to preserve the same
and then to multiply.

"Bishop Hunter is instructed to go direct to Kanesville and confer with the general authorities at that place,
and, by all means within his reach, procure every information so as to make the most judicious application of
the funds in the purchase of young oxen and cows, that
can be worked effectually to the valley, and that will be
capable of improving and selling after their arrival, so
as to continue the fund the following year.

"We will give early information to those whom we
have directed to be helped, and such others as he shall
deem wisdom, being aided in his judgment by the
authorities among you, so that they may be preparing
their wagons, etc., for the journey.

"Wagons are so plenty here that it is very desirable
not to purchase with the Perpetual Fund ; but let those
be assisted who will make wagons of wood, when they
cannot get iron, such as will be strong and safe to bring
them here, so that all the funds may be appropriated to the
purchase of such things as will improve in value by
being transferred to this place.

"The poor can live without the luxuries of life on
the road and in the valley, as well as in Pottowatomie
and other places, and those who have means to purchase
luxuries, have monies to procure an outfit of their own
and need no help.   Therefore, let such as are helped

receive as little in food and clothing, wagons, etc., as can possibly make them comfortable to this place, and when they arrive they can go to work and get their outfit of all things necessary for comfort and convenience better than where they are, and even luxuries.

"As early in the spring as it will possibly do, on account of feed for cattle, Brother Hunter will gather all his company, organize them in the usual order, and preside over the camp, traveling with the same to this place ; having previously procured the best teamsters possible, such as are accustomed to driving, and be gentle, kind and attentive to their teams. When the Saints, thus helped, arrive here, they will give their obligation to the Church to refund to the amount of what they have received, as soon as circumstances will permit, and labor will be furnished to such as wish on the public works, and good pay ; and as fast as they can procure the necessaries of life, and a surplus, that surplus will be applied to liquidating their debt, and thereby increasing the Perpetual Fund. By this it will be readily discovered that the funds are to be appropriated in the form of a loan, rather than a gift ; and this will make the honest in heart rejoice, for they love to labor and be independent by their labor, and not live on the charity of friends, while the lazy idlers, if such there be, will find fault and want every luxury furnished them on their journey, and in the end pay nothing. The Perpetual Fund will help no such idlers ; we have no use for them in the valley ; they had better stay where they are ; and if they think they can devise a better way of appropriating the emigrating funds than we propose let them go to work, get the funds, make the appropriation, set us a better pattern, and we will follow it ; and by that time we are confident they will have means of their own and will need no help.

"Brother Hunter will return all the funds to this place next season, when the most judicious course will be pursued to convert all the cattle and means into cash, that the same may be sent abroad as speedily as possible on another mission, together with all that we can raise besides to add to it; and we anticipate the Saints at Pottowatomie and in the states, will increase the funds by all possible means the coming winter, so that our agents may return with a large company. The few thousands we send out by our agent, at this time, is like a grain of mustard seed in the earth; we send it forth into the world, and among the Saints, a good soil, and we expect it will grow and flourish, and spread abroad in a few years, so that it will cover England, cast its shadow in Europe, and in process of time compass the whole earth. That is to say, these funds are designed to increase until Israel is gathered from all nations, and the poor can sit under their own vines and inhabit their own house and worship God in Zion." * * * *

On the 23rd of January, 1850, the *Frontier Guardian* sounded the call for the gathering of the camps of Israel for the march across the plains. It was in the spirit of the general epistle and it was no uncertain sound.

"The friends abroad throughout the states will do well to gather to this point as early in the spring as they can. * * * Come early to this place, and, if you are unable to go on you will be in time to put in crops; and if you are able to go on, you may start with the first companies. Let all prepare that can and be off to the valley. But we want every nook, corner, and field, put into spring grain before you start. It will probably be a forward spring, and much small grain may be put in during the month of March. The first company will probably leave here for the mountains about the 1st of May, one about the middle of May, one about the 1st of June, and one about the 15th of June— none later. Every company of emigrants will have experienced guides who know the route, who know the Indians, and who well understand the mode and manner of traveling on the plains."

The third general epistle from the valley was dated April 12th, 1850.   It reached Kanesville in time for the *Frontier Guardian* of June 12th.   It states that the colony in the Great Salt Lake valley had had no news from abroad since the previous September, a period of seven months.   The chief interest of the following excerpt is the news concerning the parties caught in the snows of the Wasatch mountains in the beginning of the previous winter.

"Some emigrants from Michigan arrived at this place on the 15th of November, accompanied by Mr. Vasques, bringing letters from Elders then going east, who were at Little Sandy, October 30th, all well.   And on the 22nd of the same month snow covered the valley from one and a half to two inches deep ; and on the 24th it was about three and a half feet in Mill Creek canyon ; on the same day Elder P. P. Pratt, with a company of about fifty men, left the most southern settlement of this valley, where they had rendezvoused the day previous for the purpose of exploring the south country to learn its geography, history, climate and locations for settlements.

"Nineteen emigrants arrived December 1st, in a very destitute situation, having left their wagons more than forty miles back, and their teams about twenty ; themselves without provisions.   They reported having left the states on the 24th of September, and having passed Elder Taylor's company at Independence Rock, November 6th, but so closely were they pressed by the snow, they did not bring us one newspaper, though they said they had many in their wagons.   *   *   *

"On the 30th of January, four men arrived from Fort Bridger, having left their goods and remaining pack animals in Weber canyon ; a portion of their horses having died on the way before reaching the canyon. This was the second attempt of the same company to pass from the fort to the valleys, and their goods remained in the canyon on the 30th of March."

CHAPTER XXVII.

THREE HUNDRED AND FIFTY WAGONS START UP THE SOUTH
SIDE OF THE PLATTE—IMMENSE EMIGRATION TO CALI-
FORNIA—PROSPEROUS CONDITION OF THE SAINTS—THE
"DESERET NEWS'"—PANORAMIC VIEW OF THE EMIGRA-
TION—RAVAGES OF THE CHOLERA—THE DISEASE IN
ITS MOST FEARFUL STAGES—GRAVES BY THE WAYSIDE
—THE LAST OF THE MORMON EMIGRATION ON THE
WAY—O. HYDE ON HIS WAY TO THE MOUNTAINS—
HIS ACCOUNT OF THE EMIGRATION—GOOD CROPS AND
FOOD ABUNDANT IN THE VALLEY—"RICH AND POOR
GATHER TO THE STATE OF DESERET"—THE SAINTS
COUNSELED TO TRAVEL ON THE NORTH SIDE OF THE
PLATTE.

THE *Frontier Guardian* of June 12th, 1850, has the
following interesting summary of the season's
operations up to date, under the head of

"EMIGRATION.

"We have attended the organization of three hundred and fifty wagons of Salt Lake emigrants, up to
Saturday the 8th inst. Captain Milo Andrus is ahead
with fifty wagons. Next follows Captain Benjamin Haw-
kins with one hundred, Thos. S. Johnson, captain 1st
division and captain—of second division. We left them
at Council Grove, twelve miles from Bethlehem, west of
the Missouri river, on the morning of the 7th. Next in
succession is Bishop Aaron Johnson with a train of one
hundred wagons, Elisha Averett, captain of first division
and Matthew Caldwell, captain of second division. Next
in order is Captain James Pace with one hundred,
Richard Sessions, captain of first division, and David
Bennett, captain of second division.

"The emigrants are generally well fitted out with wagons and teams, provisions, etc., etc.   *

"The number of California wagons that have crossed at this point, is about 4,500, averaging three men to the wagon, making 13,500 men, and about 22,000 head of horses, mules, oxen and cows.   Our own emigration to Salt Lake valley will amount to about seven hundred wagons as nearly as we, at present, can determine. They take two new carding machines, in addition to one sent last year, besides much other valuable machinery. They also take about 4,000 sheep and 5,000 head of cattle, horses and mules."

Another congratulatory editorial follows in the *Guardian* of June 25th, under the same heading of

"EMIGRATION.

"We feel highly gratified to see our emigration so well fitted out as they are. They generally have two good yoke of oxen, and from one to three yoke of cows to each wagon. The average freight of each wagon is 1,850 pounds. The average amount of breadstuff to the person, old or young, is one hundred and twenty-five pounds—bacon, sugar, coffee, tea, rice, dried fruit, and other little necessaries in proportion.

"To see a people who, three or four years ago, had to sell their all to get bread to last them until they could raise it, and now see them with from one to four wagons each, with plenty of good teams, thousands of sheep and loose cattle, horses, mules, and machinery of every kind; wagons all new and stock all young and thrifty, is gratifying in the extreme."

This is another recorded evidence of the wonderful recuperative powers of the Latter-day Saints. There were many personal experiences that would be interesting as illustrating remarkable providences which opened the way for individuals to obtain the means of gathering to the mountains. It is in accordance with the whole history of this people, that almost miraculous blessing has often attended the efforts of individuals when working under untoward circumstances for the accomplishment of some specific purpose, in the line of duty and progress.

From the evacuation of Nauvoo until the publication of the *Frontier Guardian* in February, 1849, the Church had no representative periodical on the American continent.   The first number of the *Deseret News* appeared June 15th, 1850, in Great Salt Lake City. The first was evidently intended to forward the emigration interests at the eastern end of the route across the plains, then to be abandoned.   The *Deseret News* was as evidently designed to be the leading periodical of the Church of Jesus Christ of Latter-day Saints.

As seen to-day the first volume of the *Deseret News* bears the impress of the difficult circumstances under which it saw the light.   Its editor was Willard Richards, one of the First Presidency of the Church.   The prospectus of the *News* is replete with the straight-forward, honesty and love of truth which characterized this man. Probably the peculiar circumstances surrounding the issuing of this paper will not find a parallel in the history of the continent.   The first volume is already an historical curiosity, and, with the rapidity the world has been moving, may be considered already ancient.   Its motto, "Truth and Liberty," was characteristic of a people who were under the ban of Christian civilization, for attempting to solve important social problems through the power of divine inspiration ; and for this had endured a long series of vindictive persecutions.

The following excerpt was doubtless written with a prophetic view of what the miniature sheet was to become in the future.   We "designed originally to record the passing events of our state, and in connection, refer to the arts and sciences, embracing general education, medicine, law, divinity, domestic and political economy, and everything that may fall under our observation which may tend to promote the best interest, welfare, pleasure and amusement of our fellow citizens." For forty years the paper has been considered so far the organ of the Church as to usually indicate its policies.

The following account of the journeying of a company from Great Salt Lake City to Kanesville, is from a letter of Elder Robert Campbell's published in the *Frontier Guardian* July 7th, 1850.   Its chief interest in this connection, is the excellent panoramic view it affords of the emigration, as it was met in the mountains and on the Platte river.

There was considerable mortality from the cholera in 1849, on the south side of the Platte, and several deaths from it among emigrants on the north side.   In 1850, this terrible scourge swept out on to the plains in the majesty of its power, as it had not before done. Perhaps it had more to feed it, as the emigration to California was immense.

The company with which Mr. Campbell traveled left Great Salt Lake City on the 20th of April, 1850.   May 15th, they met S. B. Crow's company of California emigrants, from Kendall county, Illinois, near Dry Sandy, the people well, and to the astonishment of the company, their animals in good condition.   They had been fed on grain until the supply was exhausted, after that flour, as their owners depended on replenishing their stock of provisions in Salt Lake valley.

The evening of May 16th, they found Denison's company of two hundred people from Ohio, encamped at the first crossing of the Sweetwater.   A few minutes later another company of emigrants rolled across the river to the west side and encamped. The animals of this company were in poor condition. The 21st of May, a few ox teams were met that had wintered at Laramie. Also a man, said to be a Dutchman, with a wheelbarrow. Several men had offered to haul his bedding and provisions. He thanked them kindly and wished to be excused, as he could not wait on the slow movements of a camp. He seemed to appreciate the fact that he had no horses for Indians to steal, and that he never lost any rest through dread of a stampede. Three hundred miles from Salt Lake City, the road was thronged with emigrants for the land of gold.

The 25th of May, the company arrived at the Upper Platte ferry and ford. From this point the road was nearly covered with emigrant wagons. Laying around on camp grounds were harness, casks, axes, augurs, stoves, etc., but these were but small in amount compared with the articles thrown away by the emigrants the year previous. These had evidently learned some wisdom from what friends had experienced who preceded them. They fitted out with light wagons and good teams and had taken no surplus property to throw away on the plains.

At the ferry was met a Mr. Hickman and others from Missouri. They were running a boat. Some of the mail company assisted the old pioneer ferryman who had come out with them, build and launch two good, substantial boats. Some of the company, going through also traded oxen for horses and refitted up a little for their journey. They left the Upper Platte ferry on the 3rd of June. They met almost a continuous train of emigrant wagons and arrived at Laramie the 10th of the month. At Laramie, a Mr. Sommerville, employed by the government to keep an account of the passing emi-

gration, furnished the company with the following items:
"Total number of emigrants passed this post up to June
10th, 1850, inclusive, 16,915 men, 235 women, 242 children, 4,672 wagons, 14,974 horses, 4,641 mules, 7,425
oxen, 1,653 cows.   Signed,
          "CALVIN C. SOMMERVILLE, Clerk."

The 12th of June, the company encamped by Robi-
dau's trading post near Scott's Bluff's.   There the
cholera was met among the emigrants.   They were
informed that the Sioux Indians had gone to White
river, for fear the white men would bring the cholera
among them as they had done the year before.   The
18th of June the animals and wagons forded the South
Fork of the Platte, but the goods were boated over.
Several of the company were attacked with disease but
recovered through the administration of Elders.   They
were daily meeting cholera in its most fearful stages.
Graves by the wayside were common, sometimes several
in a group.   They were estimated at an average of one
per mile.   Two places were seen where bodies were disinterred by the wolves, and the bones lay bleaching in
the sun.   The companies in which cholera had made its
most direful ravages were mostly from Missouri, with a
few from Illinois.   They were late and generally had ox
teams.

The 20th of June, the emigrant teams were more
scattering.   The people called themselves Oregon emigrants.   Captain Haight bought tea of a woman who
stated she had seen her father, mother and sister interred
within a few days.   A lone wagon was on the river bank.
Death had taken all who traveled with it.   A gentleman
was met with, who said he was alone in his mess, his two
companions having died.   There was thought to be
many graves out of sight from the road in camping

places on the river bank. The emigrants called this part of the route, "The Valley of Death."

The 24th of June, they passed an unorganized company of Saints and encamped in the evening with Messrs. Lorenzo D. Young and Charles F. Decker. The 25th, at Fort Kearney, they found Livingston and Kinkead's teams and Captain Lake's fifty of Saints. From this post was met the main body of the Mormon emigration of about eight hundred wagons. They were generally in good condition though cholera had made inroads among them. Mr. Appleton Harmon thought that sixty-two deaths had been reported to him. The party arrived in Kanesville about the 6th of July.

The *Frontier Guardian* of July 10th, 1850, gives us the first details of the departure of our people across the plains. It says: "By the arrival of Messrs. Johnson and Hall from the Indian country, we are informed that Elder Orson Hyde and company, of this place, left Platte river camp on the morning of the 6th inst, on a visit to the valley of Great Salt Lake. This is the last company of the season, all others being in advance. Bishop Hunter with his company, also a small company of California emigrants from Michigan, are a few miles in advance, all well. We are informed the cholera followed the California and all other emigrants for several hundred miles out, which proved very fatal. Several hundred died with the epidemic. It has, however, nearly or quite subsided, and all are moving forward."

With the season's emigration on the way across the plains, followed by Elder O. Hyde, the following letter will indicate to the reader the stirring times on the shores of Salt Lake.

"GREAT SALT LAKE CITY, DESERET.

"July 28th, 1850.

"*Dear Brother Orson Hyde:*

"The emigration poured in here to such numbers that they raised provisions to a very high price. Flour sold for one dollar per pound, which was sufficient to induce some of our speculators to sell the last morsel and go without. Harvest commenced with the 4th of July, and has continued until the present.   *   *   *
It is a general time of health with the Saints, and peace, and plenty of hard work, as every one has been so busy that they can hardly get time to eat or sleep. You speak about hurry and bustle at Kanesville ; but if you were here, to see, feel and realize the burdens, labors and responsibilities which are daily, hourly, momentarily, rolling, piling, tumbling and thundering upon us, you would at least conclude that there was no danger of our getting the gout from idleness or too much jollity.   *   *

"BRIGHAM YOUNG,
"H. C. KIMBALL,
"WILLARD RICHARDS."

Further interesting details of the movements of the emigrating companies is furnished by Elder Hyde, in a letter to Mr. McIntosh, who was temporary editor of the *Frontier Guardian.*

"UPPER CROSSING OF THE PLATTE,

July 30th, 1850.

"*Brother McIntosh :*

"DEAR SIR—We crossed the Platte yesterday. Ferried over wagons and swam our horses, leaving Captain Milo Andrus and company on the banks crossing. All well.   *   *   *   *   *   *

"Grass is very scarce though the rains through the Black Hills have been constant and powerful. But how the vast multitudes of cattle and horses are to get through, God only knows. There will be no lack of water, but grass is eaten up root and branch; and in many cases the animals have eaten out the wild sage.

"August 1st, at Independence Rock on the Sweetwater, all well. We have just passed through the "valley and shadow of death," a country of about fifty miles in extent, where the waters are deeply impregnated with nitre, saleratus, sulphur, etc., etc. There is little or no grass at all through this region, but is mostly a sandy desert. The carcasses of cattle and horses lying along the roadside are very numerous, having perished through fatigue, hunger and through drinking poisonous waters.

"This country lies between the upper crossing of the Platte and the Sweetwater river on the banks of which we are now comfortably encamped. * We are now beginning to overtake the California and Oregon emigration. They have suffered much in the loss of teams and animals; and oh! the sacrifice of wagons, clothing, firearms, beds, bedding, buffalo skins, trunks, chests, harness, and in the loss of life. The road to gold is strewn with destruction, wretchedness and woe, and yet thousands and tens of thousands follow on the way with the hope of securing the wealth of this world.   *

"There are about five hundred new graves on the south side of the Platte and but three deaths are reported at Laramie as having occurred on the north side. * If wood were as plentiful as tools, wagon tire and iron in general, on the road, we could have our hot dodger. coffee and fried or boiled bacon whenever we pleased.

"BIG SANDY, August 8th, 1850.

"The eight or ten hundred wagons of emigrants' and merchants' trains behind us have but a sorry prospect. Much of their stock must and will unavoidably perish. Cows already give but little milk, because they have but little to eat, and families whose chief dependence for food on the journey is milk and butter from their cows, will be cut short of their expectations in some respects. But if they can stand it through to Green river they will find plenty of grass, in my opinion.

"There are three hard places for stock and teams to cross over. First from Laramie across the Black Hills to the upper crossing of the Platte, a distance of 120 miles. The road is mostly over rocks, sharp gravel and flint. This is severe on cattle's feet.   *   *   * The second hard place is from the upper crossing of the Platte to Independence Rock on the Sweetwater, a distance of fifty miles. Through this section the alkali or poisonous waters may be mostly found.   * On the Sweetwater there is generally some grass; but there is more or less alkali from the upper crossing of the Platte to the South Pass of the Rocky Mountains, and whenever emigrants discover the road white with saleratus, also the banks and breaks in the land, they should be careful about letting their animals drink from the standing pools.

"The third trying part of the road for stock is from the South Pass to Green river, a distance of 65 miles. Sand and sage, sage and sand, dead horses, mules, cows, and oxen, with snow-capped mountains on your right and left, are about the variety which the eye meets in passing through this section. I would give a more flattering account of this section if I could, conscientiously. I have this assurance, however, that those who travel this road hereafter will testify to the truth of what I have written."

The following important items are from an Epistle of the First Presidency of the Church, dated Great Salt Lake City, September 27th, 1850:

"The crops have been abundant in all the settlements of Deseret this season; and we have made every exertion to have them secured for the benefit of all; and although from the best information obtained, we have reason to expect that our population will be strengthened nearly, if not quite 15,000 this season, yet we are confident, if all will be prudent, there will be seed grain and bread sufficient to sustain the whole, till another harvest. The estimated population of 15,000 inhabitants in Deseret the past year, having raised grain sufficient to

sustain the 30,000 for the coming year, inspires us confi-
dently to believe that the 30,000 the coming year can
raise sufficient for 60,000 the succeeding year, and to
this object and end our energies will be exerted to double our population annually, by the assistance of the
Perpetual Emigrating Poor Fund, and otherwise provide
for the sustenance of that population.

"Viewing the gathering of Israel, which produces
our increased population in the valleys of the mountains,
an important part of the gospel of Jesus Christ, and one
of the most important at the present time, we shall send
few, or no Elders abroad to preach the gospel this fall;
but instruct them to raise grain and build houses, and
prepare for the Saints, that they may come in flocks, like
doves to their windows; and we say, arise! to your wagons and your tents, O scattered Israel! ye Saints of the
Most High! rich and poor, and gather to the State of
Deseret, bringing your plows and drills, your reapers
and gleaners, your threshers and cleaners of the most
approved patterns, so that one man can do the labor of
twenty in the wheat field, and we will soon send the
Elders abroad by hundreds and thousands to a harvest of
souls among the nations, and the inhabitants of the earth
shall speedily hear of the salvation prepared by Israel's
God for His people."

The Epistle also recommended the route on the
north side of the Platte as the best for the Saints.

The *Deseret News* thus briefly notices the arrival of
the last companies of the season's emigration. Bishop
Hunter and company arrived on Sunday, October 13th,
1850; Elder Woodruff and company on Monday, the 14th.
Both companies were east of the second mountain on
Thursday during the snow-storm, and passed through
considerable snow in coming in, though they arrived in
health and most joyfully are the last camps of the Saints
welcomed in the valley, and particularly after so long an
absence our old friend and pioneer, Brother Woodruff.

The *Frontier Guardian* of December 11th, 1850, emphasizes the counsel of Brigham Young for the Saints to travel on the north side of the Platte the ensuing season. "The awful scenes of cholera and death on the south side of the Platte last season should be a warning to those concerned louder than thunder, to avoid a late start, and to avoid the south side of the river. More than five hundred fresh graves on the south side of the Platte between the Missouri and Fort Laramie, while from the thousands who traveled on the north side only three graves can be found that were made this season."

The efficient and arduous labors of Elder Orson Hyde, in managing Church and Emigration affairs at the eastern terminus of the route to Salt Lake valley, cannot be fully appreciated. This season the 5th of July, before the last company of emigrants were fairly on the way, he left Kanesville for Salt Lake valley, arrived there on the 15th of August, attended to the important business for which the trip was undertaken, and was welcomed back to Kanesville by his numerous friends the 18th of the following November.

Jos. E. Johnson under date of February 2d, 1851, reports his return trip from the valley. He evidently accompanied Elder Hyde, although the fact is not stated. "Started for states the last day of September with the addition to company of twelve men. Met the last of the emigrating companies, Bishop Hunter's, on the mountains west of Bear river. Met an unpleasant snow storm near the South Pass, and another gale of snow at the upper crossing of the Platte. From here kept the north side of the river the entire way down. Found the north side much better route than the south side to Laramie. From there down found many advantages on the north side; better water for camp use, more feed and better road,

buffalo abundant down as low as Fort Kearney * * *
We found no hostile Indians but they stole all the small
articles they could conceal which they could not beg.
We arrived in Kanesville on the 18th of November,
occupying fifty days in our return, being absent from
home four and a half months."

CHAPTER XXVIII.

THE EMIGRATION OF 1851—NEWS FROM COMPANIES ON THE
PLAINS—THE FIRE OF THE GATHERING—HAND-CARTS
FORESHADOWED—ELDERS EZRA T. BENSON AND J. M.
GRANT SENT TO SUPERINTEND THE EMIGRATION OF
1852—ELDER MARGETTS' TRIP FROM SALT LAKE TO
KANESVILLE.

NEITHER the *Frontier Guardian* at the eastern end of the route to Salt Lake, nor the *Deseret News* at the western terminus, furnish much news of the emigration for the year 1851. President Hyde made another flying trip to Salt Lake, doubtless to thoroughly post himself in the views and counsels of the First Presidency. He left Kanesville the 28th of June, and arrived in the valley the 17th of August attended by Albert Carrington, and a few others, all of whom were plundered by the Pawnee Indians. Elder Hyde, after a successful trip arrived in Kanesville the 17th of October, 1851.

The following from the *Frontier Guardian* of August 22nd, 1851, furnishes a few items of interest:

"A party of seven men arrived in Kanesville from Salt Lake on the 19th of August, 1851. They left there the 15th of July, making the trip in thirty-four days. They met Phineas Young and General Brown five miles east of the valley. President Hyde and company thirty-three miles west of Laramie, getting along well. * Captain —— and his company were, on the first of August, four miles west of Fort Laramie; Stevens' company five miles east of the fort; Captain Day's company in sight; Captain Cummings and company of one hundred wagons

15

ten miles west of Ash Hollow; Shurtliff's company of
fifty wagons five miles in rear of Cummings' train; Captain John Brown, with the emigrating poor twenty-two
miles east of Ash Hollow; Wilkins' merchandise train of
ten wagons, with a Scotch company in the rear, were
met near Brown's company. Gordon's company were
met the next day. They met Father Allred's company
the west side of Cold Springs, and Elder O. Pratt's company at the Springs."

The General Epistle of October, 1851, says of the
emigration:

"Elder Orson Pratt is on the way from the States;
and about five hundred wagons, mostly of these who are
emigrating to this place; but they started too late, were
hindered by heavy rains and floods, and it will be very
late before the last company will arrive."

The general epistle sent out in the autumn of 1851
as usual also gives instructions for the gathering of 1852.
It is full of the fire of the gathering and says: "The
voice of the good Shepherd is to all Saints, even to the
ends of the earth; gather yourselves together, come
home; and more especially to the Saints in Pottowatomie, the United States, Canada and the British
Isles; come home! come home!!" In the following we
see the future hand-cart companies foreshadowed:

"Some of the Saints, now in our midst, came hither
with wagons or carts made of wood, without a particle
of iron, hooping their wheels with hickory or rawhide,
or ropes, and had as good and safe a journey as any in
the camps with their wrought iron wagons; and can you
not do the same? Yes, if you have the same desire, the
same faith. Families might start from Missouri river,
with cows, hand-carts, wheelbarrows, with little flour and
no unnecessaries, and come to this place quicker, and
with less fatigue, than by following the heavy trains with

their cumbrous herds, which they are often obliged to drive miles to feed.

"Elders Ezra T. Benson and Jedediah M. Grant will repair to Kanesville, immediately after conference, and superintend the emigration the coming season. They are sent expressly to push the Saints to the valley."

It was evidently the intent by the epistle that the Nauvoo exodus should culminate with the emigration of 1852, by the removal of all the Saints on the Missouri river to Great Salt Lake valley. President Orson Hyde, who, for nearly five years had the presidency of affairs at the eastern end of the road across the plains, was directed to move his family to the valley, Elder F. D. Richards, president of the European missions was directed to send two ship-loads of Saints as early as April.

The following from the St. Louis *Weekly Union* of October 7th, 1851, indicates the interest with which many were watching the growth of the Mormon colony in the mountains :

"No body of people in the whole world, not greater in number, seems to us, to occupy a position so peculiarly prominent and powerful, whether considered in reference to religion, politics or commerce, as these people who have founded their Zion in the bosom of the Salt Lake country."

A letter from Elder Thos. Margetts to the *Millennial Star*, Liverpool, England, dated Kanesville, July 4th, 1852, furnishes the earliest information of that season's emigration that the writer has been able to find. It is a sketch of a trip across the plains with a party of Elders. It states that this party left Salt Lake on the 5th of May, 1852. At the Sweetwater, six miles above Devil's Gate, they met a small company of emigrants for California with mule teams;· a few hours after a company of packers. At Independence rock a large company with horse teams crossing the Sweetwater. From the ford of Sweetwater the emigration grew more numerous daily, until it seemed almost a continuous string of teams. This was on the north side of the Platte, for they traveled the entire distance on that side, without crossing the river at all. At every point where they could see the road on the south side they discovered that it was also lined with wagons. They all looked well. They had light loads, light wagons and strong teams. No horses were seen left, but few cattle, and only eight or ten wagons and they were broken up.

The company rolled along, answering questions, cracking jokes with the emigrants. There was a general opinion among the latter that Mormons and Indians were united in bands on the road for the purpose of robbing companies. The Elders talked and sang with them and in this way convinced them of the folly of such reports, when they would often show the change in their sentiments by the expression, "Well, the Mormons are d——d good fellows, and bring good things from their wagons and invite all to partake of the excellent fare."

At Wolf creek the company met the first sickness and saw the first graves. The number increased until they reached Wood river. From there the graves gradually lessened as they neared the Missouri river and sickness disappeared. They did not see over two hundred graves, which they thought few considering the great number of people who were traveling the road.

They met the first Mormon train, Captain Higbee's fifty, two hundred and fifty miles from Winter Quarters, and after that companies of Saints almost daily. When circumstances permitted they stopped in their camps.

After the good news from the valley were told and a thousand and one questions answered they would all turn in, in true Mormon style, to dance and sing. Including those waiting at the Ferry they met about 1,400 Mormon teams, with which traveled not less than 10,000 people. It is stated in the editorial of the *Millennial Star* of November 13th, 1852, that twenty-one companies of Saints, averaging sixty wagons or upwards each emigrated on the north side of the Platte river, and two companies besides the company with the sugar mill machinery on the south side. These estimates indicate a very heavy emigration that season. Evidently the able management at Kanesville make a very successful one.

The following items from an editorial in the *Deseret News* of July 10th, 1852, make up a vivid picture of the ravages of death on the lower Platte : "From observations made by travelers, it is supposed a thousand graves have been called into existence between the Missouri river and the South Pass, previous to the 4th of July. Bishop Smoot, with a company of English Saints, was on the south side of the Platte in the midst of cholera at the latest dates. Some cases of cholera had appeared on the north side of the river, but its ravages appear to correspond with the amount of emigration which was much greater on the south side.

"The emigrating Saints commenced leaving Kanesville about the 25th of May. The first week in June the first company, which was from St. Louis, was near the Loupe Fork. While the Saints in these valleys are enjoying the richest blessings of heaven and earth, let them not be unmindful of their brethren and sisters and their little ones who are now passing the valley of death on the Platte river. Not through 'the valley of the shadow of death,' but through the valley of death itself, where men, women and children have been left on the ground where they died, if travelers tell the truth, with no other change or covering than a few loose clods thrown over them, to hide them from the light of day, while the tent that should shelter them was hurriedly forced from its fastenings, so that the survivors might go their way. And why? For fear that death would leave the departed and cleave to themselves and not, as humanity would hope, from any want of respect to the departed."

The 2nd of June, 1852, A. W. Babbitt left Kanesville for Salt Lake, and made the trip in twenty-seven and a half days. He passed Captain John Higbee's company, at Shell Creek, the 5th of June, and A. O. Smoot's company above Fort Kearney, June 9th. Captain Higbee's company crossed the Missouri river the 30th of May. It arrived in Great Salt Lake valley about the 20th of August, the first of the season's emigration.

Ezra T. Benson and J. M. Grant returned to Salt Lake, August 11th, 1852, from the mission of gathering the Saints from Pottowatomie. They left the country almost vacated. The last family that wanted to come was brought along. The last companies of this season's emigration were late. Snowstorms in the mountains retarded their progress and made them short of provisions. Two hundred teams went from the valley with 40,000 or 50,000 pounds of flour and large supplies of vegetables which enabled them to come in safety.

The following list of names of men who led fifties across the plains in 1852, is from the *Deseret News* of September 18th. It is evidently not complete. Abram O. Smoot, captain of the Perpetual Emigration Fund emigrants from Great Britain; John Higbee, James W.

Bay, James J. Jepson, F. C. D. Howe, Joseph Outhouse, John Tidwell, David Wood, H. B. M. Jolley, Isaac M. Stewart, James McGaw, Harmon Cutler, John B. Walker, Robert Weimer, Uriah Curtis, Isaac Bullock, James C. Snow, Eli B. Kelsey, H. W. Mille, Allen Weeks, Wm. Lang, Joel Edmonds.   There were probably about 6,000 people in these organizations.

The writer has found no record of the captains of hundreds.   Elder Warren Foote led a hundred of which Elder Samuel Mulliner was historian.   The latter gave his journal to Captain Foote, and from this and the autobiography of the latter, the following narrative of the travels of this hundred has been compiled.   It is the best illustration that has come to hand of the travels of the Saints across the plains in 1852.

------—•—------

CHAPTER XXIX.

CAPTAIN FOOTE'S HUNDRED—ITS HISTORY ILLUSTRATES THE DIFFICULTIES ENCOUNTERED BY THE EMIGRATING SAINTS IN 1852—THE CULMINATION OF THE NAUVOO EXODUS —THE OPENING OF A NEW ERA—GATHERING THE POOR FROM EUROPE UNDER THE AUSPICES OF THE PERPETUAL EMIGRATION FUND COMPANY.

WHILE the Saints have been repeatedly plundered by the Gentiles, the latter have been often compelled, by circumstances over which they had no control, to minister to their necessities.   This was the case in Pottowatomie county in the spring of 1852.   The weather was cool, grass late in starting, the emigration for California very numerous, and they were compelled to wait on the frontier for grass to grow on the Platte bottom. This made farm products in good demand. Corn went up to $2.00, and wheat to $2.25 per bushel. Everything the Saints had to sell they cashed at good prices.

For some reason the most of the Mormon emigration traveled the south side of the Platte. They crossed the Missouri river eighteen miles below Kanesville, at an insignificant hamlet called Bethlehem. This hundred was organized by Apostle O. Hyde before crossing, with Warren Foote captain, Otis L. Terry captain of first fifty, and Wm. Wall captain of second fifty. The hundred comprised 105 wagons; 476 persons; 743 cattle; 19 horses; 273 sheep. June 17th, the hundred camped three miles west of the Ferry. The officers met and adopted the following by-laws for the regulation and good order of the camps. As they probably did not differ materially from rules generally adopted by the companies of emigrating Saints, we give them in full:

"*Resolved*, first—The horn shall be blown at 4 o'clock in the morning, when the people will arise, and, after the necessary preparations for starting, the horn will be blown again for the people to come together for prayers, and at half past eight at night the horn will be blown again for evening prayers, which each family will attend in their wagon.

"*Resolved*, second—That if any person while on guard at night shall neglect his duty by sleep or otherwise, for the first offence he shall be reported publicly, and if afterwards found guilty of neglect he shall again be reported and be subjected to extra duty in the day time herding cattle.

"*Resolved,* third—That any member of this camp who shall indulge in profane language shall be reported by his captain of ten, and if he shall afterwards persist in profanity he shall be published publicly.

"*Resolved,* fourth—That if any persons practice unnecessary cruelty to their animals, and after being reproved by their captain of ten, shall still persist in such cruelty, they shall be brought before the captains of the camp, who shall levy such fine or punishment as they may deem just."

These resolutions were afterwards submitted to the whole company for their approval. Accidents, births and deaths characterized human life here as elsewhere.

The 18th of June a child was born, and a boy run over by a wagon, but not seriously injured. There was much rain, making the roads muddy and creating great discomfort.

The 20th, a number of California emigrants were met returning home discouraged. They reported the cholera terrible in companies ahead. There were several cases of cholera in the second fifty. Alfred Brown died of this disease and was buried in the morning before starting.

The 21st and 22nd of June four children of Thomas Spafford died of cholera in the second fifty, and a girl had her leg broken. This was taking a family pretty rapidly, and the event must have spread a deep shadow over the company. For some unknown reason there was much more sickness and death in the second than in the first fifty. Severe storms were frequent, and a matter of considerable dread to emigrants.

The 24th, several more deaths were reported in the second fifty. A meeting was called by Captain Foote, and the Lord besought to turn the destroyer away.

The 26th, there was another death in the second fifty.

The 27th of June Elder Moses Clawson, and several others going on missions, were met. Up to this time the first fifty had enjoyed comparative immunity from the general sickness.

The 27th, about noon the company came on to the Platte bottom. That night there was a severe thunderstorm, and the next day the ground was so soft that if teams were stopped wagons often settled down to the hubs of the wheels. Water was scarce for the animals, and the sun shone very warm. Owing to almost constant exposure to wet some of the company complained of sickness in the first fifty. In traveling the third and fifth tens fell behind but came up late at night and, for the first time, the power of death was felt in the camp. A little boy belonging to John Dart, who started out in the morning to drive loose stock, died in the afternoon of the 28th with the cholera, and a sister of the lad's died early in the morning of the 29th. This threw another family into the depths of affliction. Franklin Cunningham was nearly drowned in swimming the Platte to get wood. Elders Campbell and Crosby, with a mail from the valley, were met by the company. After this visitation of the Dart family the health of the first fifty was again very good.

July 2nd, a child of Sister Hart's died. The graves of a brother Sergeant and son, from Kanesville, were passed. Brother Smallham, who was well in the morning, was brought into camp sick with the cholera. He died and was buried the following morning.

July 5th, a California emigrant, by the name of King, who traveled with the company, died of cholera. He was from Illinois and without relatives along.

Captain Wall, of the second fifty, came into camp and reported three deaths in the company within a few days. Mrs. Dart died in the evening. About 10 o'clock a. m., July 6th, the company passed Fort Kearney.

The 7th, the second ten of the first fifty wished to stop to take care of the sick.

On the 10th, buried a Sister Proctor who died the night before. Owing to much wet weather the cattle were badly crippled with sore necks and feet.

The 15th of July the company passed about twenty graves of California emigrants, and three or four of our people. From dates on head-boards these deaths occurred between the 3rd and 17th of June. Several men came into camp loaded with buffalo meat. It was the first obtained. The next day the company laid by for the hunters to bring in a good supply of meat. Apostle O. Hyde and party passed the company on their way to Salt Lake.

The 17th of July, Father Rose, who had died of cholera, was buried. The company were passing through large herds of bufialo.

July 18th, the company had passed many graves in the previous few days. They were mostly of people from Missouri, and had been made between the 5th and 15th of June. Scarcely a grave that had not been robbed of its contents by wolves, and the bones of its occupant lay bleaching on the prairie. Beds and bedding were strewn around unfit for use without cleansing.

August 7th found the company in the Black Hills, west of Laramie. In the morning they started a half mile east of what is called in the guides "The Bend in the Road," near Dead Timber creek, and as the last ten were coming into line on the road a stampede occurred with the last teams. A brother Clemens ran in before them to stop them, but he was knocked down, trampled on and a wagon ran over his bowels. Also Wm. McDonald, who was on horseback a little ahead of the stampeding teams, rode in forward of them at the risk of his life, and succeeded in stopping them before they came up to the main body of the company. The first wagons had arrived at the gulch, which caused the bend in the road, and if the stampede had not been checked, there is no doubt but the whole company would have been plunged into the gulch, which was eight or ten feet deep. Elder Clemens was so badly hurt that he died before night. A sacrifice in a noble effort to save his friends.

August 17th, the company was met by Elders Stratton and George Madsen, who had been sent out by President Young to assist the companies in finding feed for their animals, which was very scarce in some places, owing to the immense overland emigration. They also brought a very cheering letter from President Young.

Aug. 18th, the company crossed the north Fork of the Platte river. On account of heavy rains it was rising rapidly. Soon after the company were over, it became impassable.

August 19th, the company did not move. The cattle suffered with cold and hunger. It was supposed to be the last time the hundred would 'camp together. A meeting was called and difficulties were amicably settled. As a result all felt well. Heavy storms and poor feed were very hard on animals.

The 24th of August the company remained in camp to repair wagons, hunt buffalo for a supply of meat, and rest the weary and hungry cattle. The company did not move until the 28th.

September 25th, the company camped on Last

creek at the west foot of the Little Mountain. The people were again called together and all difficulties settled. The next day they arrived in Salt Lake City.

The following remarks of Elder John Taylor, in Salt Lake City, August 22nd, 1852, concerning what he saw in Kanesville and the surrounding country on his way home in the early part of the season, is a fitting close to this outline sketch of the Nauvoo exodus. It shows the season's operations to have been the crowning effort to gather the exiles and complete the fulfillment of the covenants made in the Nauvoo Temple.

Elder Taylor says, "It gave me great joy on my way home to find the Saints leaving Kanesville. It almost seemed as though they were swept out with a besom. When I was there I rode out in my carriage one day to a place called Council Point. I though I would go and visit some of the folks there, but when I got there behold there were no folks to see. I hunted around and finally found a place with something like 'Grocery' written upon it. I alighted and went into the house and asked a person who presented himself, if he was a stranger there? 'Yes,' says he, 'I have only just come.' 'And the people have all left, have they?' 'Yes,' was the answer. I next saw a few goods standing at the side of a house, but the house was empty. These were waiting to be taken away. I went to another house and there were two or three people waiting for a boat to take them down the river. These were all the inhabitants I saw there.

"When I reflected upon this removal my heart felt pained. I well knew the disposition of many in those frontier counties, and I thought that some miserable wretches might come upon them after the main body of the Saints had removed, and abuse, rob and plunder the widow, the orphan, the lame, halt, blind and destitute who might be left as was done in Nauvoo. * * * But thank God they are coming, old and young, rich and poor."

Scarcely had the last victims of the Nauvoo exodus arrived in the valley, when the first company of Saints emigrated from Europe by the Perpetual Emigrating Fund company, were welcomed home with discharges of artillery, with feasting and music. They arrived in the afternoon of the 3rd of September, 1852. "They were the poor gathering up to Zion. For this reason much interest was manifested in their arrival. The train consisted of thirty-one wagons under Captain A. O. Smoot. Captain Pitt's band met the company at the mouth of Emigration canyon, where aged Saints of both sexes, danced and sang for joy.

"The luxuries of melons and cakes were distributed. The band joined the escort and enlivened the scene with music. Following these in the procession came a band of women and children. They were weather beaten but not forlorn. The lightness of their hearts was manifest in their countenances. After these followed the wagon train, the good condition of which did credit to the excellent management of Bishop Smoot. As the procession passed the temple block it was saluted with nine rounds of artillery, while thousands of people gathered from all parts of the city to swell the joyful welcome."

There are some interesting resemblances in the histories of ancient and modern Israel. The first Israel suffered from monarchial despotism. The modern one, after thirty-three centuries, from the ignorance and prejudice of a free people; both alike destructive and cruel. Both have been hated for their religion, their social institutions, and feared for their cohesiveness, their policies and their rapid increase. Both fled from their oppressors into a desert. The former conquered a populous country for an inheritance, the latter created one. In a short time the Saints learned that to take an active part in breaking up old landmarks of religion and social conditions, was to take upon themselves as a heritage, the world's opposition.

The Saints driven from Illinois had previously experienced little else than antagonisms in the form of annoyances, plunderings and drivings. A strange thing had appeared among men. A people had arisen who claimed that the heavens had condescended to commune with men. A Prophet was among them clothed with Divine inspiration. In these facts there was power to awaken mankind from the slumber of ages, and break chains of darkness that had bound the race for centuries.

Suffering begat in the hearts of the Saints an intense desire for rest, for refuge from unrelenting enemies. As we have seen, prophetic declarations early led them to look to the Rocky Mountain region, to the unexplored deserts of the west, for the fruition of their hopes. When the route was marked out, and the place for gathering located, the getting there became a question simply of ability. On arriving there they exerted themselves to provide for their own needs, and for the sustenance of those who were to follow. In the meantime the latter struggled to make an outfit and gather to the assistance of those who had preceded them. As we have endeavored to show from the beginning of the Exodus there was a general and very efficient organization for carrying out one grand purpose, the gathering of the people to the shelter prepared for them, where they could develop the purposes of their life's mission. In this comprehensive sense they were all pioneers of

the highest type.   Those who afterwards gathered for
the first time, assisted in building the grand superstruc-
ture of which the Nauvoo exiles laid the foundation.

The gathering to Kirtland, the move westward to
the frontiers of Missouri, the Exodus from there to Nauvoo, from there across the prairies of Iowa, all origin-
ating and culminating under unusual difficulties, were so
many lessons in nomadic life. They afforded leaders
and people a vast experience in the best methods of
outfitting and of traveling with wagons, with families
and domestic animals.   The force of circumstances made
them at home in journeying during the day, and in making camp by the wayside at night.   It cultivated the
habit of suiting themselves to a great diversity of circumstances and conditions, and if possible of profiting by
those diverse conditions.

These experiences were a grand educational process
which fitted the Saints for great changes without any
weakening effect on their organization as a religious
body.   Constant efforts of enemies to weaken their
union only drew the band more tightly.

The old adage, "A rolling stone gathers no moss,"
has been reversed in the history of the Latter-day Saints.
The "rolling stone" has constantly increased in velocity
and in the same ratio, in power to contend with antagonisms.   In each succeeding change the foundation has
been laid for greater expansion, for accellerated growth.
From a country village in Ohio they held the balance of
political power in counties in Missouri.   In six years
they built a fine city and ruled a county in Illinois.

Within six months after the commencement of the
Nauvoo exodus, they moved 300 miles to the western
frontier of the United States to the lands of the Pottowatomie Indians on the Missouri river.   In less than eight-

een months they so nearly obliterated it, by planting a colony midway between the Missouri river and the Pacific ocean, that it became a reminiscence of the past. In what was then a vast, unexplored region they laid the foundations of empire and made practicable a highway for the locomotive to cross the continent, to bind together the natural eastern and western divisions of the republic.

In these moves leaders and people displayed a masterly energy. The power of Providential circumstances behind them, and an intense desire to be free from their enemies which welled up in their afflicted souls together, constituted a motive power sufficient to rouse every latent energy. The successful results of their movements, many of which, from a practical standpoint, appear like daring the fates, evidences they were led by an inspiration that made no mistakes, and that a kindly Providence overruled temporal and spiritual influences to favor them.

16

CHAPTER XXX.

IT is worthy of record that the main body of the
Latter-day Saints, in all their forced and voluntary
movements, in their journeyings from Seneca county,
New York, to the Great Salt Lake, have remained in a
geographical belt of about 300 miles in breadth, and
quite uniformly between 37 and 44 degrees north latitude,
and within the climatic belt which is generally supposed
to be adapted to developing the best capabilities of the
race.

Some notice of waymarks they have left along this
route the writer believes will be a fitting conclusion
of this sketch. The Temple in Kirtland, the first edifice dedicated in these latter times to the performances
of the ordinances of the Holy Priesthood, is still standing. Around it are numerous marks of the labors of
the Saints, and in an adjoining grave-yard lie many of
their remains. The land along the ordinary early routes
of travel is also consecrated by their sleeping dust.

The writer visited Independence in December, 1875.
He was shown the dilapidated remains of cabins occupied by the Saints when they were driven from Jackson
county. He was informed there was considerable real
estate in the county to which the present claimants had
no legal title, it being still vested in Mormons who had

purchased the lands from the general government, and been afterwards driven from their possessions.

The spot where the corner-stone of the Temple was said to have been laid was still unmolested, except being used as a play-ground by the youth of the surrounding families.

The writer did not visit other portions of Missouri which had been occupied by the Saints, but, doubtless, there are many marks of such occupancy, and many places where their dead were deposited now known only to the angels. We have already quoted Colonel Thomas L. Kane's unparalleled description of desolated Nauvoo. The *Liverpool Route*, speaking of the visit of its artist, Mr. Frederick Piercy, in 1853, says of Nauvoo and the Temple: "After the surrender of Nauvoo by the Saints, it gradually dwindled away in importance until it became what our artist found it. On the 10th of November, 1848, the Temple was fired by an incendiary, and on the 27th of May, 1850, a tornado blew down the north wall, and so shook the building that the Icarians, who had been engaged in rebuilding the edifice for their use, deemed it advisable to pull down the east and south walls, leaving only the west wall. This beautiful ruin is all that is left of what was once a work the most elegant in its construction, and the most renowned in its celebrity, of any in the whole west, and which had been built by the Latter-day Saints in the midst of poverty and persecution."

When the Mormons arrived at Council Bluffs, on the Missouri river, the country was Indian Territory. They were the "van of empire" rolling westward in that direction. The remains of their pioneering labors are fast disappearing, as well as the knowledge of them among the people who have been their successors. The writer was on a mission in that section of the country in 1876. Some of his observations will be of interest in this connection.

At the time, Utah flour was worth 50 cts. more per hundred than the home article, on account of its superior quality. Walking along the main street of Council Bluffs he noticed this difference in price marked on sacks exposed for sale. He asked the vendor what made this difference in price. He replied, "He did not know, unless it was that Utah had been settled longer than Iowa, and, therefore, had better flouring mills." This man, although of average intelligence, had no idea that the Mormons had opened farms and built the pioneer grist-mill of that country, before pioneering their way to Utah.

The writer remembers the country around Council Bluffs as quite romantic and inviting in appearance. The railroad depots, many dwellings, and most of the business houses of the city were located on the level bottom land of the Missouri river.

The great majority of dwelling houses lined streets that ran up into coves and romantic glens between the high bluffs. Many of these dwellings were fair specimens of architectural elegance, and of the refined tastes of their occupants. They afforded the advantages of a suburban residence in close proximity to the business centre of the town.

Through the western portion of the town ran Indian, *alias* Lousy creek. The latter name was suggestive of unpleasant reminiscences. Surmising there must be a cause for so unromantic a name, on inquiry, he was informed that the stream was very fickle and changeable. Today murmuring along, a harmless rivulet, perhaps tomorrow an angry, billowy flood, washing away portions of its banks, regardless of man's profit or convenience.   Running along its western bank about half a mile was Greene street, so named in honor of Mr.

KANESVILLE.

Evan M. Greene, who was one of the first residents in the locality.   He was an early pioneer, and the first post master of the place, then called Kanesville, in honor of Col. Thos. L. Kane, the philanthropist.

In the immediate vicinity, but on the east side of Indian creek, was the residence of Mr. Wm. Powers and his amiable lady. From their garden the latter pointed out the location of this primitive post office, and also that of the Log Tabernacle, in which the Priesthood of the Church of Jesus Christ organized its second First Presidency, soon after the return of B. Young and others of the pioneers from Great Salt Lake valley, in December, 1847, and also in which the writer was ordained a Seventy in the spring of 1849, under the hands of President Joseph Young.

On the south-east side of the town is a cove which, in the early days, was occupied by Apostle George A. Smith and family. It is still known by many as "George A's Hollow." In 1876 it was occupied by a couple of fine brick residences.

Twice he strolled into Fairview cemetery. This is a well-laid-out, modern cemetery on the slope of a high bluff just out of town, on the north-west side of Indian creek. He had been informed that the "Old Mormon burying ground" was on this hill. Rambling over the inclosure he failed to recognize it. Inquiring of a laborer on the grounds, he was informed that he would find the object of his search on the summit of the hill, and that modern improvements had not encroached on the sacred place.

The summit affords a fine view of the city and surrounding country. The surface of the ground was in such a shape that no reliable estimate could be formed of the number buried. The boards and billets of wood which had been placed at the heads of graves, the former in some instances with the indistinct remains of lettering in memory of the departed, were gradually disappearing, leaving only little knobs of earth covered with rank grass, scarcely distinguishable from the surrounding surface, to indicate where weary wanderers found a resting place.

No carving was found in memory of the dead dating farther back than 1850. The corroding influence of the elements had obliterated everything of earlier date. One inscription on a head board, which had decayed at the surface of the ground and fallen over, on account of family ties and personal friendship, interested him more than the few others. It bore the following inscription: "John P. Greene, infant son of Evan M. and Susan Greene, died March 3rd, 1852, aged 8 months and 16 days." Memory reminded him that the grandfather, and namesake of this little waif, was prominently connected with the early history of the Church. Inquiring of one who was a citizen of Nauvoo at the time of the exodus, he was informed that Mr. Greene sank under excessive labor and exposure in protecting the Saints during their persecutions, and that he found a resting place on the bank of the Mississippi. Perilous times were the heritage of the little one that bore his name, and we trust it was a kindly Providence that early released it from sorrow which it was not fitted to endure.

One more reminiscence of Fairview cemetery. This city of the dead had its pioneer as well as the neighboring one of the living. A marble headstone, broken off near the surface, and lying on the ground, marks the place of deposit. The erasure of the name and date, from the inscription and general appearance of the stone, indicated that it was a stray from some other locality. Malicious reports were once in circulation that it had been stolen from another grave. Whoever circulated them failed to give due weight to the consideration that one who would incur considerable expense and trouble to gratify the impulses of affection, might be expected to have a proper regard for the tender sentiments of others.

A person was found who had previously made some inquiries concerning this grave, and was informed that the headstone was purshased at Trader's Point, some ten miles below Council Bluffs, of the owner of an old burial place that had been ploughed and its monuments removed. The grave was the resting place of a daughter of Elder Silas Richards. Mrs. Mary Powers informed the writer that she visited the ground in an early day when this was the only grave there. The epitaph on the stone would alike be appropriate over a grave near a frontier trading post, or over the resting place of a Mormon pilgrim on the top of a high bluff on the bank of the Missouri river, 40 years ago.

"Here, lonely and sad, in this wilderness land,
    Thy parents, resigning, deplore thee ;
Sweet, sweet be thy rest, till thy Savior's command,
    In beauty and youth shall restore thee."

The 12th of May, 1876, the writer visited Elder John Mahood and family, about six miles east of Council Bluffs. The prairies were becoming green with the fresh verdure of spring. The wild fruit-trees and shrubs were in full bloom, and forest trees in all stages of development from the bursting bud to nearly the full-grown leaf. Mr. Mahood's residence was enveloped in the forest. From sunset until early dawn, whenever sleep gave way to consciousness, might be heard the echoing notes of the whip-poor-will with a peculiar curt accent on the last note, as if the wakeful night-bird was angry with itself for the everlasting monotony of its song. When at early dawn it retired from active life, it was succeeded

by the ceaseless twitter and merry-making of such a
variety of birds that every tree and shrub of the forest
seemed alive with the music of their song.   It was
an earthly paradise, well fitted for the activities of life or
for a resting place when its energies were exhausted.
On a farm, then owned by Mr. Joshua Gregg, a little
over a mile from Mr Mahood's, was a quiet cove, open
on the east but otherwise quite surrounded with timber.
Abruptly jutting out into this vale, on the south side,
was a prominent, well-defined point.   The ground
between and around a few large linn trees that had lived
through the storms and prairie fires of a century or
more, was covered with a thick growth of small timber.
About half-way up the point was a large linn tree with
several smaller ones growing from its roots.   About ten
feet south-east of these were the remains of a black walnut head-board.   It had decayed at the surface of the
ground and fallen over.   The following inscription,
carved in the wood, was still legible: "In memory of
Solomon Hancock, who died December 2nd, 1847."
Although his name is historical, as he was an active Elder
in the Church, it is probable that this passing notice is
the only record of the place of his sepulture.   There
were indications of several other interments on the spot.
Two or three stakes, indicating places of burial, were
still standing, and several more, partially decayed, were
lying around.

Several families of exiles from Nauvoo built their
cabins in this sheltered nook, and mutually assisted each
other in raising food with which to recruit their wasted
energies.   Evidently quite a heavy per centage of them
found a resting place in this lonely, romantic spot.

This little mausoleum, now being rapidly hidden in
the growth of a young forest and its annual fall of leaves,

is a silent and impressive way mark of these pioneers of western civilization. There are, doubtless, many similar burial places in the country, the signs of which are obliterated by the plough or covered in a new forest growth, beyond the recognition of the living.

The following sequel to this story was learned from the aged widow of Solomon Hancock, Mrs. Phebe Hancock, in the autumn of 1888. She informed the writer that her husband went west from Winter Quarters with the company of Miller and Emmett and, with them, went into camp for the winter near the mouth of Running Water river, late in the autumn of 1846. He and his family did not remain there long, being advised by those in authority to go, with others, to Rush Valley on the Missouri river to assist in taking care of the cattle belonging to the Saints in Winter Quarters. It was harrassing business, as the Indians were troublesome and stole a large number of cattle.

Elder Hancock had been much afflicted with chills and fever and continued to suffer, more or less, with the disease when herding the cattle. In the spring of 1847 the camp of herders was broken up and Elder Hancock, with his family, located near the secluded spot where he was buried, in company with twelve or more families. The hamlet was presided over by Elder Brownell and it was called Brownell's Settlement. After planting some crops of vegetables for his family to look after during the summer, Elder Hancock's health being much improved, and the necessities of his family great, went down into Missouri to seek labor.

He took a job of chopping timber, labored very hard, and when he had nearly completed it he was again taken sick. The Missourian, under the plea that he had not completed the job, refused to pay him anything for his labor.   He returned home as destitute as he left it, and after a sickness of about three months found rest; his spirit in the abode of the faithful, his worn-out body in the lonely but lovely spot we have described.   The black walnut board, which had fortunately served to perpetuate his memory and the place of his sepulture, was cut from the headboard of the bedstead where he had rested during life, and where he had breathed his last. He was a member of Zion's Camp, a faithful preacher of the gospel, shared with the Saints the persecutions of Missouri and Illinois and now rests beneath the luxuriant growth of a modern forest.

The 16th of May, 1876, the writer visited Florence, on the west bank of the Missouri river, six miles above Omaha.   It occupies nearly the same ground as the Winter Quarters of 1846-47.   For several years after the culmination of the Nauvoo Exodus, it continued to be the outfitting point for the emigrant road on the north side of the Platte.   It became quite a flourishing village. When no longer an outfitting point it went rapidly to decay.   In 1876 the few tenements, the appearance of which indicated thrift in their occupants were generally the residences of successful cultivators of the soil.

To meet the storms of the coming winter of 1846-47 log cabins, "dugouts" and shelter in any and every available form were hastily constructed by the exiled Saints.   These very imperfectly sheltered their inmates from the severe cold and storms of that latitude.   In the bodies of many the seeds of disease had been already sown by hunger, exposure to the elements and excessive toil.   To obtain food severely taxed their slender resources, and when obtained it was often inadequate for their needs both in quantity and quality.   The only observable mark of this dark period of the history of the

Saints was the cemetery over the hill west of the town. About all that indicated their use of it were the many little inequalities of the ground showing that it had been disturbed.   Those were no times for chiseled urns or marble momuments in honor of the departed.   Many of the weak, debilitated survivors were barely able to perform the rights of burial, and an unhewn stake, or rude headboard was all they could afford to mark the spot where remains of loved ones were deposited.   Decay and prairie fires had destroyed nearly the last vestige of these.   The piece of ground has been designated as a burial place by the citizens of Florence and in 1873, they inclosed about two and a half acres of it with a good fence. · It is supposed that several hundred of the Saints found a resting place there.   In addition to the thousands who found rest on the prairies of Iowa between the Mississippi and Missouri rivers and at Winter Quarters many laid down their lives along the road "To the West" where lay the final object of their toils—a place of refuge from their enemies.   Well might the Prophet Joseph when he saw the valleys of the mountains in vision, and the sufferings of his people in getting there exclaim in anguish of spirit, "Oh, the dead that will lay between here and there!"

ERRATUM.—On page 27 instead of Section 110 read Section 105.